Sandy
Cove

NORTH AMERICA

•Boston
Norfolk
Bermuda Is

EUROPE

ATLANTIC
OCEAN

AFRICA

Panama Lorica
Galápagos Is

★Corona

Ascensión I

St. Helena I

SOUTH AMERICA

Juan
Fernandez I

Cape of
Good Hope

Falkland Is
Cape Horn

hunderbird

THE RETURN OF THE THUNDERBIRD

Also by Charlotte Baker

KINNERY CAMP: A Story of the Oregon Woods

SUNRISE ISLAND: A Story of the Northwest Coast Indians
        Before the Coming of the White Men

MAGIC FOR MARY M

THE VENTURE OF THE *Thunderbird*

The Return of the Thunderbird

STORY OF A VOYAGE

From Canton, China
to Norfolk, Virginia
in the Ship Thunderbird, commanded
by Samuel Heflin
Begun in 1801 and termi-
nated one year later

TOLD AND PICTURED BY

Charlotte Baker

Published at the Sign of the Thistle by
DAVID McKAY COMPANY. INC.
NEW YORK CITY

To

ROSE DOBBS

who brought the *Thunderbird* to a safe berth
between the covers of this book

VAN REES PRESS • NEW YORK

Contents

I.	NEW YEAR'S EVE	1
II.	THE FEAST	13
III.	NEWS	26
IV.	UNDERWAY	33
V.	MACAO	40
VI.	CHINA	49
VII.	ADVICE	59
VIII.	THE MASQUERADE	67
IX.	THE FACTORY	78
X.	THE CHASE	93
XI.	BEHIND THE WALL	103
XII.	THE TRAP	111
XIII.	THE SONS OF HAN	120
XIV.	DIRTY BUTTER BAY	130
XV.	THE SPICE ISLANDS	140
XVI.	BATAVIA	154
XVII.	STORM	164
XVIII.	CALM	179
XIX.	THE RETURN	191
XX.	THE RESCUE	202
XXI.	THE TEA SET	211

Author's Note

I am grateful to Leo William Nilon, Rear-Admiral, U.S. Navy, Ret., for checking the nautical material in this book.

For ease in identifying the various foreign places mentioned in the story, modern spelling has been used in most cases.

THE RETURN OF THE THUNDERBIRD

The earlier adventures of Roy and Jerry are
set forth in the recently published *The Venture
of the "Thunderbird."*

CHAPTER I

NEW YEAR'S EVE

IT WAS THE last night of the year 1800.
Leroy and Gerald Lacey sat on the deck of the *Swan*, their backs propped against the fife rail just abaft the mainmast. Their eyes were fixed anxiously aft, where a light shone from the Captain's cabin. It was toward the end of the second dogwatch, and they had been waiting thus for nearly two hours. Mimbo, Jerry's dog, lay at his feet, waking from his slumber now and then at some urgent sound or fragrance from the shore.

The village of Waikiki lay there, dark, but not yet sleeping. The water-front houses were lit with smoky lanterns, and a flare of torches moving along the reef showed where a party of night fishermen was setting out. A few pin points of flame from native huts pricked the restless shadows of the palm groves. The land breeze brought to the ship an exciting aroma compounded of wood smoke, roasting pork, seaweed, and the blossoms of the hala trees.

The boys, however, did not allow their attention to be distracted by the enticements of the shore. They were more concerned with the light in the Captain's cabin, with the sound of voices speaking there, and with the faint odor of tobacco that drifted forward.

Jerry shifted his position. "They must be haggling over the price," he said. "This Captain Brown would have taken his leave long ago if he did not intend to make the purchase."

"Yes, they say he is a man who knows his own mind," Roy agreed.

1

"All we've heard has been to that effect. 'Captain Brown never has a slack hand on his ship.' 'Captain Brown's cargo is always first-chop.' 'Captain Brown gets the trade first.' Why, to live up to his reputation, he'd have to be ten feet tall and breathe fire!"

"I wish we could have seen him when he came aboard," Roy said. "Well, we won't miss him when he leaves. He'll not get away until we have a chance to say our piece."

"He'll not get away from Captain Quincey until he buys the *Swan*," Jerry said. "Our Captain Quincey has had enough of trade with the savages of the Northwest Coast of America. If I ever saw a man in a panic of fear, it's our Captain Quincey. He hasn't stopped shaking since the Indians attacked the *Swan* at Tlatlasikoala. He'll get rid of the *Swan* if he has to give her away."

"He can't do that. He has his owners in Boston to account to. And if Captain Brown will not buy the ship, where can he turn? The Sandwich Islands may be the Paradise they say, but that kind of money doesn't grow on trees, even in Paradise."

Jerry grinned. "Selling the *Swan* is Captain Quincey's affair. We have other business with Captain Brown."

Roy smiled back. The two boys looked much alike, their sunburned cheeks creased into deep dimples, their blue-gray eyes sparkling. They sobered at once when the cabin door opened and Captain Quincey came out on deck, followed by the man they knew must be Captain Brown. As the two came forward, Roy and Jerry stepped up smartly.

Captain Quincey peered at them, then said, "Oh, yes. Captain Brown, these two members of my crew—not regular members, indeed; in fact, somewhat irregular—"

"Just what do you mean, sir?" Captain Brown interrupted.

"Why, only that they are not ordinary seamen, Captain. One of them, Gerald Lacey, I found cast away on an island in the Galápagos, although he told me that he was not *exactly* a castaway...."

Captain Brown looked hard at Jerry, and Jerry looked back, but he could make out little of the face in the shadow of the hatbrim.

"The other lad, his brother Leroy, came aboard at Tlatlasikoala, on the Northwest Coast of America, on the night of the attack of which I told you. He was attired like an Indian himself, and was accompanied by one of the savages, bearing the name of Ching."

"I beg your pardon, sir," Roy said, "Ching is no Indian, but Chinese."

"Only another brand of heathen. There is also in the party, I believe, a dog and a—a—crow."

Roy felt that Captain Quincey could have phrased their introduction in more favorable terms. He addressed himself to the visitor. "Captain Brown, will you allow us a moment of your time? My brother and I—"

Captain Brown seemed to make a habit of interrupting. "I'll not be kept standing here on deck," he said brusquely. "If Cap'n Quincey can spare you, you may come ashore with me, and I'll listen to you in the comfort of my own quarters."

The boys looked to Captain Quincey, who nodded sourly. Roy, Jerry, and Mimbo followed Captain Brown into the waiting boat, which pulled away at once for the shore.

Captain Brown's quarters turned out to be a room in the rear of one of the water-front huts. Mimbo and the boys followed his broad back through the outer room, where a motley crowd of foreigners and natives was gathered about the tables. A counter along one wall served the double purposes of trade and refreshment, and shelves behind it were heaped with bolts of cloth, candles, canisters of sugar and tea, trinkets, firearms, and clothing, as well as bottles and jugs. There was an impression of noise, smoke, and pungent odors; then the door was closed behind them, and they stood in a plain, bare room, walled in with lashed poles and thatched with grass in the native manner. Clean mats covered the earthen floor. A sailor's hammock hung in one corner, with a sea chest underneath it. The only other furniture was a trestle table and a chair. Captain Brown removed his hat and jacket and sat down on the one chair; the boys were obliged to stand facing him while he looked them over.

They looked back at him in astonishment. In the light of the ship's lantern on the table Captain Brown was revealed as a very young man. He was not as tall as Roy or Jerry, but was stockily built, with heavy shoulders and chest, a thick neck, and a jutting chin. His face was tanned to the color of old leather. Under broad brows his bright brown eyes appraised his visitors. His hands rested easily on the table as he watched them in an unhurried silence; still he somehow gave the impression that he might leap upward at a moment's notice.

Jerry and Roy looked at each other, taken aback. Captain Brown's youthful appearance confused them for a moment. The young captain regarded them with a lopsided grin that showed strong white teeth. He was aware of the initial surprise his appearance caused, and had often used it to his own advantage. This time, however, he himself was puzzled by the lads who stood before him. He said so, frankly. "Great, overgrown pups, aren't you?" he drawled. "With your blond locks and your dimples and your drawing-room speech; any lady would love you! Yet you stand here barefoot, in seamen's trousers daubed with tar, and your pretty faces burned like a rare bit of beef. With some wild tales to tell of desert islands and savages, too, it seems. Well, let's hear what you have to say."

Roy flushed, and Jerry began to simmer and clench his

fists; he didn't like this speech. Roy said hastily, "We want to ask, sir, if you will buy the *Swan,* and if you are bound for China."

"What business is it of yours?"

Roy spoke up again, for he knew Jerry's temper and wanted to forestall unpleasantness. He had the instincts of a diplomat, even after five months among the savages. "We have no wish to intrude upon your business, Captain Brown. It's only that we must get to Canton and will ship with you if you are willing."

Captain Brown stared deliberately at Jerry. "What have *you* to say? Can you not use your tongue?"

Jerry blurted, "I have nothing to say, sir. Come, Roy, there will be other ships bound for China."

Roy looked from the crimson face of his brother to the quizzical face of Captain Brown. He was on the point of following Jerry to the door when the Captain said, "Hold on there, lads. I'm only sounding as I go, to see what sort of bottom I have to anchor in. Surely you don't expect a seaman to enter unknown waters without casting the lead!" He leaned back in his chair and spread out his hands with a frank, boyish smile.

Jerry's face cleared. He stepped forward eagerly, "You'll find us handy enough on a ship, sir," he said. "We've picked up a bit of seamanship, and we're both strong. We've been told that you're bound for Canton, and we'd be grateful for a chance to sign with you."

"Very well. I can tell by the look of you that you've soaked up enough salt to be seaworthy." Captain Brown rose from his chair with the suddenness of a steel spring. "But here it is New Year's Eve, and we're all a long way from home, and there's nothing to do with ourselves unless we want to redden our eyes and addle our brains carousing with that crew in there." He jerked a thumb toward the outer room, from whence came the sound of drunken voices. "So before you sign the articles, and we become Captain and crewmen, let's hear what brings two young gentlemen so far from— where *do* you come from, by the by?"

While Roy answered, the youthful captain dragged his sea chest out into the room, gestured Jerry toward it and Roy toward the chair. He himself hopped nimbly into the hammock, where he sprawled with his legs hanging over, his hands clasped behind his head, and an expression of polite attention on his rugged features. Mimbo, who had been nervously watching each one as he spoke, breathed a gusty sigh and arranged himself at Jerry's feet.

Roy began, "Why, we come from Virginia, sir; the Laceys have owned land there for a hundred years. Our home place is called Rivergarden."

"I'm a New Englander myself," Captain Brown observed. "Boston. *We* don't hold with owning black men like cattle."

"You hold with freighting them by the shipload and growing fat on the profits!" flared Jerry. He swallowed, then brought out, "Sir!"

"Those days are over, thank God," the Captain said, unruffled. "But you've hit on the right answer to our pious criticisms. As for the 'sir,' until we take our places on the quarterdeck and in the fo'c'sle, we're too much of an age for me to expect a sir from you. Which one of you is the older? I can't make out."

"We've both had birthdays since we left home," Roy told him. "I'm seventeen. Jerry's a year younger."

"I'm nineteen, but I've been six years at sea, two years of that as First Officer. We start young in my trade. Now I'm master of the brig *Margaret,* and part owner, too. I'll own a fleet before I settle ashore."

Jerry demanded, "Are you purchasing the *Swan*?"

Broderick Brown laughed. "That's what Captain Quincey

would like to know. Here's the proposition I offered him: I'll take the *Swan* off his hands, sail her to Canton, market her furs, and take on a cargo. When I reach Boston, my firm will pay for the *Swan* from her profits and those of the brig. If I make no profits, the *Swan* goes back to her owners."

"What did he say?"

"That I was a dirty robber. Of course he'd rather have hard coin in the hand. But he'll take my offer. There's a whaler in the islands now readying for her home voyage; Captain Quincey won't forgo the chance of a passage on her. He'll agree to my terms, but he's not happy about it—that's why he was in such a sour mood when we left him."

"It was the Northwest Coast savages that turned his stomach," Jerry said. "He's the perfect picture of a captain at sea; I'll vouch for that. He just couldn't deal with the Indians. He was afraid of them, and they knew it. When he picked me up in the Galápagos—"

"Yes, let us get back to the story. What's all this about the Galápagos? You were shipwrecked there?"

"Oh, no. I had myself put ashore there from the Panamá tortoise boat."

Broderick Brown sat up to stare at him; the hammock rocked wildly. "You *what?*"

"I asked them to leave me there. It was for that purpose that I shipped to the Galápagos from the City of Panamá, so that I could get out of Spanish waters and into the path of the traders."

"But how did you come to Panamá City?"

"From the Gulf of San Miguel."

"And by what route did you arrive at the Gulf of San Miguel—wherever that is?"

"Why, I came afoot across the Isthmus, of course." Jerry's dimples deepened with mischief. The mystified expression on Captain Brown's face was as good as a play.

Captain Brown sank back into his hammock. "I'm baffled; I admit it." He turned to Roy. "Can you enlighten me?"

Roy laughed. "I can't tell you anything about Panamá or the Galápagos," he said. "I was on the Northwest Coast at the time, the slave of an Indian Chief."

The hammock rocked like a boat in a gale, and Captain Brown sank into its depths, only his boots left in view. His voice came to them muffled. "Come, come. I don't care who tells the story; but tell it! Out with it!"

Roy and Jerry looked at each other. Jerry raised one eyebrow questioningly, and Roy nodded. They had debated beforehand as to whether they should reveal their complete story. They had decided to tell the whole truth if, after meeting Captain Brown, they felt they could trust him.

They had met Captain Brown, and, though he was very different from what they had expected, they liked him immensely. His candor, his youth, his bright brown eyes and formidable shoulders—oh, yes, they liked him immensely! But both boys remembered how jolly they had thought their Cousin Audley at first, and how dearly they had paid for that mistake. They were cautious now. Still, they had to trust someone. So Roy nodded, and Jerry began:

"We must begin at Rivergarden. That's where we have always lived, with our father. Our mother died before we can remember. We had a tutor, Richard Morris, and everything was as pleasant as could be. When Father married again, it was even pleasanter; Rivergarden is the kind of place that needs a lady—and our stepmother is the most beautiful lady you ever saw, and gracious as a queen. But then Father died."

"He died suddenly one night," Roy explained. "Mr. Morris told our stepmother that Father had shot himself. His story was that Father had played at cards with him and gambled away the farms, the slaves, and Rivergarden—everything he owned. He said that Father shot himself in shame at having lost our inheritance." Roy could not tell this part of the story without his throat tightening with anger. He rose from his chair and walked up and down, while Jerry bounced up from the sea chest.

"It wasn't true, though! I knew it wasn't true, and it wasn't!" Jerry shouted. Finding Captain Brown's eyes snapping at him from over the edge of the hammock, he went on more calmly, "Later on I learned the truth from Benjamin, Father's manservant, who had been with him that night. He said there was no game of cards. While he was away for a few moments, Mr. Morris killed my father and made up the story. Then he threatened Benjamin into running away, so there was no one to dispute his claim. Mrs. Lacey was forced to believe what he told her. She kept it secret from the world, giving out that Father had died of a stroke. She tried to come to terms with Mr. Morris, but he would not alter his demands, so she turned to her cousin—her only male relative—for advice.

"That was Cousin Audley. Captain John Audley, he is. He came to Rivergarden, after visiting Mr. Morris in Baltimore. They had come to an understanding, the villains! What a meeting of rascals! I wish—"

Roy came to his brother's aid. Broderick Brown was sitting up now, giving sober attention. "We were completely taken in by Cousin Audley," Roy said. "He proposed a venture that he said would satisfy Mr. Morris. He proposed that we buy the ship he had sailed on a recent voyage, the *Thunderbird*, which was already equipped with trade goods, and take her to the Northwest Coast to trade for furs. Then here to the Sandwich Islands for sandalwood, then on to Canton to exchange our wares for tea and porcelain, nankeen, and such goods as are in demand at home. Cousin Audley would be master of the vessel, and Jerry and I were to go as owners and supercargoes. He assured us that the profits would be sufficient to ransom the estate from Mr. Morris. We believed his every word."

"It seems a plausible plan," Captain Brown said. "He offered you a sporting chance, at least."

"That is the way he put it to us," Jerry said bitterly. "We did as he said. We bought the *Thunderbird* and set forth with high hopes. Not until we reached the South American port of Corona did we learn of his real plan."

Broderick Brown urged the boys back to their seats. He remained on his feet, balanced as if on a rolling deck. "I know Corona. What happened there?"

"Cousin Audley had me killed."

Captain Brown threw up his hands and turned his back on Jerry.

"He did, Captain Brown! He left me for dead. It was no fault of his if I struggled back to life. Providentially, I fell in with Benjamin then, and together we made our way to the Isthmus. We were looking for a way to get to the Northwest Coast, for I was determined to find Cousin Audley and the *Thunderbird*—and Roy—but Benjamin fell prey to a tropical illness, and I was forced to go on alone. As I told you, Captain Quincey picked me up at the Galápagos in the *Swan*, and we did find Roy on the Northwest Coast, where Cousin Audley had sold him as a slave to the Indians."

Roy rounded out the story. "Cousin Audley tried to kill me in Corona, too, but he failed. As a substitute, he hit upon the plan of abandoning me to the Indians, thinking they'd soon make an end of me and save him the trouble. I met Ching in the Indian village. He had been a slave among them for years, but had never lost hope of getting home to China. If it hadn't been for his faith, I'd have given up a hundred times. But we managed to be with the group who went to Tlatlasikoala to trade. The night they attacked the

Swan, we escaped to the ship. That's how Jerry and I found each other."

"I don't pretend to follow all of this Odyssey," Captain Brown said, "but I begin to understand why you are determined to make the voyage to Canton."

Roy nodded. "We must find Cousin Audley and bring the *Thunderbird* safely home. We must save Mrs. Lacey from Cousin Audley and Mr. Morris. They aim to own Rivergarden, and she stands in their way. We must regain Rivergarden and make those two villains pay for their crimes."

The young captain clapped him on the back. "Hurrah!" he exclaimed. "You have the spirit for it—but do you know the difficulties? Coming up with a ship is one thing. Taking her is another. However, you do not need to deal with the latter problem until you solve the former. Where do you reckon the *Thunderbird* to be now?"

"She left me on the Coast five months ago," Roy said. "She was bound for these islands then, to take on a load of sandalwood and ready herself for the voyage. She might still be at one of the islands—but she is probably even now at Canton."

Jerry reported, "We've inquired wherever we touched in the *Swan.* The *Thunderbird* spent a week here at Waikiki four months ago, but there's no recent news of her."

Captain Brown pondered, "The *Margaret* is taking on provisions at the southern island of Hawaii. If Captain Quincey accepts my offer for the *Swan,* I shall set out tomorrow to join her, since I wish to bring her here in order to transfer her cargo to the *Swan.* She will then return to the Northwest Coast for more furs, while I take the *Swan* to Canton. Perhaps you two would like to accompany me, and see what you can learn of Captain Audley's whereabouts?"

Roy and Jerry forgot themselves in their excitement. Jerry was pounding Captain Brown on the back, Roy was pumping his hand, and Mimbo was dancing around between their feet when they realized what they were doing. They fell back, abashed.

Broderick Brown ignored their embarrassment. "Come ashore in the morning; I expect to finish my business with Captain Quincey early, and then be off," he told them. He strode to the door and banged the flat of his hand against it. "Bring the drinks!" he bellowed. He had a voice like a foghorn when he let it out.

A native boy came timidly through the door, thrust a tray at them, and retreated. Their host raised his hand. "Now for a New Year's toast," he said. "Here's to the return of the *Thunderbird!*"

On the tray were three coconuts, their eyeholes pierced. Captain Brown put one to his mouth, and the boys followed suit. The fresh coconut milk slid down their throats, wonderfully cool and delicious.

A sailor's song was raised in the next room. When it died out, a throbbing of distant drums could be heard from somewhere beyond the palm groves. Underneath all other sounds was the ceaseless whisper of the surf breaking on the reef. But Roy and Jerry were not listening to the sounds of the islands. Their thoughts had turned back to Rivergarden, where they had celebrated the arrival of the New Year only a year ago.

"To the return of the *Thunderbird!*" they echoed.

CHAPTER II

THE FEAST

THE BOYS WENT ashore early next morning in one of the native canoes that came out to the *Swan* with a load of bananas. With them went Mimbo, Ching, and the raven, Kowí, so that when Captain Brown met them on the wharf he found a strangely assorted group awaiting him.

He stopped, his hands on his hips, and looked them over in his disconcerting way. Roy and Jerry greeted him with bright faces, and Mimbo waddled over on his short legs, wagging his tail as if to an old friend. Captain Brown examined the other members of the party. Ching bowed from his waist, his hands folded over his concave middle. His hair, which had grown wild during his years among the Indians, was now shaven except for that portion allotted to his queue, neatly braided with narrow black ribbon. His black eyes sparkled, and his yellow face creased into smiles as he tried to express his gratitude to the young captain who was going to take him home to China. "My t'ankee; my go China-side. My make largee t'ing wood, my work," he said.

Captain Brown nodded. "We can use a good hand in the carpenter shop," he told him. "You'll pay your way." Ching bowed again and again, chuckling. Roy could tell that he approved of their new friend.

Kowí returned the Captain's gaze with suspicion. Unsettled by Ching's bows, he flopped from his shoulder and established himself on Roy's, making a resentful noise in his throat.

"The Kanakas will be here shortly with the canoes,"

13

Captain Brown said. "The journey we plan is counted a long one in these parts, and they are going through some ceremonies of preparation in their heiau yonder. Why don't you take a stroll about the town and stretch your legs before you must jackknife them into a canoe?"

Before the boys could answer, Ching pointed to the water. "Look-see."

A boat was coming off from the *Swan,* and they recognized in the bow the upright figure of Captain Quincey, dressed in his black broadcloth and starched linen and surrounded with baggage. Mr. Hart, the first mate, sat beside him.

Jerry grinned. "You were right, Captain Brown. He's brought all his gear ashore."

Captain Brown strode to the landing to meet the *Swan's* officers. The three men spoke briefly and moved off to the Captain's quarters. Roy, Jerry, and Ching amused themselves watching the sailors unload Captain Quincey's gear, the scene being enlivened by the arrival of two native canoes, larger than the usual craft that plied back and forth in the bay. The natives, fine, strapping men girded for travel in kapa loincloths, had scarcely drawn their vessels on the sand when the two captains came out again, one very gay and the other very dour. Mr. Hart wore a self-conscious look, as if he were trying to keep his feelings hidden.

Captain Quincey spoke stiffly to the *Swan's* seamen standing by the boat. "Captain Brown is the new master of the *Swan,*" he told them. "Since he is making a journey to the southern island, Mr. Hart will be in command until he returns. During that time every man will have his turn at shore leave."

The sailors raised a cheer, which Captain Quincey shut off with a gesture. Captain Brown then spoke to the men. "I understand that all of you signed on for the voyage to China and return to Boston; therefore I assume that most of you will stay with the *Swan* despite her change of masters. But if any man does not care to accept a new master, he will be paid off, with no questions asked, and no hard feelings. I want no man aboard my ship who is not willing—and able."

The men nodded, shuffling their feet under their new captain's sharp appraisal. "Mr. Hart has my orders," Captain Brown went on. "It will be his task to make the ship ready for sea. You will have to sail her, so it behooves you to see that she is seaworthy. Very well, Mr. Hart; carry on."

Handshakes over, Captain Quincey stalked away, followed by a squad of native boys carrying his baggage. Captain Brown turned to Kalana, the headman of the Kanakas, and they spoke together in the native tongue. "Look lively, lads," the Captain then told the boys. "Passengers in the starboard vessel, luggage and provisions in the other."

Having no baggage to speak of, Roy, Jerry, Ching, Kowí, and Mimbo stowed themselves away without fuss. Captain Brown delayed but a moment to oversee the final loading; then they were afloat, paddling rapidly out of the tangle of canoes and shipping that obstructed the bay.

The sea wind felt glorious. The sun danced on the water, and, looking back, the passengers saw the shining beach, guarded by the long breakers crashing on the reef. The canoes paralleled the shore; ahead of them rose a beetling mass of land that cut off the prevailing northeast winds sweeping from the vast spaces of the Pacific through Kaiwi Channel. Now the Kanakas hoisted sail.

Captain Brown watched them approvingly, noting many ingenious combinations of native and European methods. "There's not much these fellows don't know about seamanship," he observed. "They make the best sailors in the world. If any dissatisfied citizen decides to leave the *Swan*, I've only to nod at one of these islanders to replace him."

As the day wore on, Roy and Jerry saw more and more

reason to agree with Broderick Brown's high opinion of the natives. Their seamanship was superb. The canoes rode the water like ducks. Faster and faster they sped, heeling over so that their outriggers rose out of the water. Accustomed to the more stately motion of ships, Roy and Jerry clung to the cross booms lashed across the gunwales, expecting to be spilled into the bottle-green brine at any moment. Ching squeezed his eyes shut, and Mimbo crawled between Jerry's legs. Up and up rose the float. Roy wondered why Captain Brown did not put in a word. But just when the canoe seemed to tilt beyond recovery, several of the Islanders sprang nimbly onto the booms, forcing the float down with their weight. They balanced there, laughing, while the water hissed under their bare feet.

"Bueno!" applauded Jerry, who still used some of the Spanish words he had picked up during his adventures in the Caribbean.

"They're splendid fellows," Roy agreed. "My friends on the Northwest Coast build fine canoes, too, and are handy on the water. But they seldom use sails, and I never had a ride like this with them! What's your opinion, Ching? This more better, eh?"

Ching opened his eyes cautiously, ducked his head, and smiled. "More better sunshine, more better smilee," he said.

Roy drew in the bright, mild air, and nodded. The smiling faces and musical voices of the islanders were indeed different from the scowls and gutturals of Chief Tom-Tom's people. As different as the soft fragrant breeze of the islands was from the chill fogs of the Northwest Coast.

Jerry was watching his chance. When the outrigger rose again, he was ready, and as the first Kanaka climbed out along the boom, Jerry was close behind him.

"Ahoy!" cried Captain Brown, turning just in time to see what he was doing.

He was too late to stop Jerry. Jerry was poised on the long spar connecting the float with the canoe, his hair blown into his eyes by the wind, his arms flailing to keep his balance. The Kanakas, agile as dancers, shifted their places to compensate for his clumsy weight. They called to one another and to the crew of the other canoe, gesturing comically between gales of laughter.

Jerry laughed, too, but he saw his fate coming speedily. The canoe skipped like a flung pebble; Jerry tipped backward. His feet came up; his head went down; the next moment he was swimming for dear life, with the canoe already an astonishing distance beyond him.

Jerry expected a tongue-lashing from Captain Brown and would have taken it meekly, for he felt he deserved it. But the young captain, like the islanders, was in a holiday mood, and the worst Jerry got for his folly was his wetting. The friendly sunshine dried him long before they came to shore.

The winds were less boisterous when they left Kaiwi Channel astern and sailed under the lee of Molokai. Soon they had four islands in their view. A warm note of pride rang in Kalana's voice as he called their attention to his home island, "Maui!"

"We stay at Kalana's village tonight," Captain Brown told his passengers. Later he pointed to smoke rising above the green forest a short distance inland. Already they could see canoes coming out through the tumbling surf to meet them.

Kalana and his men began to sing. The music of their chant was thrilling, emerging exultantly from their deep chests in time to their movements as they furled the sails and set themselves to bring in the canoes by the strength of their own arms. Answering calls echoed across the water. Roy and Jerry looked with some apprehension at the seething white water ahead. To them it appeared an impossible barrier. But their islanders drove forward without a moment's hesitation. Skillfully the canoes rode the incoming rollers and raced through the foam crashing all about them. For an instant the world was all tumult: dizzying motion and noise that deafened the ears. Then they glided into green, quiet waters inhabited by a race of merry mermen. Splashing and laughing, the villagers swam alongside the canoes to greet the new arrivals.

Two small wet hands fastened on the gunwale beside Roy and a mermaid rose into view—a girl, naked to the waist, with streaming brown hair. Her laughing face took on an expression of amazement as she saw Roy. She stared at his fair hair and blue eyes, her mouth shaped into a startled O. Roy, just as surprised, stared back. Her eyes darted to Jerry, then back again to Roy. Her astonishment apparently more than she could contain, she slid back into the water as suddenly as she emerged. With one backward glance full of mirth, she ducked beneath the surface and disappeared.

Roy leaned far out. "Where did she go? Where did she go?" he cried. The water was full of sleek, seal-like heads, and everywhere he looked were bright, mirthful eyes and flashing smiles. But the girl was gone.

Jerry laughed till he choked. "If only you could see your face!" he crowed. "I wouldn't have believed it could possibly turn redder than the sun has already cooked it! Have you never seen a girl before?"

"Of course I have! But I— But she—" he made such hard work of it that Jerry laughed louder than ever.

"What would Rosalie think?" he teased.

"Now, look here—" Roy seldom lost his temper, but something in the incident had covered him with confusion, and the mention of Rosalie's name was the last straw. Rosalie McAllister had become so much more than the playmate and neighbor she had always been to him and Jerry at Rivergarden. Every mile he had traveled away from her had strengthened her hold on his heart. He half rose from the thwart on which he sat. "Look here!"

Broderick Brown interfered. "Belay that!" He spoke in his quarterdeck voice.

Roy sank back, but his face was set. Jerry muttered, "Can't you take a joke?"

"I'll have no joking about Rosalie," Roy said.

"Pshaw!" said Jerry. "I would not use her name lightly for all the tea in China, and you know it. What's the matter with you? Just because an island girl in a state of nature cuts her eyes at you—"

"Let be!" Broderick Brown interposed again. "Older heads than yours have been troubled by the charms of these dusky sirens. I lost a good Boston man to the islands on my last voyage. I saw what was in his head and tried to knock some sense into it; but he deserted the ship one night off Kauai and has never been heard of since."

Willing hands drew the canoes up the beach. Mimbo was the first to leap ashore, where he ran back and forth on the sand, torn between his yearning to explore the many-scented land and his loyalty to Jerry. Captain Brown followed, then Jerry and Roy, their dispute forgotten in the interest of their surroundings. Ching stepped out gingerly and looked about him, Kowí on his shoulder. But the clamor was too much for Kowí. With a hoarse cry he flapped upward and took refuge in the nearest tree.

A stately palm grove stretched before them, some of the long-fringed leaves almost overhanging the water. The sun, setting out to sea, stretched long shadows like guiding pointers toward the village half-hidden in the depths of the grove. Barking dogs, dancing children, and a crowd of men and women surged around Kalana and his men. Greetings were exchanged as friends and families were reunited.

Nor were the foreigners overlooked. A tall, portly man stepped from the crowd and gravely offered Captain Brown his hand. He wore, in addition to the kapa loincloth, which was the common dress of all the men, a handsome cloak of brilliant colored feathers. His body, wherever it was left bare, was seen to be covered with the most intricate patterns of tattooing, and a small human figure carved in bone hung around his neck. His voice, when he spoke, was deep and resonant. *"Aloha oukou."*

Captain Brown answered, *"Aloha olua."* Although the island chief was twice his age and towered over him, Jerry and Roy thought their new friend, the young captain, looked quite as much a chief as he in his own way. He stood erect and sturdy, meeting the chief's direct gaze with equal frankness, and conversing confidently, if haltingly, in the native tongue. He introduced his companions, and Ching and each of the boys received in turn a warm pressure of the hand and a gracious welcoming address of which they could not understand one syllable.

"Ask him if he has seen the *Thunderbird*," Jerry reminded Captain Brown.

Captain Brown put the question, and the islanders discussed it among themselves. "They appear to have heard the name," the Captain reported. "They say they have heard of such a ship from friends on Hawaii, but that she has not touched at this island."

"On Hawaii!" repeated Roy. "Then surely we can find news of her there."

The Chief spoke again. "The Chief, Koa, invites us to his village," Captain Brown explained. "It is still the *Makahiki* season, a time of feasting and games. He invites us to remain a week and take part in the festivities."

They followed the Chief and his party, while the merry villagers scampered on ahead or lingered in the rear to stare curiously at the foreigners. Roy was captivated by the grace of their movements and the soft music of their language. As dusk fell, small smoky candlenut flames came alive in the village, and the tantalizing fragrance of cooking drifted abroad. A fire burned in a clearing about which the thatched huts were grouped. Silhouetted against its glow the lithe figures of men and women moved back and forth.

"I would like to stay," Roy thought. But the memory of the *Thunderbird* overpowered all other desires. "Captain Brown, you will not delay here?" he asked, his voice charged with urgency.

At his shoulder Jerry echoed his anxiety. "You promised you would set sail as soon as possible. You must not—"

Broderick Brown laughed shortly. "The master of a ship little likes the word 'must,' even on a holiday ashore. Use it less and live longer, my lad." He let this reproof take effect, then said, "Spare yourselves any concern in the matter. My resolution is taken, and no island frolic will tempt me to change it. We will proceed at daylight."

Relieved, the boys found themselves entering into the festival spirit of the occasion. In the clearing a bountiful feast was taking shape before their eyes. The women had disappeared like smoke, yet their voices could be heard not far away, laughing. Koa, Kalana, and other principal men of the village led the way to the mats spread on the ground. As they took their places, Captain Brown, Roy, Jerry, and Ching were allotted spaces beside them. Before them were spread great freshly washed green leaves, and on the leaves a feast that must have been poured out from some tropical cornucopia.

With much talk and laughter the men and older boys fell to. All the bounty of the sea was there: fish and shellfish, crabs, shrimp, eels, squid, and turtle. All the fruits of the land were added: gourd bowls full of poi and pudding, sweet potatoes, plantains, yams, breadfruit, bananas, coconuts. For meat there was succulent roast pig and chicken.

Jerry ate so heartily that he soon had to lean back and rest. "It has been a long time since I have had such good food, and in such plenty," he sighed. "When I left the Galápagos, I thought I would never again care to eat fish—but these islanders have the art of preparing it to a king's taste! And all the meats as well. What is that you're eating, Ching?"

"Dog," replied Ching, with relish.

Jerry looked away hastily. He felt Mimbo behind him, leaning against his back. He had not strayed far from Jerry since coming ashore; there were too many dogs in the village. He had been well fed from Jerry's share, and now lay at ease, sampling like a connoisseur the variety of odors on the breeze. Jerry looked up at the sky above the clearing, spangled with stars.

Roy had overheard. He knew Jerry's soft heart and squeamish stomach. "Never mind," he told him, "Eat some fruit and think of the beauties of the place. When I recall the stinking houses and rotting fish heads that fell to my lot on the Northwest Coast, I'm most grateful for the cleanliness of this food."

Jerry mustered a smile. "It *is* beautiful," he agreed. "It confirms all the stories we have heard describing these islands as an earthly Paradise. But there's something wrong with Paradise if dogs are used for food."

"That only proves that it's an *earthly* Paradise," Roy replied. "Apparently there's no spot on earth free from ugliness or evil. Even at Rivergarden—" His voice grew hard. "Even at Rivergarden there is treachery and murder."

Jerry forgot his stomach. "Roy," he said, "I'm fearful for the safety of our stepmother. With us far away, she's at the mercy of Mr. Morris! Would he dare attempt to do her further harm?"

Roy had thought a great deal about this question. "I think not," he said. "Mrs. Lacey is no frail girl, but a mature woman of intelligence. She is warned against him. She doesn't know of Cousin Audley's treachery, but we'll be able to send letters home by Captain Quincey, telling her the truth. And we can write to Rosalie, and to her father. Mr. McAllister will help us."

"Wait. Is it wise to write the truth to anyone other than Mrs. Lacey? Until we return, nothing can be proved, and should Mr. Morris hear in advance of our plans, he would be armed against us."

Roy pondered. "Perhaps you're right. He supposes us to be dead. . . . Yes, you *are* right. It's to our advantage to keep him in ignorance." Roy felt a keen disappointment. He wished ardently to write to Rosalie. He wanted her, at least, to know he was still alive and on his way back to Rivergarden. On his way back—but by what route? When would he and Jerry see Rivergarden again?

"I've often heard of the skeleton at the feast," Captain Brown broke in upon their thoughts. "Here we have two of them, if skeletons can be supposed to consume such quantities of food as I have seen go down your gullets tonight. Enough of solemn conversation! We are guests of honor, and Koa and Kalana have gone to considerable trouble to amuse us." He nudged Jerry in the ribs. "But why do I waste my breath? It's time for the dancing. I defy you to keep a solemn face five minutes longer!"

Koa rose and led the party to another clearing. Only a few palm trunks rose between them and the starlit beach, where the white surf churned murmurously. The women were there before them, some seated in groups, some dancing languorously as the musicians took their places.

The only musical instruments were drums of many sizes, but no lack was felt when the singing began. The blending of male and female voices was perfectly harmonious, and some individual voices were distinguished by their range and sweetness. Accompanied by the throbbing drums, the rhythmic murmur of the surf, and the whisper of the palm leaves, the effect of the whole was magical.

But the real weavers of magic spells were the dancers. With the movements of their bodies they created every emotion. The maidens, decked with flowers, shaped stories from the air with the gentlest, most insinuating of gestures: stories of ancient goddesses and ancient lovers, stories of the fern trees and the waterfalls. The young men performed war dances and mimic games exhibiting virile feats of agility and skill. The older men and women enacted legends of their race, grave dramas of great antiquity.

There were comic dances, too, whose broad humor sent gales of laughter round the circle of spectators. An old scarecrow of a man and a fat, foolish-faced young woman were the favorite buffoons. After dancing until they were spent, they lay down and pretended to sleep, while the young men and girls danced over them. Now and again the sleepers would seize a skirt and unfasten it, or trip a dancer so that he sprawled on the earth. Highly amused at first, Jerry began to tire of the festivities, and to think longingly of bed. Roy, on the other hand, had no thought of rest. The throbbing drums and leaping figures had his blood in a ferment. His eyes searched among the dancers. All evening he had been looking for that girl.

There were dozens of girls. They all had clouds of dark hair, small, graceful hands, golden bodies, and mirthful eyes. How could he tell which was the girl who had clung to his canoe? And why should he care?

He felt that he could sit still no longer. He could not hear

the drums for the throbbing in his temples. He started to
rise.

Broderick Brown put his hand on his arm. His smile in-
cluded drowsy Jerry and restless Roy, seeming to understand them both. He spoke with surprising gentleness.
"Come, we must not offend our hosts. Courtesy requires that
they recite their genealogies, and that we listen to them.
Even the commoners can trace their families back five hundred years. A chief like Koa follows his line back to the Original Void."

"*Caramba!*" groaned Jerry. "Let me find a palm trunk to
prop myself against, and I'll have a nap."

CHAPTER III

NEWS

JERRY DID NOT get his nap until after midnight, when the villagers retired and the foreigners were left to rest in one of the thatched cottages that made up Koa's establishment. Lying on soft kapa, lulled by the music of wave and breeze, and tired by their long day of travel, the party lost no time in sinking into a sound sleep.

True to his promise, Captain Brown roused them before daylight. Kowí rejoined them when they reached the beach, and at dawn the canoes were pushed off from the dark shore into the pale radiance of the sea. A few hours later they left astern the green bulk of Maui and sailed toward Hawaii across the open water.

As they sailed, Kalana and his crew sang an ancient chant of their voyaging ancestors. Captain Brown translated fragments for his companions. "... Hawaii of the green back ... a land made in the waters ... drawn up from the depths ... caught on the fisherman's hook ... the great fisherman, Kapu-he'e-ua-nui."

"What does it mean?" asked Jerry.

Captain Brown questioned Kalana. "It is said that these islands were fished up from the sea by a legendary hero of the race." He passed on the information as Kalana answered. "Hawaii was the first and largest of the islands. It was named for its discoverer, Hawaii Roa, who sailed from far to the south. Accustomed to range far in his fishing expeditions, one day he sailed even farther, led by the Pleiades and the Morning Star. He passed from the Sea-Where-the-Fish-Do-Run into the Many-Colored-Sea-of-Kane. Still far-

ther he went, into the Deep-Colored Sea, where he found a
green island. So desirable did it seem that he returned to his
home for his family and his followers. They were the first
people to set foot on these shores."

The wind had freshened, and the soft clouds that had
hung over the heights of Maui when they took their departure now raced after them and blanketed the sky. The sea
ran high. The islanders wrapped their kapa cloaks about
them, while the foreigners hunched their shoulders under
their jackets. The rain, driven by the wind, stung the flesh
and filled the eyes; it churned the surface of the sea until
it seemed that as much water rose up as fell down. The canoes, tossed and pelted, wrenched and driven, began to fill
with water.

Sails furled, all hands fell to bailing, with the exception
of Mimbo, Jerry, Kowí, and the steersmen. Mimbo and Jerry
were overcome with seasickness, and had all they could do
to stay aboard the struggling canoe. Kowí, buttoned within
Roy's jacket, moped resentfully. The steersmen battled to
keep their craft head on into the seas, which rose, lifting the
bows of the canoes skyward, then fell away suddenly, leaving nothing beneath them but backbreaking space.

Roy, Captain Brown, and Ching baled steadily, warmed
by the labor in spite of the icy rain. Kalana shouted instructions to his crew. At intervals a conch shell was blown as
a signal to the other canoe, no longer visible. Faintly
through the tumult they could hear a mournful but reassuring note in reply.

The storm passed as quickly as it came. The raindrops
scattered, the clouds drew apart; and the sea subsided into
long glassy swells. The baggage canoe was sighted on their
starboard quarter at no great distance. Jerry, opening his
eyes at last, forgot his misery. Dead ahead loomed the island
of the song; Hawaii of the Green Back, with misty clouds

just breaking away to reveal a snow-capped peak gleaming in the sunlight. Between the canoes and the island quivered the ghost of a rainbow.

All day they sailed within sight of the west coast of the island. Not one snow-covered peak, but two, crowned the distant heights. The landscape offered every variety, from wild jungle to cultivated grove; hot lava waste and beetling crag; cool waterfall, dusty path, peaceful village of peaked thatched huts secluded in the shade. Looking down over the gunwale of the canoe, another landscape of equal interest was revealed in the clear shallows. There were strange forests of moss and seaweed, precipices and caves of coral. This underwater land had its inhabitants, too: legions of fantastic fishes and living creatures shaped in the likeness of flowers and stars.

Twice the rain clouds gathered and drenched them, but in the lee of the island they were able to weather each squall without shortening sail. The late afternoon sun was smiling again when Ching, whose keen eyes were always first to sight the goal, raised his arm and pointed, "Look-see. Two-piecee bamboo!"

Rounding a low, barren point of land, they saw a wide bay. Behind the black volcanic cliffs of the shore were many cultivated enclosures and clusters of native huts shaded by coconut and breadfruit trees. These cultivated plots gave way to dense forests as the land rose toward the backbone of the island; the forest, in turn, giving way to the naked rock and the snow-capped peak of Mauna Loa. A vast number of canoes moved back and forth across the bay, and amid them rose the two masts of a European style vessel, the first the travelers had seen since quitting the *Swan*. "It's the *Margaret*, right enough," Captain Brown said. "All's well, it seems."

Kealakekua Bay was the most populous place Roy and

Jerry had yet seen in the islands. At the largest of the villages that bordered its shores, Mr. Haverhill, the first mate of the *Margaret*, had established his headquarters. He met Captain Brown's party on the beach and led them to his hut at the end of the village. Nearby were tents put up for the *Margaret's* men.

"I had to pay for the property," Mr. Haverhill said. "The natives have learned a lot about business since the day Captain Cook sailed into the bay and they thought he was a god. It cost me an ax for the subchief, a coat with brass buttons for the chief, a musket for the King's councilor, and a real silver timepiece for the King himself. But we've made good use of it. The sick are recovering nicely, and each watch takes its trick ashore. The sailmaker and the carpenter have set up their shops yonder. We've made good progress with the repairs to the brig, and we've been supplied with provisions in plenty."

"Is she ready to sail?" Captain Brown broke in.

Mr. Haverhill had shown no surprise at the appearance of Roy, Jerry, Ching, Kowí, and Mimbo, and remained unmoved by the Captain's sudden question. "She is if you say she is, sir," he answered, dryly. He was a tall young man with a stiffness in his back that made him list forward. This, together with his weathered face and his dry, unhurried manner of speech, gave him the look of premature age.

"Put her in readiness, then, to make sail tomorrow as soon as may be. You will put us ashore at Waikiki, and return in the brig to the Northwest Coast, as master. I shall take command of the *Swan*, and proceed to Canton."

"Aye, aye, sir," said Mr. Haverhill, receiving his promotion without batting an eye. He touched his cap and turned to go.

Jerry could stand the suspense no longer. He blurted, "Sir, we are seeking news of the ship, *Thunderbird*, out of Norfolk, John Audley, master. Have you seen her?"

A spark of interest brightened Mr. Haverhill's narrow gray eyes. "I've not seen her, but I've heard of her," he replied.

Roy's heart gave a jolt. He and Jerry spoke at once. "Where is she?" "Did she touch here?" "When?" "Where was she bound?" Their words tumbled over each other.

Broderick Brown took command. "Belay-oh!" He silenced the boys. "Mr. Haverhill, we'd be obliged if you can give us any information about the *Thunderbird*."

To Roy and Jerry, Captain Brown's "we" had a grateful sound. Although they were determined to pursue the *Thunderbird* and attempt her recovery with nothing but their own bare hands, they were well aware of their weakness in the face of such a task. They did not expect Captain Brown to put himself out to help them—yet he had used the word "we"! They waited eagerly for Mr. Haverhill's reply.

The master of the *Margaret* seated himself upon one of the nail kegs with which he had furnished the space just outside the door of his hut, indicating that his guests should do the same. Ching preferred to squat upon the ground, his back against the thatched wall. Kowí had taken wing at the sight of strangers, but he came back now and perched warily in a nearby clump of bamboo. Mimbo trotted around the yard, sniffing contentedly.

"What I've heard of Captain Audley ain't good," Mr. Haverhill came directly to the point. "If he's a friend of yours I wouldn't noise the fact abroad, for it won't make you popular here. The story goes that he first came to Kealakekua a year or so ago, leaving behind a couple of men to cut sandalwood. These men spent most of their time in the hills with a crew of natives; when they'd cut all they could carry, they'd bring it down to the village yonder. They built a shed to house the wood while it was waiting. They'd gather up a new crew then and go back for more. Everything was peaceful; Captain Audley was in the good graces of King Kamehameha's councilors, and the men both took native wives for themselves and acquired in-laws of the higher class. But the King is no fool; he came to the conclusion one day that if the sandalwood was of value to Captain Audley, it was of value to him, too. He told the men they could deliver the wood they had already cut to the Captain when he came, but could take no more. Then he invited them to cut wood for him.

"Well, the seamen saw no harm in that. They had to await Captain Audley's return in any case, and were as willing to be employed by a king as by anyone. They built another shed for King Kamehameha's wood, and the priests put a *kapu* upon it.

"Well, by the time Captain Audley arrived in the *Thunderbird*, the King's shed was as full as the Captain's. He—"

"When was this?" Jerry interrupted. Roy nudged him. "Sir?"

Mr. Haverhill considered. "About three months ago, I reckon. The incident had not been forgotten when I came. The natives were still in a suspicious mood. It was only with difficulty that I—"

"What incident? What happened?" This time it was Captain Brown who interrupted.

Mr. Haverhill squinted at his audience, then at the sunset over the bay, refusing to be hurried. "It seems," he went on at last, "that Captain Audley claimed all the sandalwood for himself. Before the natives knew what he planned, he broke the *kapu* and had the wood stowed aboard the *Thunderbird* at night. The two men wouldn't go with him, though; they made for the hills. When the Captain sent a search party for them, their native friends gathered to help them. They escaped, but two of the natives were killed, and the bay was buzzing like a hornet's nest before the *Thunder-*

bird got underway. Captain Audley will find no welcome here as long as the King lives."

"I understand that King Kamehameha now rules all the islands with the exception of the two most northerly," Captain Brown said. "His power grows hourly. It is likely that the *Thunderbird* did not dare touch land after escaping this place, unless she did so at Kauai or Niihau. I venture to say she sailed for China within the week, and reached her destination at least a month ago."

Roy exclaimed, "Then we may expect to find her still there! Captain Audley intended to remain on the China coast until spring; he said one could not complete a cargo in less time."

Jerry could not contain his joy. He gave vent to a smothered, "View halloo!" and began to dance a shuffle he had learned in the quarters at Rivergarden as a child. Mimbo raced to join the fun, barking at his heels.

Broderick Brown, Roy, and Ching laughed at their antics, while Mr. Haverhill rose stiffly. "I'll go pass along the orders," he said.

Jerry paused, panting, and Captain Brown told him, "That's right. Save your breath for the dancing at the feast tonight."

"Feast? Another feast?" Jerry gasped.

Captain Brown gestured toward the path that led to the village. Already it was dusk, and a procession of islanders was coming toward them, carrying torches. In the lead were a group of chiefs, splendidly clad in feather capes and helmets. "Here they come now, to invite us."

Jerry grinned. "Let 'em come!" he cried. "I'm ready. I'm in a mood to dance tonight!"

And at the feast, he proved it; after eating six kinds of shellfish and a whole hen, he and Roy danced a minuet, to the great delight of the island audience.

CHAPTER IV

UNDERWAY

"NO MORE FEASTS and no more minuets," Jerry grumbled. "From now on it'll be 'Show a leg!' and 'Lay aloft!' and cussing fore and aft and 'thwart the ship."

Roy nodded. They were back on the *Swan;* back in their places as the youngest and least experienced hands aboard. Again they took up their cramped quarters in the fo'c'sle, a dark, malodorous hole in the eyes of the ship where a ray of sunshine never penetrated. Kowí was denied even this shelter, having long since been exiled because of his thievish raids upon the sailors' pantry. He was tolerated only in the carpenter shop, where Ching assisted a taciturn Scotsman. Ching held long conversations with Kowí in his native Cantonese, which Kowí appeared to understand, at least as well as he understood English.

Mimbo resumed, with zest, his self-appointed duty of hunting rats. His success made him popular with the sailors, who cursed him only mildly even when he woke them in the midst of a chase.

The crew, in general, was an easygoing lot, less ruffianly than the crew of the *Thunderbird.* But on the *Thunderbird* Roy and Jerry had been the owners, observing the men at a distance as a necessary part of the ship; now they were common seamen themselves, or tried to be. Their companions felt something different in them, and some resented it. There had been unpleasant incidents when Jerry had first come aboard, and Roy and Ching had met the same hostility. But the novelty soon wore off; the newcomers kept their

33

own council and worked with a will; so that finally they were accepted, more or less.

Roy and Jerry found the fo'c'sle buzzing with talk about the new captain of the *Swan*. They had no sooner left the village of Waikiki astern than they were assailed with questions about Captain Brown.

"I've heard he can lift a sea anchor with one hand," said Peter Blue, a young New Englander with fuzzy cheeks and an Adam's apple that worked up and down when he talked.

"Ha!" jeered black-browed Joe García, whose origin was unknown, "and *I* 'ave 'eard dat 'e's so yong 'e don't shave yet, and don't dreenk nothing but de meelk of coconuts."

The bo'sun spat and wiped his hand across his mouth. "Some people believe everything they hear," he remarked to no one in particular. "I've knowed men that served under Captain Brown. They say he can sail rings around a hurricane and outwit a Barbary pirate, and he gets his ship there, and he fetches it home again. That's enough for me."

"Here's the lads that get took for pleasure jaunts with the Captain," a voice drawled from the darkness of an upper bunk. "They're the ones to give us information about the bloomin' aristocracy."

"Come on, speak up!" demanded other voices. "Is he as young as they say?" "Is he as strong as we hear?" "Is it true he takes a bath every morning before breakfast?" "Is it true he don't drink spirits, nor have nothing to do with females?" "Why, I heered he had a harem in Batavia."

Roy for once was at a loss for the right thing to say, but Jerry laughed, and answered, "We only rode in the same canoe with the Captain. He didn't tell us his life history."

A head was raised out of the upper bunk, a sneer on its face. It was the sailor called the Duke, from the fact that he was forever mimicking what he called the "upper clawsses." He was thought to be British, but professed to hate the

"limeys" and their ships. He persisted, "Oh, come now, is
that all you can say?"

"From what we saw on board the *Margaret,* he's a good
seaman. He keeps a strict ship, but he's fair with all hands."

"A verrytubble parygone," drawled the Duke, unpleasantly.

The bos'un set an example by swinging himself into his
hammock. "We'll know all about the Old Man by the time
we sight the China Coast," he said. "Anybody that wants a
wink of sleep before we reach Niihau had better turn in."

At Niihau the *Swan* took on a good supply of the yams for
which the island was famous, besides a quantity of coconuts
and some hogs, which excited Mimbo beyond endurance.
Next day the ship bore off and made all sail for China.

Pleasant northeast trade winds, strong favorable currents,
and a smooth sea gave promise of easy days for the seamen,
but they were soon disillusioned. The first day out was de-
voted to the killing and salting of twenty large hogs. A few
hours at this distasteful task tried Roy's and Jerry's spirits
more than a week of rough weather. The deck became a
slaughterhouse. The bones must be removed from the meat,
and the latter salted and laid between two hatches upon
which a heavy weight was left overnight. Next morning the
meat had to be examined and packed away in barrels of
brine; the barrels had to be stowed away, and the decks had
to be swabbed and holystoned to meet the exacting eyes of
Mr. Hart—and the more remote but even more exacting eyes
of Captain Brown, who seemed only to glance forward at
rare intervals, but saw everything.

The days wore on, with not a squall to mar the horizon,
but Roy and Jerry found all their spare time occupied in
cleaning furs. All the furs that had been aboard the *Margaret* had been transferred to the *Swan,* which already carried
a considerable store. Many had been imperfectly cleaned,
others not at all, while even those that had already had at-

tention must now be hauled out, inspected, and exposed to the sun and air.

Ching, Roy, and Jerry sat in a row under the break of the fo'c'sle head, solemnly engaged in combing and scraping a pile of stinking furs. Suddenly Ching began to chuckle. "Allee same monkey!"

Jerry grinned sourly. "A monkey would do a better job. I wish Breakfast were here—you remember, I told you about the monkey I had in Panamá. He would have made short work of these vermin."

"Why didn't you bring him along?" Roy asked.

"I knew it would be too cold for him on the Northwest Coast, so I left him with Benjamin. Perhaps I'll meet them both again some day. Benjamin promised to follow me as soon as he got well."

"He'll do it, too, if he promised," Roy said. He closed his eyes and inhaled cautiously. "I can imagine that I am back in Chief Tom-Tom's house right now. Doesn't the fragrance seem familiar, Ching?"

Ching wrinkled his nose. "Allee same olo fish."

Roy laughed. "There were some good smells, though. The smell of the forests and of wood smoke and of bear meat sizzling on a stick. There were good friends, too. You and Yumqas and Numis and even Chief Tom-Tom, in his way. And Kowí."

"Kowí!" exclaimed Jerry. "I'll fetch him. He's just the one to help us at this work."

Kowí did, indeed, prove to have a talent for the work. He would cock his head, then pounce with unerring aim upon the crawling inhabitants of the furs. When the sailors saw him demonstrate his art, his status aboard the *Swan* changed overnight. Kowí was welcomed wherever he chose to alight; indeed, his services were purchased with titbits from the mess kids.

On Captain Brown's ship there was always work, no matter what the weather. On fair days the lockers were cleaned and all rope stores were roused up on deck to sun. When it rained, the ropes and canvas that had been wet with salt water were brought out for a washing. Between other tasks there was oakum to pick or cargo nets to repair or practice in making knots or splices.

Jerry took his seamanship seriously. He applied himself to the mastery of the bowline knot, the clove hitch, the marling hitch, the carrick bend, the eye splice, the short splice, the long splice, and the manufacture of grommets and cringles. Whenever he was not put to work elsewhere, it was his delight to station himself in the leadsman's chains and swing the lead. This required an experienced hand, and more often than not Jerry got himself and the line thoroughly entangled with the foreshrouds, an object of ridicule to his fellows.

Roy joined in the laughter. "Heaven only knows how many fathoms of water lie between us and the ocean bed," he told him. "No lead in the world could sound these deeps. Why do you waste your time?"

"You have the mind of a planter," Jerry retorted good-naturedly, untangling the kinks from his line.

"I *am* a planter," Roy agreed. "I intend to be a planter the rest of my life, if ever we reclaim Rivergarden. You speak as if—surely you're not thinking of remaining a sailor?"

"Sometimes I think I shall. I shouldn't mind becoming master of a ship in a few years, like Captain Brown. There's one thing I do mind, though, and that is being rousted out for the watch. Then I dream of my bed at home, where I used to sleep until the sun awoke me, as nature intended."

"Nature intended for you to live in your father's house and cultivate your father's farms," Roy said earnestly. "Why must you dally with the idea of following the sea?"

Jerry had his line clear and prepared again to cast the lead. "Why must you waste your time worrying about the future?" He laughed, swinging the lead back and forth. "Tomorrow I'll tell you what I'm going to do tomorrow. In the meantime I'm a sailor, and I intend to be a good one!"

Although there were some small islands in these far empty reaches of the Pacific, the *Swan* sighted no land for weeks. The world had been reduced to water and sky. The impatience with which Roy, Jerry, and Ching had embarked at Waikiki had subsided. They no longer talked or even thought often of China or the *Thunderbird*, but only of the ship, the sea, the sky, and the weather. But one day during the forenoon watch the lookout called, "Land ho!"

Mr. Hart sprang to the rail. "Where away?"

"Two points on the starboard bow, sir!"

"That would be the Bashee Isles," Mr. Hart said.

Captain Brown was on deck as the islands came into view. He watched until their pattern became familiar—a far-flung chain. "We'll not be able to weather them with the wind from the northeast," he told Mr. Hart. "Bear off to run between Grafton and Monmouth."

With the cries of the sea birds and the smell of land, excitement again took possession of Roy and Jerry. Their watch was below when the *Swan* came between the islands, doubled Grafton, and luffed close under the lee of Orange Isle. But the boys were on deck, leaning over the rail and straining their eyes through the darkness to see the land. They could see fires on shore, but that was all. Turning to go below, they found Ching at their elbow, as wakeful as they.

The next day they saw the island of Formosa lying east by north at twelve leagues' distance. And the next day they saw the mainland of China.

Ching stood on deck, his face creased into a beatific smile, his hands, idle for the first time in weeks, tucked into his sleeves. No one recalled him to his work, and he did not seem aware of his immediate surroundings as his gaze wandered happily afar to the blue mountains of his native land, across the yellow-tinged waters of the China Sea.

Jerry, too, was happy. At a word from Captain Brown, he was sent to heave the lead as the *Swan* made her way against a fresh northeast monsoon. The brisk breeze, the choppy sea, the bright sunshine, and the nearness of his goal would have been exhilaration enough; but added to these was the pride he felt in being entrusted with such an important task by Captain Brown, who had been remote as Olympus during the voyage from the islands. To be sure, another seaman was taking soundings on the port side, but that did not prevent Jerry from feeling that he carried the whole responsibility of the ship.

"China! There it is at last!" thought Roy. The *Thunderbird*, which had faded from his waking thoughts, sailed back into his mind to tease him. She was somewhere just ahead, and with her was Cousin Audley, the villain who had betrayed their stepmother, besmirched their father's name, robbed and attempted to kill Roy and Jerry.

Their progress seemed maddeningly slow. Another day dawned before Piedra Blanca, the conical white rock famous to western sailors, was sighted. At noon another landmark, the island of Grand Lema, came into view. The water was dotted with hundreds of fishing junks, and other islands lay ahead as far as the eye could see. Guns were manned and the lookout alerted for pirates, but the only incident was the peaceful one of taking aboard a Chinese pilot.

Nightfall found the *Swan* still making her way among the islands, where she was obliged to stand off and on until dawn. By the first light she spread canvas, and in a few hours dropped anchor in Macao roads.

CHAPTER V

MACAO

IMMEDIATELY upon coming to anchor, Captain Brown summoned Roy, Jerry, and Ching to his cabin. It was the first time they had been in his presence alone since their departure from the Sandwich Islands.

He was dressed in his shore clothes and stood before a small mirror, tying his neckerchief. He turned and smiled at them as they came in. "Well, now, Ching, your journey is almost at an end," he began, as if they had been conversing pleasantly all the way across the Pacific. "But Roy and Jerry, your mission is just beginning. I have asked you here in order that you might make known your plans."

Roy and Jerry looked at one another blankly. They realized that they *had* no plans—nothing but wild dreams. "Why, sir," Jerry blurted, "we must find the *Thunderbird*."

"And what then?" Broderick Brown smiled grimly.

"Why, then we must take her, and bring Cousin Audley to justice."

"How?"

Jerry was silent. Roy, too, could find nothing to say.

Captain Brown turned to Ching. "Well, Ching? You savvy what *you* wanchee do?"

Ching bobbed his head, his queue swinging. "My go Canton chop-chop. My look-see find house, find brudder, farmi-lee." His eyes sparked at the thought. For a moment the years of exile and slavery slipped from him, and he looked again like the young man he must have been when he shipped aboard the *Argonaut*. His companions had died or remained enslaved in the land of fog and giant trees—only Ching had returned to his homeland. Captain Brown clapped him on the shoulder. "I would not delay you one hour," he said warmly. "You can hire a fast boat and reach Canton long before the *Swan* can make her way through the official rigmarole. You are due your wages." He dropped a fat little purse into Ching's hands.

Ching bowed so low his joints creaked as he straightened. "Too muchee! Too muchee!" He hefted the purse, struggling to express all that he felt, but his pidgin English was not equal to the task.

Captain Brown waved him away. "Bimeby you find your people, maybe-so you wanchee work; you come Mr. Wilson's house in Macao."

"My come," Ching said, solemnly. He made a brief bow to Roy and Jerry.

They shook hands wordlessly, then Roy said, "You take good care of Kowí." They had arranged that the bird should go ashore with Ching, since he was a reluctant sailor.

"My take care."

Ching was gone. Roy swallowed a lump in his throat. On the Northwest Coast he had been his only friend, keeping alive his faint hope of freedom. He had relied upon Ching perhaps more than he knew. The uncertain future seemed even more menacing without him at hand.

He was roused from his melancholy thoughts by Captain Brown, who stood poised for action. "One of my owners, Mr. Wilson, of Wilson and Company, resides in Macao," he told them. "I am on the point of calling upon him. If you wish to bear me company, I suggest that we tell Mr. Wilson your story and ask his advice. He has spent many years here and knows the conditions with which you must deal."

The boys accepted this suggestion gratefully and set out with the Captain for shore. Macao lay four miles off, at times hidden by one or another of the islands that thrust rocky slopes above the muddy coastal waters. The roads were alive with sampans and fishing junks, with here and there the tall masts of a European vessel. Could one of these be the *Thunderbird*? Or was she hiding, just out of sight, behind that shoulder of land, or that one? Or had Cousin Audley finished his business and already set sail for home?

In a fever of impatience, the boys watched as they drew near Macao. In Macao there would be news, they felt sure; the Boston traders made it their business to know what other American ships came to Canton.

The city lay before them, a wide semicircle of white beach and sea wall, and behind, the domes, roofs, trees, and towers of the town. At right and left two fortified hills guarded the approach from the sea. In spite of these forts, the place had an open and hospitable air. This impression grew stronger as the boat drew alongside one of the jetties, and Roy and Jerry followed the Captain up the steps to a spacious promenade fronted by a row of substantial European buildings, the first the boys had seen for many a month.

Captain Brown gave them no time to gawk, but led them at a fast clip up a narrow street paved with worn stones, past crumbling old houses with glimpses of luxuriant gardens, and across a church plaza overgrown with grass. Then, halting abruptly, he knocked at an iron gate set into a high colonnaded wall.

A Chinese servant answered the knock and led them across a garden. They were left standing on a shady veranda. Roy breathed a deep, happy sigh as he looked about at the brick floor, the plastered walls, the wrought-iron railing, the solid painted door with its sparkling side lights. After the huts of savages this European house seemed incomparably gracious and comfortable.

The servant returned and showed them, not into the

house, but up a short outside staircase. They came out upon an upper veranda overlooking the bay. One end was made into an outdoor sitting room, protected from the sea breeze and warmed by the sun, and there a man awaited them, lying upon a rattan chaise longue, three spaniels at his feet.

He greeted Broderick Brown cordially, but without rising more than two inches from his recumbent position, and acknowledged the introduction of Roy and Jerry with a limp handshake. He collapsed again immediately to the flat of his back, and with his chin on his chest he looked up at his guests with a charming smile.

Soon they were made as comfortable as he, seated in easy chairs, supplied with footstools, shaded by bamboo curtains, and refreshed with cups of fragrant tea. All the while Mr. Wilson chatted pleasantly in a cultivated, breathless voice.

At first the boys thought their host slightly ridiculous, but they soon found that under his indolent manner an efficient mind was at work. He drew from Captain Brown all the pertinent history of his voyage in short order, and although he asked no questions concerning them, he examined the captain's strange companions with shrewd attention.

When Captain Brown had completed his brief report, he sat forward in his chair and said, "Sir, my young friends here are in need of good advice. I could think of no better source of this commodity than yourself."

Mr. Wilson smiled affably. "Speak up, young sirs. As a father, I am perfectly aware that most young men of your age are in need of advice, but I have usually found them to be unaware of the fact. As Captain Brown says, I have a fund of it. It is at your disposal."

Encouraged by the indulgent twinkle in his eyes, Roy began his story of the events which had brought him and Jerry to Mr. Wilson's veranda. Mr. Wilson sipped his tea, rubbed the spaniels' ears, gazed out to sea—but a question now and then let the boys know that he was listening closely. Jerry put in when the tale came to his own adventures, and together they laid before their listener the whole fantastic story. As they talked, they grew more eager for action, until at the end they were both on their feet, their faces flushed with emotion.

Mr. Wilson, his chin still on his chest, smiled and observed, "Your story, if written down, would read like one of the novels that my daughter contrives to secrete in her room. By the way, my daughter, who acts as my hostess, would be most pleased to receive you this evening at tea."

Jerry exploded. "But—but, Mr. Wilson, sir! We are in a situation of the greatest urgency. We cannot wait! We—"

Even Roy forgot to be diplomatic. "We have come a long way to find the *Thunderbird*. If you cannot help us—"

Mr. Wilson sighed. "My dear young gentlemen, I cannot produce a rabbit from a basin, in the manner of a Chinese sleight-of-hand artist. But I shall make it my pleasure to inquire, between now and teatime, whether the *Thunderbird* is on this coast, and I am satisfied that I can produce this information. As to taking possession of the ship, that is another matter, and one in which I fear I can be of little assistance. I suggest that if we discover that the ship is here, you seek the advice of the American Consul, Mr. Kincaid, who is still at Canton."

The boys were immediately ashamed of their outburst and tried to express their gratitude for his courtesy. Mr. Wilson waved them into silence. "Captain Brown has matters of business to discuss with me. I suggest that you go into the town and obtain suitable clothing for your call upon Mr. Kincaid. I shall send a servant with you. He will obtain sedan chairs and show you to a shop that can turn you out acceptably."

Roy looked ruefully at his tar-daubed trousers, but shook his head. "Sir, we are aware that we look more like shipwrecked mariners than like Virginia gentlemen. But until we regain our inheritance we are as destitute as Crusoe, and we shall have to continue looking like him."

"Don't deprive me of the pleasure of risking a little of the firm's money in this romantic adventure. If your story is true, and if you find the *Thunderbird*—"

"*If* our story is true!" cried Roy and Jerry together.

Mr. Wilson sighed. "I am too many years your senior for you to challenge me to a duel, so save your indignation, lads. You must realize that the gentlemen at Canton will find your story hard to believe. And your present appearance will make it even more difficult."

Jerry thrust out his chin stubbornly. "They must take us as we are. We ask your help, sir, but not your charity!" With these ringing words he strode across the veranda and stood beside Broderick Brown, who was looking over the balustrade.

Jerry followed his gaze. Slowly his angry scowl changed and disappeared. A blush like a stormy sunrise rose from his neck and spread over his cheeks to his ears. After a long moment of silence he shuffled his feet and muttered, "Well, perhaps, sir—after all—"

"It's not a bad idea, after all," Broderick Brown helped him out. Jerry nodded gratefully.

Roy, astonished, protested. "But, Jerry—"

"I think we should accept Mr. Wilson's kind offer," Jerry mumbled.

Mr. Wilson exerted himself so far as to ring for a servant and give him instructions. Roy went to the railing beside Jerry and Captain Brown and looked down.

Below was a garden that followed the contour of the rocky slope. A profusion of shrubs and small trees left only space enough for a small plot of well-kept lawn, upon which was a bench, a table, and a tiny, tinkling fountain. On the table lay an open book, face down. At the fountain a pet deer drank daintily. And near the bench stood a young girl, poised like a bird, watching the deer. As he lifted his head, she held out her hand, offering a tangerine.

It was an enchanting tableau. Roy, however, felt an overwhelming desire to laugh. Jerry looked as if lightning had struck him. Jerry was the one who was always teasing Roy about girls! Girls were all right, he often remarked, but they were only girls. Now, it appeared, things were quite different. One glimpse of his hostess, and Jerry decided to dress for tea!

At teatime two elegant young gentlemen descended from sedan chairs at Mr. Wilson's gate. They were admitted and ushered into a spacious drawing room full of rare and curious objects. Broderick Brown was there before them, and presently Mr. Wilson came in, proving, somewhat to the boys' surprise, that he was able to stand erect. With him was his daughter Felicia, and as they bowed over her hand, both Roy and Jerry were glad that they had exchanged the garb of Crusoe for that of Virginia gentlemen.

Felicia was as fair as her name. She had milk-white skin and large dark blue eyes fringed with silky lashes. Her hair was light brown and smooth. As smooth as silk? thought Jerry. No, smoother than silk. Much, much smoother than that.

While they were served with many delicacies welcome to a sailor's salty palate, Mr. Wilson conversed pleasantly about Macao's colorful history. The boys choked back their impatience as best they could, wondering when he would get around to the subject nearest their hearts—the *Thunderbird*. Felicia remarked that in another month or so they would find the society much more animated in Macao, "since all business ceases at Canton, and many of the gentlemen of the foreign factories take up residence here." Jerry pictured her playing hostess to the gentlemen of the factories and felt a pang of jealousy.

In the midst of this inconsequential chatter Mr. Wilson at last spoke the words that had Roy and Jerry sitting on the edge of their chairs. "There *is* a ship called the *Thunderbird* now anchored at Whampoa. Her master is John Audley, who is purchasing a cargo at Canton. I am told he brought a lading of prime furs from the Northwest Coast. This is all I have been able to learn."

Roy cried, "It's quite enough, sir. We're most grateful."

"He can't escape us now!" said Jerry.

Broderick Brown rose. "It seems clear that your next move is to proceed to Canton. I know you will wish to discuss the matter with our host. While you are engaged, I shall claim the pleasure of keeping Miss Felicia company." He gave Jerry a maddening grin over his shoulder as he offered Felicia his arm. "I remember from a previous visit a very pretty terrace and an observatory. Is the air too cold this evening for a stroll in that direction?"

A rustle of skirts, an inclination of a silken head, a flutter of lashes, and they were gone through the wide glass doors that opened on to the veranda.

Mr. Wilson settled into an easy chair. "Tomorrow the *Swan* will sail for Whampoa. From there you will be able to reach Canton without delay, and make known your plight to Mr. Kincaid."

"Surely he will help us!" Roy said.

"He will undoubtedly listen sympathetically. But I must warn you that he has no legal powers in a case of this sort. He is only a business representative. Still, it will do no harm to state your case to him, and he may be able to give you good advice."

The boys felt that they needed action more than advice,

but they expressed their gratitude with as much grace as they could muster. When Mr. Wilson suggested a game of chess, Roy obligingly offered himself at the chess table. Jerry wandered restlessly to the doors looking out beyond the veranda to the bay. Little lights were sparkling from the boats and ships at anchor, and a servant was lighting the lanterns hung along the garden paths. But Felicia and Captain Brown had not returned.

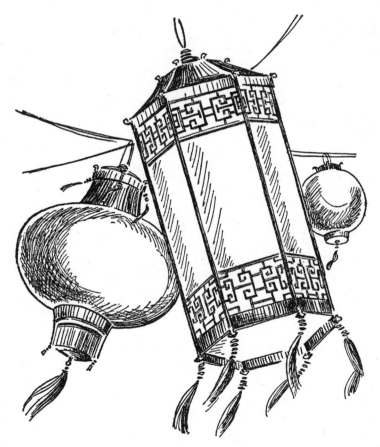

CHAPTER VI

CHINA

AGAINST THE northeast monsoon the *Swan* made snail-like progress. Roy and Jerry were back at their work, and steady work it was, too, with the vessel constantly in stays. The morning was overcast, with a raw chill in the wind. Even after they were well into the Pearl River, they were unable to see the opposite shore, so that from all appearances they might be still at sea.

"The closer we come to our goal, the slower we advance," Jerry complained, rubbing his rope-chafed hands. He had been in a gloomy humor since last night, and the weather, the labor, and the unfriendly looks of the other sailors had combined to make it worse.

"But we know the *Thunderbird* is there, only a few leagues upstream," said Roy. "That thought should make you cheerful." He, too, was impatient, and he disliked the drudgery of the ship more than Jerry did, but he tried to take his own advice and fix his attention on the future.

"If I were cheerful it would do me no good in the fo'c'sle," retorted Jerry.

"You can't blame the men for being suspicious of us. They must stay aboard the ship while we hobnob with the Captain and his friends ashore. They see us leave wearing sailor's jackets and trousers, and return in broadcloth and linen. They don't know what to make of it."

"We never made any secret of our story."

"Most of them are good enough fellows. It's only that by

49

habit they like to keep the fo'c'sle and the quarterdeck far apart. And Duke is forever stirring up trouble."

After a day of zigzag progress, the *Swan* anchored for the night below Lintin Bar. The Chinese pilot, relieved of the day's duties, leaned over the rail and haggled happily with the occupants of a sampan that came off from shore. A number of these native boats clustered about the ship, offering vegetables, rice, fish, and a variety of other commodities for sale. They were small, shallow craft propelled by one or more oars, and partially roofed over with matting. From under these shelters whole families peeped up at the ship, some calling their wares, some arguing with their competitors, others unconcernedly going about their domestic affairs.

"For the first time I feel we are really in China," said Jerry, his mood somewhat softened by the picturesqueness of the scene. Lintin Island presented a high conical peak against the fading light, its lower hills covered with trees, among which could be seen the roofs of a village. Across the turbid water came a confused murmur—the voice of China. Listening intently, the boys identified among the sounds the dipping of oars, the faint clanging of gongs, and the cries of domestic fowl.

Another day of beating up the wide, muddy river past the hazy, flat, alluvial shore. They met great, seagoing junks, the cold northeast wind making weird music in their sails. Smaller vessels carried cargo and passengers between Macao and Canton. Most of the traffic was going down-river, reminding Roy and Jerry that the season was on the wane. Many of the foreign vessels had already completed their cargoes and sailed for home; in a month or two all would be gone. The *Swan* was late; she could not linger long. The *Thunderbird* might already be preparing to sail. Still the monsoon held them back from Canton.

In the evening the shores on either side of the river sud-

denly closed in. The *Swan* sailed between projecting head-
lands into the tiger's mouth. The Portuguese who had opened
this route to trade had named this place the Bocca Tigris.

The jaws of the tiger were fortified, and several islands
within also bore forts of formidable construction. In an ample
bay the *Swan* dropped anchor, leaving Roy and Jerry to
fume and fret away the night as best they could.

Next morning anchor was weighed, and their laborious
progress was resumed under the frowning rocky buttresses
of numerous islands. From now on the river grew more
complex and constricted, and at the same time more animated. Forts and villages, cultivated fields, temples, and
resorts lined the shores, while the water formed a highway
for all kinds of shipping.

Not many miles beyond the slender tower of the Second
Bar Pagoda, the river narrowed still further and made a
turn. With the wind on their quarter, they could have shown
it their heels, but the channel became intricate with sand
bars and small islands. The pilot left off smoking his everlasting pipe and the leadsmen were sent to the chains. Jerry
was not experienced enough for this work, and in any case
his mind was too preoccupied with his own thoughts. One
of the islands ahead was Whampoa, beyond which no foreign ship was permitted to pass. Already he and Roy had
sighted the flying colors of European ships riding at anchor.

Soon the *Swan* was one of them. Roy and Jerry eyed them
anxiously. Most had only their mainmasts standing, their
topmasts being lowered or stored for the long stay in port.
Others were in readiness to sail. Here and there they recognized with a thrill the Stars and Stripes whipping on the
alien air. But they did not see the *Thunderbird*.

The Duke came up to them as they stood by the rail. He
made an exaggerated bow. "The Captain presents his compliments, gentlemen, and requests the pleasure of your pres-

ence, gentlemen, in the drawing room, gentlemen," he drawled as offensively as possible. Deliberately he kicked at Mimbo near Jerry's feet.

Jerry clenched his fists. Roy seized his arm. "Not now, Jerry. Don't waste time on him. Let's see what Captain Brown wants." Reluctantly, Jerry allowed himself to be drawn away.

When they presented themselves in the cabin, Captain Brown was superintending the laying out of refreshments on the table. "The Great Hoppo will arrive directly," he explained. "He will have the vessel measured and levy the customs tax—and collect the usual cumshaw for himself. Not until then can the unloading of the cargo begin. I must remain to oversee the operation and to engage a comprador, but after the Hoppo's visit there is nothing to keep you from proceeding to Canton. Since your business is urgent, you may wish to do so."

"Yes, we do!"

"Then rig yourselves for the journey and stand by. I will join you at the American factory as soon as I can."

The approach of the Great Hoppo was heralded by a salute of nine guns, which made the *Swan* shudder. The Hoppo's sampan replied with its own brass cannon, and the mandarin came aboard to the tune of his own orchestra, which emitted sounds entirely inharmonious to the western ear. Captain Brown had his crew drawn up on deck with the style of a man-of-war, to the evident satisfaction of the Great Hoppo and the lesser mandarins who accompanied him. Captain Brown, with the two mates, waited to receive him on the quarterdeck, where greetings were exchanged through a Chinese interpreter, and everyone concerned shook hands with himself and sought to discover who could bow the lowest and the greatest number of times. This over, the Hoppo accepted the hospitality of the cabin, while the inferior mandarins, hardly less imposing than himself, set about measuring the ship and figuring the customs tax with the aid of a long measuring rod, a many-colored abacus, and a bevy of solemn clerks.

The process was carried out in the most leisurely manner possible, but at last it was over, presents were offered and accepted by the Hoppo, and the procession of dignitaries departed over the side. As their fleet of sampans drew away from the ship, Broderick Brown produced a letter that he handed to Roy and Jerry. "Give this to Mr. Kincaid. I am vouching for your characters, but I have not told him your story; you must do that yourselves. You will be offered hospitality as employees of Wilson and Company."

He gave them each a warm handclasp and delivered them into the care of a Chinese boatman. Mimbo, of course, was one of the party. He tucked himself under the seat between Jerry's legs but stuck his nose out inquisitively so as to take stock of his surroundings.

Their frail little craft slipped like a water bug between the tall ships and in and out of the clutter of native craft. From the level of the yellow water, Roy and Jerry looked up as the black, weathered hulls of foreign ships loomed above them, searching for the familiar shape of the *Thunderbird*, which they had come so far to find. The low shores of Whampoa Island, crowned by its nine-storied pagoda, drew near.

Then they saw her, the long-sought *Thunderbird*, lying at anchor ahead. They must pass close under her side. Roy felt himself grow tense, and saw that Jerry's lips were tight. They looked at each other wordlessly, then back at the ship. There were figures moving about the deck. Would they see any faces they knew? Among the rascally crew all were not enemies. Hyppolite, the cabin boy, was gone, but old Hawks, the carpenter, had always been kind to them, and the second mate, Mr. Heflin, with his tragic eyes, was an enemy only to himself. There must be others who were not completely controlled by Captain Audley.

Her bow was close enough to distinguish the carved figure of the Thunderbird under the bowsprit. Roy said suddenly, "If we are recognized, we'll lose the value of surprise. We'd better keep out of sight."

"I won't hide!" protested Jerry.

"Nobody asked you to hide. But we don't have to show ourselves until we're ready. Come on!"

They drew back into the shelter of the cabin. The boat, small though it was, was fitted out with some pretension to luxury. Roy, Jerry, and Mimbo looked curiously about the interior, with its carved, painted, and gilded woodwork, its tasseled paper lanterns and floor covered with fragrant matting. The boys sat stiffly on lacquered chairs, feeling miles away from the bright, noisy river from which they were separated by the frailest fabric of split bamboo. Through the cracks of the awnings they could see the river glare suddenly blotted out by a monstrous shadow, and they knew that the *Thunderbird* loomed over them. For a moment or two they glided under her side. This was their ship, in which they had invested great hopes and treasure— the ship that was to save Rivergarden. And here they were skulking like criminals in a sampan, while Cousin Audley was in possession of their inheritance.

When they emerged, the *Thunderbird* was behind them. They were traversing the narrow channel south of Whampoa Island, with the pagoda on their right hand. Other pagodas were in sight, and the roofs of farmhouses and villages. There were people everywhere; boatmen and fishermen on the water, coolies carrying loads along the bank, crowds about the door of the joss houses, women working in the rice fields. People everywhere—yellow, pig-tailed, busy, and

Canton ~ where Roy & Jerry learned about treachery & tea

Whampoa ~ where the Thunderbird anchored

First Bar

Honam I.

French I.

Large Second Bar pagoda

Small Second Bar pagoda

Second Bar

Ty-Cock-tow I.

Boca Tigris

Chuenpee

PEARL RIVER

N

W   E

S

Lintin I.
where the duel did _not_ take place

Macao
where Jerry met Felicia

noisy. Roy suddenly thought of Ching. He had disappeared somewhere into this swarming beehive of humanity. Would he ever see him again?

Jerry was laughing at Mimbo, who was distracted almost to frenzy by the ripe and racy smells of the river. A drove of pigs, a boatload of fish, a scavenging sea gull, a nameless bit of flotsam floating by under his very nose—he tried to investigate them all at once. Jerry kept a tight grip on his collar. "Good old Mimbo!" he thought. "He has traveled a long way since I found him turning the spit at the Rainbow Tavern. . . . For that matter, I've traveled a long way, myself."

Imperceptibly the activity on the shores of the river had changed from rural to urban. The venerable stone wall of the City of Canton showed here and there among the trees and suburban houses that had grown up outside. Towers, peaked tile roofs, and the tall red poles marking the residences of gods or mandarins rose above the houses that lined the water front. The river became congested with traffic beyond belief; still their boatmen smiled and pushed and darted between the other craft to make good speed. They passed a crenelated stone fort rising from the water itself, and soon after they saw a row of white buildings along the water front, where the flags of western nations flew.

Their boatmen, shouting and threatening with their oars and poles, slipped with consummate skill to a landing. Climbing out on the stone jetty, Roy and Jerry set their course toward the flagstaff proudly lifting the young flag of the United States. A large three-storied building of plain businesslike design confronted them. At their left yawned the dark, clamorous opening of a Chinese street, so narrow and overshadowed by signs and balconies that the lanterns were already being lit before the shops. On either side of this opening the foreign factories faced the river, each displaying the flag of its homeland.

Just inside the door a corps of Chinese servants took over the baggage, while a roly-poly young Oriental advanced to greet them. "My Jim Dandy," he introduced himself, chuckling amiably. "My linguist; all Meleika merchant allee same my flen. Can do all thing you wanchee. You wanchee dinner?"

Roy presented his letter. "We wanchee see Mr. Kincaid. You tellee him we chin-chin he."

Jim Dandy retired, returning promptly with the message, "Misser Kincaid, he chin-chin you. He say you come dining room chop-chop."

First, however, the boys were ushered to their rooms. To reach them they passed through the building that they had entered, and crossed a courtyard to a second building immediately behind. The apartment allotted to their use consisted of several well-appointed rooms on the third floor and had its own private entrance through a small garden.

They did not linger but returned at once to the dining room in the first building. It was a large, paneled room with windows overlooking the water front. At a long table some two dozen men were seated, pleasantly engaged with knives, forks, and wineglasses. A portly gentleman at the head of the table arose and came to meet them. Wheezing asthmatically, he shook hands and led them to the table. This was Mr. Kincaid, who they hoped would help them in their difficult undertaking.

One by one Roy and Jerry acknowledged introductions: a Dutch merchant, a Norwegian sea captain, a group of British supercargoes, the staff of the American factory. At the right hand of the American Consul, as he came back to his seat, was an elegant Chinese gentleman in plum-colored

silk, Fouqua, the celebrated hong merchant. His servant
stood behind his chair.

Then the room and the people and the bountifully laden
table with its lighted candelabra began to swim before the
boys' eyes. Roy and Jerry were introduced to the gentleman
at Mr. Kincaid's left hand. He was John Audley, master of
the *Thunderbird,* as florid of face, as frank of eye, and as
jolly of manner as ever.

CHAPTER VII

ADVICE

WHILE THE BOYS were trying to collect their wits, Captain Audley sprang from his chair and came toward them, face beaming with joy, arms outstretched. "Leroy and Gerald Lacey!" he cried. "Dear lads! Cousins! And I believed you both to be dead."

Roy and Jerry took postures of defence. They could not believe their ears. They were even more astounded when Captain Audley turned to the company, whose attention was arrested by the dramatic scene. "Gentlemen, you have known and heard much of the marvels of the sea. Here you witness one of the most marvelous. These lads, young stepsons of a female cousin under my protection, set sail with me from Norfolk little more than a year ago. One met with a hunting accident on the coast of Brazil. I was informed that he was killed, and, unable to rescue his body, was forced to sail without it. Yet now I see him alive before me! The other was kidnapped by the savages of the Northwest Coast, destined, it seemed, for certain death. I was helpless in the face of superior numbers, only escaping, myself, at the risk of my life and that of my crew. Yet he, too, survived to rejoin me here. Dear lads! My dear lads!" And turning back to the boys, he opened his arms still wider, as if to embrace them.

Both the boys stepped back. As usual in times of emotion, Jerry turned very red, Roy very white. Roy said quietly, addressing the assembly, but looking Captain Audley in the eye, "Gentlemen, Captain Audley lies!"

A shocked murmur went around the table.

59

"He lies! He knows he lies!" cried Jerry, seeing disapproval and unbelief on the faces staring at them. "He had his men stampede the wild pigs at me at Corona, and he sold Roy on the Northwest Coast to the Indian chief as a slave. Make him tell you the truth!"

Captain Audley was silent, his mobile face expressing deep distress. "What *is* this?" one of the Americans was heard to say. "Wild pigs?" muttered one Englishman to another. "What nonsense!"

Mr. Kincaid, who had just lowered himself into his chair, with difficulty heaved himself out again. "Gentlemen!" he protested. "This is unseemly. Most unfortunate."

Captain Audley bowed. "You are quite right, sir," he declared. "This *is* unfortunate, and to me, quite incomprehensible. What can have turned my young relatives against me? But this must be discussed in private. I shall give myself the pleasure of waiting upon them after dinner."

Jerry sputtered, "I—! You—!"

Mr. Kincaid advanced upon the boys and urged them out of the room. "This won't do, you know," he protested fussily. "Breaking in upon a genteel group at dinner with such fantastic exaggerations! Intolerable!"

Roy said, earnestly, "Sir, I assure you, every word we have told you and Captain Brown is the truth. Captain Audley intended to kill us. He thought he had killed us. How can he have the face to claim innocence before all those people? But, yes, I see his plan. This is the cleverest thing he could do. Already he has turned everyone against us."

Jerry demanded, "Can't you see in his face that he's a blackhearted murderer?"

"John Audley has every appearance of a gentleman," Mr. Kincaid said, stiffly. "I find nothing to reproach in his conduct. But the whole situation is embarrassing. I feel quite uncomfortable about it."

"Then don't let us detain you longer," said Jerry, bitterly.

Mr. Kincaid was obviously controlling his temper with difficulty. "You will not be able to complain of injustice here," he said. "I shall call at your rooms after dinner with Captain Audley and will hear your story in full."

Back in their rooms, Roy sat unhappily on the edge of a chair. "We haven't conducted this affair with much skill," he said.

"I suppose you mean I shouldn't have lost my temper!" Jerry paced up and down, hands in his pockets, kicking at the carpet. He was ready for a quarrel, but, getting no answer, after a moment or two he hung his head. "I *am* sorry, Roy."

Roy produced a pale smile. "Don't apologize to me. *I'm* the one who overturned the applecart, accusing Captain Audley of lying in front of all the fine gentlemen. It looked to them like pure insolence to a respected sea captain from some young pup nobody ever heard of."

"What could we do, though? Let him weep over us without speaking up for ourselves? What *could* we have done? What are we *going* to do?"

"I don't know. Well, I suppose we *could* just sail home on the *Swan* and wait until our return to establish our claim to Rivergarden. It isn't really Captain Audley and the *Thunderbird* who matter; what we must do is to prove that Mr. Morris killed our father and stole our inheritance."

"That sounds very well. But if we leave Cousin Audley free, he is likely to reach home before us. What might he not do to help Mr. Morris get his way?"

Roy interrupted. "The truth of it is that Cousin Audley would never let us sail away on the *Swan*. He doesn't intend for us to reach Rivergarden again.

"Our only chance is to convince Mr. Kincaid and the other American merchants that our story is true. They could arrange for a master to sail the ship home, with Captain Audley in irons. Otherwise our lives aren't worth a continental."

"I'll be very calm and quiet," Jerry promised. "You present our side of the case and I won't chime in unless you call on me. I only wish Captain Brown were here! *He* believes us."

"Even he might begin to doubt after hearing our smooth-tongued cousin."

Jerry shook his head. "Not he. Not Captain Brown. He'll believe us, and he'll help us, too."

"Well, he won't be here until tomorrow. In the meantime—"

There was an abrupt knock. Jerry opened the door and stood aside as three gentlemen entered, as silent and grave as a jury. They accepted chairs, and Roy and Jerry sat down facing them.

Cousin Audley had chosen an ample chair near the fireplace. He gazed at the boys wistfully, his eyebrows raised above his nose and slanting downward in the expression they remembered so well. Mr. Kincaid was tightly confined in an armchair too small for him, drawing his breath with difficulty after his climb up the stairs. On a straight chair sat their third, and unexpected guest, the Chinese merchant mandarin, Fouqua. He was very slender, very erect, and his narrow, hollow-cheeked face wore an unvarying, gentle smile. His plum-colored outer robe fell apart on his crossed knees to expose an underrobe of lime-yellow brocade. When he moved, the whisper of silk against silk could be heard in the quiet room.

Mr. Kincaid opened the proceedings with an official wheeze. "Leroy and Gerald Lacey, you have made some serious accusations against Captain John Audley. There are no courts of law here to which either of you can appeal, but all American citizens concerned in trading with the Great Empire of China"—he made a slight bow toward Fouqua—

"have a moral duty to protect the interests of other Americans in this trade. For this reason I have consented to hear your story. We are also honored by the presence of the distinguished representative of the Chinese Empire"—he made a deeper bow in the direction of Fouqua—"who, as security merchant for both the *Thunderbird* and the *Swan,* and as a proven friend to the Americans on these shores, has expressed a desire to learn more of this matter."

Fouqua inclined his head graciously. Captain Audley, asking permission with a gesture, lit his pipe and settled back in his chair. With a wave of his hand, Mr. Kincaid gave Roy the floor.

Slowly and clearly, and as calmly as possible, Roy reviewed his story: how Mr. Morris had murdered their father, making the death appear to be a suicide caused by the loss of his estate; how he had rid himself of the only witness by frightening Mr. Lacey's body servant, Benjamin, into running away; how he had demanded the estate as payment of a debt of honor. His audience listened with polite interest, but the western faces were as impossible to read as the Oriental.

Roy continued. He told of the arrival of Captain Audley at Rivergarden, summoned by his cousin, Mrs. Lacey. Of his message from Mr. Morris, that if the boys purchased and outfitted the *Thunderbird* and brought her trading voyage to a successful conclusion, he would accept the proceeds of the voyage in lieu of the estate. "Now it is clear that this was only a scheme to rid himself of us," Roy came to the crucial point of his tale. "Captain Audley betrayed his cousin's trust and became a hired killer for Mr. Morris, undertaking to dispose of both Jerry and me in return for the *Thunderbird* and her profits." Again he described the manner of his abandonment among the savages, and Jerry, with a valiant effort at restraint, told of his narrow escape from death at Corona.

"That's what happened," Roy ended. "We ask that Captain Audley be removed as master of the *Thunderbird* and sent home in irons. Once we are safely home, we can trust our rights to the Virginia courts."

Mr. Kincaid tapped his finger tips together. "This is a fantastic story, John," he turned toward Captain Audley. "Just how much of it is true?"

Roy's heart sank. He knew at that moment that their cause was lost. Jerry, too, heard their death knell in his words. The sweat broke out on his palms. If no one believed them, they were at the mercy of Cousin Audley.

Cousin Audley looked benevolently at the boys. "Their troubles have given them wild fancies," he explained, as if eager to excuse their behavior. "Let me clarify the situation. In the first place, they were severely shocked by the discovery of their father's ruin. Who can blame them? Next, Gerald suffered a tragic accident at Corona. A group of my men were with him, saw him get in the way of the stampeding wild pigs, saw him trampled, gored, and broken. They were convinced of his death. Who knows what permanent damage might have been inflicted at that time? What warping of memory and reason? Naturally, leaving his brother for dead was a dreadful experience for Leroy. I myself nursed him through an illness weeks in duration. I know what he suffered! Upon arrival at the Northwest Coast, the Indian chief with whom I traded took a fancy to Leroy. He often expressed his desire to own him as a slave. I did not take him seriously. But on the night of our departure, when I had only a few men ashore, the chief seized him by force. There was a struggle in which the cabin boy was killed. The rest of us had all we could do to get away with our lives. I made every attempt possible to recover Roy, but at last was in-

formed that the savages had killed him as he attempted to
escape. I was obliged to think of my men; it would have been
idle to risk them in a vain effort at reprisal. My only course
was to continue the voyage, make it as profitable as possible,
and return to the aid of Mrs. Lacey. This I have done so far.
And now I have the unspeakable joy of welcoming back the
real owners of the *Thunderbird* and of assisting them to
complete the venture upon which they embarked."

Roy said, hopelessly, "It isn't true, Mr. Kincaid. Sir—" he
did not know how to address the mandarin.

Mr. Kincaid inquired, "Do you have any proof of your
claims? Any witnesses to these alleged acts of violence?"

"Hyppolite knew what was going on," Roy answered. "He
was with me when I was nearly pushed off the tower at
Corona. He warned me not to drink the chocolate, afterward. And he seemed to suspect what was going to happen
the night I was abandoned to the Indians."

"Who is Hyppolite?"

"A cabin boy aboard the *Thunderbird,* but he is dead. He
was killed trying to help me."

Mr. Kincaid tapped more and more impatiently. "Do
you have any witnesses to your story, Gerald?"

"I have a paper signed by Benjamin, telling what happened the night of our father's death," Jerry said, eagerly.
"I'll show it to you."

"Just a moment. Who is Benjamin?"

"My father's body servant. I told you about him."

Captain Audley smiled. "Oh, yes. The runaway slave."

"He didn't run away! He—"

"Now, now. A slave. . . . What about the hunting party
who were with you when the wild pigs attacked?"

"I will be happy to call them before you," Captain Audley
offered. "If I remember correctly, they were: Ross, Ole,
Jim—Jim, however, died since then, in the islands—"

"The worst ruffians on the ship!" cried Jerry. "They would not speak a word of truth!"

"They were the very same who stood by and let Chief Tom-Tom take me!" Roy joined in.

Mr. Kincaid lifted his hands from the arms of his chair and let them fall.

"I cannot take a hand in this matter," he said with finality. "There is no evidence to support the accusations you have made. I advise you to forget your prejudice against your cousin, and continue your voyage without further ado. However, if you are unwilling to do this, your letter of introduction states that you have berths on the *Swan* and may keep them as long as you do your work. There is nothing whatever to prevent you from returning in her to America, where you can take whatever measures you wish in your local courts."

He pulled himself out of his chair like a cork from a bottle, bowed, and went to the door. "That is my advice."

Captain Audley lingered, but, since Fouqua remained serenely in his chair, he took his leave. "I shall be entirely at your disposal," he said to the boys with a forgiving smile.

Last of all the mandarin rose and glided in his soft-soled slippers toward the door, outside which the gentlemen waited. As he came opposite the boys he bowed, shook hands with himself, and said, in a whisper like the rustling of his silks, "Fouqua have five, six boy my house allee same you." They thought he was going to say something else, but he did not. With a slow, sweet smile he left the room.

The door closed behind them. Roy and Jerry were left alone, except for the faithful Mimbo.

CHAPTER VIII

THE MASQUERADE

CAPTAIN BROWN was now their only hope. Roy and Jerry fretted through the hours before his arrival, sustained only by the thought of his bright brown eyes and iron jaw. Breakfast was served in their rooms, so they did not see Mr. Kincaid until dinner. He treated them with perfunctory courtesy, and they were spared the effort of making conversation by the presence of a number of guests at table. Captain Audley was not in evidence, much to their relief.

They returned to their rooms, shot the bolt, and faced each other glumly. "We can't lurk forever behind locked doors," Jerry complained. "We must do something!"

"Captain Brown will be here before nightfall," Roy said for the hundredth time. "It would be folly to make any decision before we talk to him."

Jerry flung himself on the sofa with a violence that made it creak. "All right," he grumbled. "But what if he is like all the rest? What if he begins to doubt us, too?"

Scarcely an hour had elapsed when they heard a light, vigorous step in the hall, and the door vibrated to a sharp knock. It could be no one but Broderick Brown. Roy hurried to open the door, and the young captain was hardly inside before he burst out, "Well, now there's hell to pay and no pitch hot! I've just been talking to Kincaid. He thinks you're either liars or lunatics. What did you say to turn him against you?"

"We only told him what we told you. It was Captain Audley who did the mischief. He has been here long enough

67

to make friends with Mr. Kincaid and the gentlemen of the factory. He forestalled us and presented his case first. After that we looked like cads, trying to ruin the reputation of an innocent man."

Broderick Brown paced the room as if it were his quarter-deck. "Yes, that's understandable," he admitted. "Your story is outlandish, you know. In fact, I can't see why I believe you, myself!"

"But you *do*?"

"Certainly I believe you," Captain Brown said, impatiently. "But the question is, what is to be done?"

Roy and Jerry, a load taken from their minds, sat down, urging their guest to make himself comfortable. But he said, "I think better on my feet."

"I've been thinking all day," Jerry said. "There's only one thing to do. Take the *Thunderbird* by force, and put Captain Audley in irons."

"Do you know what you're suggesting?" demanded Captain Brown. "Piracy! Well, I'm no pirate; I'm an American merchant, and the safety of all other American traders depends upon our behavior in these waters. If I were to help you carry out such a plan, I would be ruined, my company would be ruined, the factories would be closed, and Fouqua would be strangled in the public square. No, thank you!"

The boys were abashed. They had not thought of the consequences, only of their own necessity. Roy said at last, "Then we must take Mr. Kincaid's advice and go back on the *Swan*. That is, if we can get aboard her before Captain Audley finds a way to silence us for good."

Captain Brown slapped his thigh. "I've got it! You must tell Captain Audley that you will go home on the *Thunderbird*."

"What?" exploded Jerry. "Once aboard the *Thunderbird*, and we've signed our death warrant."

"Exactly. And if Captain Audley believes you intend to sail on the *Thunderbird* with him, he will not molest you until he has sailed. I'm certain he would prefer to have nothing unpleasant happen here. You will be quite safe while the *Thunderbird* is in port, and the moment we have word of her preparing to sail, you can slip aboard the *Swan*. He'll fume and fret, but he can't wait here forever, and so you'll be quit of him till you reach home."

"But would he believe us? After all we have said?"

"If you act the part well enough."

Jerry protested, "I'm no actor!"

"Anyone can act if it is a matter of life or death," Broderick Brown said grimly. "And it is."

"I can see some advantages in the idea," Roy began to smile. "If we are reconciled with our Cousin Audley, we become owners and supercargoes of the *Thunderbird* again; he will have to restore our clothes and other belongings and make our money available to us, so that we can repay Mr. Wilson for his generosity, and live like gentlemen. After all his protests of affection for us, he will be forced to put up a good front."

Jerry laughed. "It might be worth it, at that!"

"And it would save your lives," added Broderick Brown.

"We'll do it!" cried the boys. "How do we begin?"

They began by appearing at supper with solemn, chastened faces, and afterward seeking an interview with Captain Audley. Captain Brown had explained to Mr. Kincaid that the boys had regretted their obstinacy and were now ready to listen to reason. Accordingly, he met with them in the common room. After shaking hands all around and expressing his satisfaction that the affair was brought to a gratifying conclusion, he went to the billiard table at the end of the room, leaving Captain Brown to mediate between the boys and their cousin.

The young captain opened the subject. Leroy and Gerald Lacey, he said, had thought over the advice of their elders and had resolved to profit by it. He himself had reinforced their decision by making it clear to them that a man of Captain John Audley's character, enjoying, as he did, the esteem of his colleagues in the China trade, was not to be suspected of such actions as they attributed to him. After searching their own hearts they had admitted that they had no proof of any wrongdoing on the part of Captain Audley, that they could have been mistaken and misled by imaginations overwrought by the hardships they had passed through. They wished to apologize to Captain Audley for their ill-advised actions and to accept his kind offer to continue their common venture in the *Thunderbird*.

Captain Audley listened, beaming and nodding as Broderick Brown's explanation progressed. At the end he arose and clasped each boy's hand in turn. "Any distress I have felt at being misunderstood is swept away by my joy and gratitude in having you restored to me after these months of sorrow," he told them. "Let us dispense with apologies and press forward toward our goal."

Roy's heart almost failed him as he felt Captain Audley's large warm hand close over his and smelled his brandy-scented breath. Could he keep up a pretense of friendliness with this monster? Yet such was the charm and naturalness of Cousin Audley's manner that he felt himself smiling in response.

Jerry thought for a moment he was going to be sick. He, too, wondered if he could possibly play his part. Then he remembered that Cousin Audley was playing a part, too. What an ornament he would have been to the stage! The thought put him into a good humor, and he produced a smile.

"Good! Good!" cried Captain Brown. "I shall have to say farewell to my clumsy young sailors from the *Swan*, then, and salute the owners and supercargoes of the *Thunderbird.* We shall see much of each other during our residence in the factory, where gentlemen always find good company." He looked pointedly at Captain Audley.

That worthy responded promptly. "I'm sure that our stay in port will be most pleasant." To the boys he said, "Perhaps you would like to go to the ship at once and collect some belongings?"

"No, thank you, sir," Roy answered, resolutely holding his voice steady. "But we will be obliged if you will have our things sent for."

"I will send a boat to Whampoa directly. There is no reason why you should not be comfortable here, since we shall be kept in Canton some weeks longer. Our cargo is not yet completed."

"Business cannot be hurried in the Celestial Empire," Captain Brown observed. "Because of my late arrival I shall be lucky indeed if I dispose of my goods at a favorable rate. In one way, however, I am more than fortunate. To have Fouqua for security merchant is assurance of fair treatment."

"He has done well for me. For *us,* that is," Captain Audley nodded to the boys. "The bulk of our return cargo is already stored in his godowns. We await only the tea deckers from upriver, and the delivery of the chinaware, most of which is being decorated here. Since the chinaware will make the flooring of the ship, nothing may be loaded before it. One thing must wait upon another, while expenses mount."

Captain Brown agreed. "And *what* expenses! Only the genius of the Chinese could invent such a variety. To tonnage dues, the Hoppo's fee, and fees for the superintendent of the Treasury, must be added a percentage for converting specie into bullion, the cost of transporting it to Peking and weighing in government scales, and, if you please, an additional percentage to make up the difference in weights between Canton and Peking! I sometimes think our ships are like great cows that we drive up the river to be milked by every merchant, comprador, pilot, bumboatman, official, and official's servant in China!"

Roy saw an opportunity to introduce a matter that had long been in his mind. "Now that we are able to take up our unfinished venture, Jerry and I should begin to be useful," he said. "We undertook to discharge the duties of supercargoes, but I fear we have as yet scarcely seen the books. Will this not be a convenient opportunity to make us familiar with the business transacted so far, so that we can begin to be of service?"

It required an effort to keep a serene face under Cousin Audley's shrewd stare. He could follow perfectly the thoughts inside of the Captain's curly pate. "Ah ha! The young pup thinks he has me dancing like a trained bear! He makes his requests in public, where I cannot well refuse. But what does it matter? Changee for changee; black dog for white monkey! I can humor them now, and when I have them on the *Thunderbird* again, they will dance to my tune!" Aloud, Captain Audley said, "An excellent idea! As a step toward acquainting yourselves with the cargo, you might care to accompany me to the shop of the china merchant Syngchong, whom I have engaged to visit after breakfast tomorrow."

This invitation was accepted, and so the momentous interview was closed. Roy and Jerry retired wearily but with a feeling of satisfaction; as for Cousin Audley, he, too, appeared to be in the best of good humors.

Before breakfast next morning a servant knocked at the door announcing the arrival of sea chests belonging to Messrs. Leroy and Gerald Lacey, and the boys stood grinning to watch them brought in, delighted to see their familiar possessions again. Roy opened his own chest and tossed the keys to Jerry. "At least we have our own clothes again. And here is my sketching paper and my pens and ink and brushes! I only hope I haven't forgotten how to use them!"

"Well, don't get your hands in the inkpot now. It's time for breakfast, and immediately after that we are to take the air with Cousin Audley—remember?"

Freshly scrubbed, brushed, and polished, the boys met their cousin at the time agreed upon. He was awaiting them in one of the public rooms of the factory, conversing with the interpreter who was to accompany them on their visit. This was Jim Dandy, one of the innumerable employees of Fouqua, who furnished every necessity and convenience— at a price—for the merchants whom he secured.

Although the factory was a busy place, leaving it was like swimming out of a quiet pool into a cataract. Immediately they were in the heart of China. The broad open space between the factories and the water front was nominally reserved for the foreigners, but the mouth of Old China Street, opening at the side of the American factory, overflowed with humanity. Porters and vendors, soldiers, boatmen, idlers, and merchants blocked the way, making it necessary for Jim Dandy to clear a path for his party by going ahead of them, shoving and shouting at the top of his lungs. They did not turn into Old China Street, but walked along the fronts of another series of foreign factories to the next opening, that of New China Street. This they entered, turning their backs to the river. In the narrow passage between the buildings, the din was terrific. Every tongue in the crowd seemed to be wagging, and the vendors in the street strove to get the trade away from the shops by crying their wares into the very ears of the passers-by. Itinerant barbers advertised their trade by twanging enormous tweezers. Beggars offered their baskets, ringing bells or blowing horns.

The odor of the Orient was as overpowering as its sound.

All in one breath the boys inhaled the smells of fruits and vegetables, poultry and fish, peppers, tobacco, dried sea horses, and smoked sausages, sandalwood, cats and dogs, parrots, raw silk, opium and tea, tung oil, castor oil, gunpowder, wax, and humanity.

Roy and Jerry, trying to see everything, hardly took in what they saw. The shops opened directly into the street, but the street was obstructed by so many bales and baskets, so many thatched booths and squatting vendors, so many hanging signs, balconies, and lanterns, that it was next to impossible to see what went on within.

Suddenly the boys realized that their companions, who had been in the lead, had disappeared. For a moment they felt helpless and confused. Looking hastily about, they discovered Captain Audley and Jim Dandy standing within the shop they had just passed, enjoying a laugh at their expense.

"Meleika chintelemun turn heads so-fashion like owl," Jim Dandy chuckled, tracing a circle in the air with his fat finger. "Too much look-see, too little watchee!" He savored his joke, his eyes squeezed tight with mirth.

Captain Audley observed, "You can't see it all in one day. Come, you must meet Syngchong; he's one of the most important china merchants in Canton."

The china shop was more spacious than it seemed from the street. The ceiling was lofty, supported by slender columns and ornamented with wooden fretwork. A few customers sat at the counter on bamboo stools, while clerks exhibited the wares displayed on the shelves. One of these left his work at a word from Jim Dandy and returned in a moment with their host. Greetings were exchanged, introductions were made, and they were invited to follow him down a corridor into a reception room where little teakwood tables waited, laden with fruit, tea, and delicate cakes.

As they sampled these refreshments, Roy and Jerry tried to follow the business being discussed by Captain Audley and Syngchong through the medium of Jim Dandy. Their attention wandered, however. Roy's was attracted by the gleam of fine porcelains from niches in the wall—vases and bowls of elegant shapes and jewel-like colors quite unlike those of the wares in the shop. Jerry's ear was caught by the murmur of voices just beyond the wall, a sound like the hum of a busy schoolroom.

Captain Audley was checking a list which he took from his pocket. "Fifty blue and white dining sets, one hundred and seventy-two pieces each," he read. "Why have they not yet arrived? When I ordered them, I was told that they could be had promptly, since they did not require special decoration here."

Syngchong replied slowly and deliberately, stroking two drooping wisps of mustaches. Jim Dandy interpreted. He explained at length, making up with gestures and grimaces what he lacked in vocabulary, that the porcelain was all made at the city of three thousand furnaces, Ching-teh-Chen, four hundred miles to the northeast. Some was decorated there, especially the blue and white, since that color could be applied before the glaze. When ready, the porcelain would be brought by porters and pack horses over the Mei-ling Pass to Saochow. From there it would come by river junks and be unloaded directly into Syngchong's godown. By that time, Jim Dandy promised, "tea sets, coffee sets, choc-lat sets, punch bowls—all allee-samee leaddy; all allee samee go ship-side, one time, chop-chop."

"And these special orders? Surely they are nearly finished?" Captain Audley inquired.

Syngchong inclined his head toward the wall from whence came the humming sound. "You likee come see?" Jim Dandy asked.

Syngchong led the way behind a lacquer screen, through a curtain of swinging beads, and into a long gallery. Here the porcelain painters sat, row after row of them, old men, middle-aged men, youths, and children. While their brushes moved, their tongues kept pace. The boys stepped close to watch one child busy with a wafer-thin saucer. His hand poised over the piece like a butterfly, giving it a flick from his charged brush too rapid to follow. He had drawn a tiny, perfect circle. Without a pause he passed the saucer to his neighbor and took up another. This process was followed all along the line, each painter adding the few strokes at which he excelled. Porters carried the finished product from the room and brought in loads of blank ware on long planks balanced over one shoulder.

Passing from table to table, Roy's eye was caught by a familiar design. There it was—Rosalie's tea set, which he had promised to bring home to her when he said good-by under the old mulberry tree so many months ago. This was the design—a wreath of roses encircling Rosalie's initials—that he had finished and given to Cousin Audley just before going ashore at Sandy Cove to be enslaved by the Northwest Coast savages. He kept his head down, hoping that his memories did not show in his face. When he stole a look at Cousin Audley, it was met with a bland smile. "I believe your project will turn out rather well," the Captain said. "It should be an ornament to any lady's tea table. Well, there is nothing to be gained by lingering here. As you see, the Chinese have their own ways of doing things and cannot be hurried."

They returned by a longer route, Cousin Audley having undertaken to give his young friends a view of the sights. They followed New China Street to Thirteen Factory Street, which ran behind the foreign hongs separating them from the forbidden city of Canton. Turning into Thirteen Factory Street, they came to the vast establishment called

Consoo House, where all public business between the Foreign Devils and the hong merchants took place. In front of Consoo House they turned again, this time toward the river, and found their way along the clamor of Old China Street to the American factory. At the door Jim Dandy took his leave, and Cousin Audley expressed his intention of paying calls at the East India Company. He did not invite the boys, and they were glad enough to be relieved of his presence.

"Whew!" exclaimed Jerry. "I've had my fill of play-acting already. And to think there are still weeks of it to come!" He loosened his collar, for he had grown unused to wearing the garments of civilization.

"I don't know whether I can keep up this masquerade or not," Roy agreed, his usually clear blue-gray eyes dark as a storm cloud. "When I saw Rosalie's tea set, I was sorely temped to pick it up piece by piece and break it over that old hypocrite's head!"

CHAPTER IX

THE FACTORY

ALTHOUGH the shadow of Cousin Audley loomed large over the next few weeks, Roy and Jerry found themselves enjoying a busy and pleasant existence as residents of the American factory.

This establishment consisted of four large buildings one behind the other, separated by courts. Roy and Jerry occupied rooms in Number Two, and had the satisfaction of knowing that Cousin Audley was some distance away in Number Four, while Broderick Brown was just next door.

The mornings began with a discreet knock announcing a native servant with hot water and the offer of breakfast. Jerry ordered breakfast with relish, and dismissed the servant, but Roy called after him, "—and plenty of hot water and towels for shaving! It's lucky I brought Father's razors along," he added to Jerry, fingering his chin. "What are you grinning about? I *do* need a shave! Look!"

Jerry examined his brother's sunburned jaw. "It does look somewhat like a peach," he admitted. He rubbed his own cheek, then reached for a mirror. "My word! I believe *I* need a shave, too, Roy! Look!"

While they were passing the mirror from hand to hand, a small barrage of knocking was heard at the door. Upon opening it, their caller was found to be a slight, dapper young man, with round blue eyes and unruly hair, who informed them:

"I'm Worth. Anyone will tell you I'm not worth much; still, Bullfinch and Company pays a modest sum for my services and hasn't sacked me yet. I was chosen by the fellows to welcome you to the factory, and since we are told that it will be some weeks before your ship sails, to invite you to take part in our poor amusements, such as they are. How about a row on the river this afternoon? We want you on the Blue team. Those infernal rascals, the Reds, snagged Captain Brown for their side, and he's as good as two men, any day."

The boys accepted readily, but before either could complete a sentence, their guest went on, "You'll meet all your teammates at tiffin, and our opponents, too; they're all a splendid lot of fellows. Some of them you've met already, and others live in the other factories—we take a strong arm wherever we can find it, no matter what language the owner of it speaks. There are a number of us still young enough to enjoy life, and we see to it that we do. We practice fencing in the court after business hours and have regular tournaments at billiards and whist, and of course there is always the best of conversation at dinner, and now and again the hong merchants invite us to chopstick dinners; three days a month we are allowed to visit the Flower Gardens at Hwa-to and the Honam Temple. Too bad regulations forbid rowing on the river."

"But you said—"

"Oh, of course we *do* row on the river anyway, but it's against regulations, and every so often the hong merchants give us a scolding and make us stop for a while. Then we're at it again."

"Who makes the regulations?"

"The Son of Heaven, the Emperor, himself. The hong merchants are duty-bound to make us keep them; they fuss over us like a flock of mother hens, and do everything for us but feed us with a spoon. I must say their system is nothing short of marvelous, and the Foreign Devils in Canton are the best fed, best protected, and enjoy the most orderly and profitable business in the world." He ended this oration flushed with enthusiasm, but after a moment's pause added gloomily, "However, no ladies are allowed in the factories, and existence without the fair sex is bound to be a dreary one." He gazed pensively out of the window.

Another knock announced the arrival of breakfast. "Won't you breakfast with us?" Roy invited Worth. He liked the talkative young man, who beamed with good nature.

"Oh, I've already eaten; still, we shall have a busy day today, for Captain Elliot's making up his cargo. That bacon looks ever so good."

Jerry placed a chair for him, and they fell to with good appetite. During the days to follow they saw much of Worth, who was always talkative, always hungry, and always good-natured. He was scarcely twenty. Among the clerks—they were called pursers—there were some even younger than he, and Roy and Jerry found them a congenial company. After business hours they entered into the rowing, the fencing, and the visiting back and forth; they became acquainted in the French, Dutch, Swedish, and East India Company factories, finding a welcome everywhere. At meals they had the advantage of mixing with men of business of all ages, including the taipans—the chiefs of the business houses— and the officers of the ships that came and went. There was much talk of tea and silk, of buying prices and selling prices, and of weather, uncharted shoals, Malay pirates, and typhoons. There was news from America and Europe not six months old. Roy and Jerry heard for the first time of the success of the American Peace Mission in its negotiations with Napoleon Bonaparte. These international matters, which would have seemed very far away from Virginia, were of personal interest to them now.

While their new friends were occupied in office and

countinghouse, Jerry strolled with Mimbo in the square in front of the factories, where there was always entertainment to be had watching the life of the water front. Roy delved into the factory libraries, overjoyed to find books available again. During their first free hours they had composed another long letter to Mrs. Lacey, repeating all that they had said in the letter left with Captain Quincey. After conferring with Jerry and Captain Brown, Roy sat down to write to Rosalie, but since they had all agreed that she should not be told the whole of their story, lest word leak out to alarm Mr. Morris, it was hard work. He filled it with light anecdotes of life in Canton, and with scribbled sketches of the scenes he glimpsed in the square.

At intervals they called upon Cousin Audley and went over long lists of teas, learning the distinction between young hyson, hyson, and hyson skin, gunpowder, imperial, souchong, and superior souchong. They went with him to Fouqua's godowns to sample bales of nankeen, sarsenets, satins, and lustrings, and to the shops to choose camphorwood chests and lacquer trays. Cousin Audley laid all the business of the ship before them with a lack of reserve that should have been gratifying. His frankness, however, only reminded the boys of their peril. As Jerry said, "What does he care how much we know, since he intends us never to reach home with our knowledge?"

The *Swan* was beached on Dutch Island to be graved and overhauled, and the boys often accompanied Captain Brown when he went to oversee the work. The *Thunderbird* had already completed this process and was afloat, but her holds were being fumigated and prepared for the sensitive cargo of tea, the bilges being sweetened with limewater. Roy and Jerry visited her one day at their cousin's invitation, secure in the belief that his trap was not yet ready to spring. They wandered about the familiar decks and renewed acquaintance with such of the crew as were aboard. Fat Pork, the Portuguese cook, Codder, the New Englander, Jock, the Cockney, and old Hawks, the carpenter, all came forward to pay their respects. The boys got only a hard, sardonic stare from Mr. Griff, the first mate, still chewing his cud of tobacco; but they wanted nothing and expected less from him. He had never neglected a chance to show his contempt for the *Thunderbird*'s young owners, and Roy had a vivid memory of his ugly face looking on as he was delivered over to the savages. Ole and Ross, whom Jerry remembered best as his would-be murderers at Corona, were on leave ashore. "Thank heaven!" Jerry thought. "If I were to see them, it might be the end of this pretty masquerade!"

Roy thought sadly of Hyppolite, the cabin boy who had tended him so faithfully and who had died for his sake on the other side of the world. Altogether it was a difficult visit, one to get over with. Memories were of no use to them now; they needed all their attention for the future.

There was no news of Ching at the *Swan*, nor had he been heard of at the factory. "I know he would have come back if he could!" Roy complained. "China seems to have swallowed him up without a trace."

Worth nodded sagely. "The Chinese Dragon is quite capable of doing so. Just as Higginbotham's dog disappeared one day from the East India Company and was never heard of again. Higginbotham posted a reward card, but the comprador said, 'All finishee. Some man have chow-chow he.'"

Worth made a dive for Mimbo with imaginary chopsticks, his meaning so clear that Mimbo whined and crawled under Jerry's chair. Everyone laughed. Mimbo came in for a good deal of teasing from the young pursers, but in return he claimed the titbits from their tables and seemed to thrive upon both. A group of what Worth called "splendid fellows" were gathered now in the common room, awaiting dinner. The weather being exceptionally cold, the blazing fire and drawn curtains were doubly welcome. As usual, someone was knocking the balls about on the billiard table at the end of the room, several were reading months-old newspapers, and the rest were carrying on a much-interrupted conversation as newcomers arrived. Broderick Brown made one of the group. He was a great favorite with both the pursers and the taipans, being qualified for the one society by his tender years, and for the other by his position of authority as owner of the *Margaret* and master of the *Swan*.

The oldest of the company was Nathaniel Miller, an ancient of twenty-five, who had already spent a decade in the Canton trade. A guest from the East India Company was a lantern-jawed young Scot named Mackie, his host being Jacob McChesney of New York.

Nathaniel Miller, looking into the fire, mused, "The season's nearly over. Captain Elliot has sailed; there are only four American ships left at Whampoa. The *Thunderbird* will be next, I hear."

"The *Swan* will not be far behind her," Broderick Brown said, quietly.

"Yes, soon they'll all be rolling down the China Sea, and we shall pack ourselves off to Macao."

Worth cried, "We can't let the season close without some sort of celebration. We must give the last ships a rousing send-off. What shall it be?"

"Let's go to the Hwa-to Flower Gardens, have an alfresco banquet, with plenty of toasts and speeches. You must compose a farewell poem, Worth."

"Must? No one could prevent his doing it, you know," muttered McChesney.

"Nothing could be easier," said Worth, airily. "I shall retire to yonder desk and commence at once."

He took a chair at the nearby desk and made a great show of spreading out papers and sharpening pens. The talk went on without him until presently he turned around, his hair in his eyes and an ink blot on his nose, and said, "I say! I have a splendid beginning, but I'm stuck for a rhyme."

"Read it!"

Worth cleared his throat and declaimed:

> "Farewell, Celestial Land, farewell!
> Farewell, O sons of Han!
> Whose teas and silks our purses swell—

"Can anyone think of a word to rhyme with Han?"

Mackie said, promptly, "Mon."

"Mon? What's that mean?" Worth inquired.

The Scotsman flushed. "Why, mon, did ye no' hear aright? Mon! Mon!"

"Oh! You mean man," said Worth. "It won't do. It doesn't rhyme."

Mackie rose slowly. He towered above Worth, who looked up at him with round eyes. "How can ye say it doesna' rhyme, when ye hear me speak it distinctly? Mon—Han. Han—Mon." He turned to the company. "Can any mon here say it doesna' rhyme?"

"Never mind, Mackie," cautioned his friend McChesney. "It doesn't matter, one way or the other."

"The mon is either deaf or daft," Mackie persisted hotly. "In any case he's no versifier, for he doesna' ken a rhyme when he hears it."

Worth sprang up, his hair fairly bristling. "I may be deaf, and I may be daft," he cried, "but I'm as good a versifier as the next man, and I pronounce it *man*."

"With all the things there are in the world to quarrel about, why quarrel about one little word?" asked Broderick Brown.

The others laughed, but Worth and Mackie still glared at each other. "It isn't the word, it's the principle of the thing!" declared Worth. "He insulted my poetry!"

"He insulted the whole race of Scotsmen!" thundered Mackie.

Nathaniel Miller made an effort to smooth things over. "Come, now, no one has insulted anybody. Nothing has been said that cannot soon be forgotten."

"Then I say it now," challenged Mackie. "Your verses are poor, and you are no gentleman!"

Worth drew himself up and flung his words back at him. "If you, sir, are representative of your race, then the whole race of Scotsmen are no gentlemen!"

"That's done it," sighed Broderick Brown.

Mackie spoke through his teeth, "Oblige me by naming someone to act for you. My second will wait upon him to-morrow."

"Nathaniel, will you make the arrangements?" Worth turned to Miller, who rose, bowed to both, and resumed his seat and his cigar.

Mackie bowed and stalked out of the room.

The projected duel was the talk of the factories. In the morning Miller was waited upon by a black-browed young gentleman from the East India Company, and it was agreed that all arrangements as to time, place, and weapons should be made by letter, since all parties concerned were much occupied with business during the last weeks of the season.

Every day or so Miller reported the progress of these ne-gotiations. "The choice of weapons is difficult," he explained, "since we are not allowed to bring firearms into the factories, nor would we be permitted to fire them if we had them. Worth is all for swordplay, but Mackie has never held a sword in his life, and insists on pistols."

"The challenged has the right to choose weapons," some-one observed.

"Yes, but who challenged whom? No one seems to re-member. It's a difficult matter." And Miller went off shaking his head.

So the days passed, full of interest and amusement for Roy and Jerry. They had not forgotten their danger, but they were content to ignore it until they must meet it face to face. Their quarters in Number Two had become home-like; Broderick Brown was the best of companions; the weather was turning milder, and the *Swan* was afloat, cleaned and painted, and ready for her cargo. As they came downstairs one morning, Roy, Jerry, Broderick Brown, and Mimbo, the future looked bright enough.

As usual, the courtyard was astir. Like an army of ants the coolies were emptying the godowns under the super-vision of the comprador and his assistants with their brushes and paper, their tally sticks and abacus. In front of the iron doors of the treasury, the Schroff and his helpers were weighing heaps of silver in their copper scales. The clinking of it echoed through the broad arched passageways, a con-stant accompaniment to life in the factories.

The office of Mr. Kincaid was reached through a large outer room, where busy pursers worked despite the con-versation of two ships' officers, a comprador, and a linguist who were settling some affair at a desk by the window. Mr. Kincaid being engaged, Broderick Brown and the boys waited.

"Have you heard the latest concerning the duel?" Mc-Chesney leaned from his work a moment to ask. "The weap-ons are settled now; it's to be pistols smuggled up from Macao. But the place is not so easy to decide. Where can they go that will not be under the eye of the Futai, the gov-ernor of the province? Fouqua has heard talk already, and says he is as good as strangled if the duel takes place here. Worth suggests some place at Macao, but Mackie swears he won't risk being killed in a town where there are thirteen Roman Catholic churches. I—"

The door of Mr. Kincaid's office opened, and Captain Audley came out, ruddy and smiling. At sight of the three waiting, he advanced heartily and clapped Roy and Jerry on the back. "Well, lads," he cried, "it's homeward bound for the *Thunderbird*. What say you? We sail today week if all goes well."

Broderick Brown covered an awkward silence by saying, "We'd all best follow your example, or we'll lose the monsoon. You may be sure you won't leave the *Swan* far astern."

The duel was overshadowed now by plans for the farewell party at Hwa-to. Worth, of course, was the ringleader in the affair and went into lengthy conferences with the comprador and the cook over the menu. Arguments were heard throughout the factory as to the relative merits of "fly gooso" (wild duck) and "sit-down gooso" (tame duck), and as to the selection and sequence of wines.

Meanwhile Roy and Jerry braced themselves for the moment of trial. They put their belongings in readiness for transfer to the *Swan*, and one of the *Swan's* boats stood by near the landing. But they must not make their move too soon. "Wait until Captain Audley gives you notice of departure," Broderick Brown advised. "Then get your luggage aboard the boat and get away at once for the *Swan*. The men have orders to take you there at any hour of the day or night, whether I am at hand or not."

So the boys awaited the *Thunderbird's* sailing with confidence. Two days before the day Captain Audley had set, the promised excursion to the Hwa-to Gardens took place.

The party embarked at Jackass Point, late in the afternoon, twenty-odd gentlemen in a festive mood, dividing themselves between two magnificent flower boats fit for any mandarin. These were followed by a large sampan bearing servants and the feast. The little fleet moved off up the river, passing the foreign factories, and soon nothing could be seen to recall the western world except the flutter of the flags on the tall flagstaffs. The banks were lined with houses, their carved balconies overlooking the river, their steps leading down to the water. Wide spreading banyan trees and drooping willows shaded a network of canals that led off from the main stream.

Most of the guests sat within the cabins, content to catch glimpses of the view through glass windows while sipping hot rice wine. Roy, Jerry, and Broderick Brown preferred the deck, where they could see all the sights, and Worth sacrificed his comfort to keep them company. They entered a broad canal, clamorous with the cries of the boatmen bringing their craft to their moorings for the night. Aboard the numberless sampans about them fires were lighted to cook the evening meal. Lanterns began to glow from the houses ashore, multiplying themselves by reflection, and a great yellow moon cleared the horizon astern.

There was still an hour of light by which to see the gardens. While the servants busied themselves about the pavilion in which the banquet was to be served, the guests sauntered along the paths, over the little bridges, and in and out of fantastically constructed grottoes and artificial ruins. Groups of Chinese were taking the air also, brought out by the Festival of the Full Moon: stately fathers of families in fur-lined robes, carrying pet birds on sticks; bustling nurses with roly-poly, well-padded children; and shy ladies with lacquered hair and toddling crippled feet. Their servants were setting up fireworks displays, brewing tea, and making ready lanterns for the dark.

When dusk closed in the party from the factory gathered

at the pavilion, made comfortable with screens, charcoal braziers, and foot warmers, and gay with many lanterns. "A toast!" cried Worth. "To departing friends!"

This was the first of many toasts. Voices rose, faces glowed, and tongues became loose. Roy and Jerry, after responding to the first toast, turned their attention to their food. They had seen many men in their cups, and they had seen their father remain sober in spite of ridicule. Comparing the drunken with the sober, it was not hard for them to choose between them. They only grinned when the others teased them, and went on enjoying the crab soup and roast capon. Broderick Brown also refused to intoxicate himself; but as for the rest, most of them were soon befuddled, not excepting Jim Dandy, who was charged by regulations with the responsibility of the Foreign Devils. Prominent among the upraised hands and tilting glasses were those of Captain John Audley, whose ruddy face lit up like a lantern as he drank to the successful homeward voyage of the *Thunderbird*.

Outside the sky was lit by a shower of colored sparks, and the beating of gongs and twanging of musical instruments celebrated the Festival of the Full Moon. "Let's see what's going on," Jerry whispered to Roy. "I must walk around before I can eat any dessert, and no one will miss us here."

They looked at Broderick Brown, but he was deep in conversation, so they did not disturb him. They walked down a path leading from the pavilion to the water's edge, where a landing gave them a view up and down the canal. Here they could see the fireworks bloom like flowers in the sky, lighting up the busy scene below before they shattered and fell. The canal was crowded with boats, some filled with merrymakers and others plying their accustomed trades. By lantern light they displayed for sale cooked foods, fireworks, toys, lanterns, incense, or caged birds, or offered the services of boatmen, barbers, musicians, or fortunetellers. Over all the full moon hung in the east, growing smaller and paler but brighter as it rose.

Some distance away up the canal, lanterns were being dropped into the stream, from whence they floated past the gardens on the current. Roy and Jerry leaned out to see them come drifting toward them, fairylike globes of rainbow colors. A voice chirped unexpectedly almost under their noses. "You wanchee see more better, chintelemuns? Allee same come on sampan, you like."

It was a boy on one of the sampans moored at the landing. He beckoned to them, smiling. Jerry stepped on board, and Roy followed him. They stood looking at the bobbing lanterns, and Roy asked, "What for those men do so-fashion?"

"Allee-same full moon pidgin. Number one good luck," said the boy. "You wanchee savvy good luck? This sampan got number one fortuneteller. He savvy much thing. He tellee you, you come?" Again he beckoned, this time toward the cabin.

Jerry laughed. "No, thanks, we no likee. Come on, Roy, I think I can eat that dessert now."

They crossed the deck, but as they passed the opening into the cabin they heard the rattle of fortunetelling sticks. A dry old voice spoke softly in Chinese. The sampan boy put his hand on Roy's arm. "He say Meleika chintelemuns take larchee journey. He number one fortuneteller; he tellee you good-luck stars for journey. You come?"

Roy shook him off. "It wouldn't take a number one fortuneteller to guess we are going to take a journey," he said to Jerry. "Every foreigner in Canton is bound to take a journey, if only to Macao."

The old voice spoke from the dark opening. The boy

translated, "He say, velly funny ting. He say two bird take larchee journey. He say Meleika chintelemuns allee same go with one bird, not savvy which one. My no savvy this talk; too much fool."

Roy and Jerry looked at one another. "Bird?" exclaimed Jerry. "My word, Roy, he's talking about the ships—" he did not finish the sentence, but Roy had the same thought. Two birds were going to make a long journey—the *Thunderbird* and the *Swan*.

The question came to them softly, in Chinese and pidgin English, "Maybe so you likee know which one?"

Roy made a move toward the cabin. Jerry said, "Oh, it's all foolishness. Let's go back to the pavilion."

"Of course, it's only foolishness," Roy agreed. He started toward the gangplank, but Jerry said, "But if he knows—if he could tell—"

While they hesitated, they heard the little sticks rattled in their cup again, and a lantern inside the cabin was moved. In its light they could see a cup shaken and a flat bamboo stick fall out upon a table draped in cloth. Behind the table sat an old man huddled in a black gown. A cap was pulled forward, shading his eyes. He held up the stick between his thumb and forefinger.

As if hypnotized, Roy and Jerry bent their heads and entered the cabin. They felt the presence of others in the shadows, but their attention was fixed upon the hand holding the stick. The old man began to mumble a long, singsong speech. A helper popped up from nowhere, sitting cross-legged on the mat at the fortuneteller's side. He held a book and searched busily through its pages. The cabin was full of incense, seeming to grow thicker as the boys waited.

"Now he allee same read sign in Book of Classics," the interpreter explained. "Truly, he savvy all thing. You wait. He tellee all thing you wanchee know."

Suddenly they felt a movement under their feet. For a moment they were puzzled, then the cause became obvious. The sampan had been pushed from the bank and was now swinging rapidly into the current. Roy and Jerry awoke from their dream and rushed for the door. It was closed, and before it stood two menacing forms they recognized at once as their old enemies from the *Thunderbird:* the giant Scandinavian, Ole, and Ross, with his apelike stance and polished bald pate. Behind them three other figures came closer into the lantern light. These were brawny Chinese rivermen.

"Yell, Roy!" roared Jerry. But up on deck a gong set up a din that drowned out their voices.

Ole said, "Ve can gag yu, an' tie yu oop. Vy give us such trobble? Yust sit down nice an' enchoy de ride to Whampoa."

"Are you crazy?" Jerry demanded. "Don't you know our friends will discover our absence? Don't you know they will trace us to the *Thunderbird*?"

"Your friends will miss you, sor, I have no doubt," answered Ross. "As for tracing you to the *Thunderbird*, let them! She sails the moment we're aboard."

CHAPTER X

THE CHASE

"VELL," sneered Ole, hefting a marlinespike in his big fist, "yu goin' to fight or be gude?"

Roy was stunned by the sudden turn of events. At last his mind began to function. The sampan must have already passed the pavilion now, he thought. It was useless to struggle against Ole and Ross and three Chinese boatmen; and as for crying out, no human vocal chords could compete with the bronze gong on deck. He ignored Ole, but said to Jerry, "We might as well be comfortable."

Jerry nodded. He had been following the same line of thought, and although he itched to put a fist into Ross's ugly smile, he decided to save his strength. He turned his back on the two seamen. "Are there any chairs in this place?"

The fortuneteller still sat at the table, his helper and the interpreter squatting at his feet. A glance around the cabin revealed no other chair, so Jerry with a shrug sat down on the matting, his back propped against one wall. Roy followed suit. Thus established, they fixed a calm gaze on Ole and Ross, who presently dropped their eyes and began to shuffle their feet. They were confused by their captives' behavior and would much have preferred a good fight.

Seeing this, Roy and Jerry stared the harder. Ross could stand it no longer. "Look here," he blustered, advancing with his apelike crouch, "get a civil look on yer high-and-mighty faces, if you don't want a taste o' me knuckles."

"I can't help it if you don't admire my type of beauty," Jerry grinned maddeningly. "Ah! Careful there! You know very well our Cousin Audley told you not to lay a hand on us. Why else would you have brought those Oriental bully boys along? No, our Cousin Audley wants us kept nice and tidy until we are well out of reach of Canton."

Ross muttered obscenely, drawing back his arm. Ole caught it. "Dot's true," he said. "Dot's vat Capt'n said. No use to make Capt'n mad wid us, Ross."

"Then let me get out of sight of 'em," growled Ross. "I can't stand the sight of their pink faces!" He snapped an order to the silent Chinese guards. "You watchee good; you sleep, I slittee your throats; you savvy?" They looked at him uncomprehendingly until the boy who had enticed Roy and Jerry aboard translated this into Chinese. Then they nodded and ranged themselves along the opposite wall. Ross and Ole went on deck. The boys could hear them settle down just outside the door.

The Chinese gazed at nothing, their eyes half-closed, but watchful. "We'll never stare *them* down," Jerry murmured to Roy.

The fortuneteller said something to the boy, who rose and placed a pile of coins on the table. He counted them into three portions before the two others and himself: a little heap of copper cash and one silver dollar for each.

"The price of our lives," Roy said bitterly.

"It's not much, is it?" muttered Jerry. "I would have thought Cousin Audley would put a higher value on us."

The boy at the table spoke to them over his shoulder. His face and voice were expressionless, but his words sent a thrill of excitement tingling through the captives. "My only man this place savvy Foreign-Devil talk. S'pose Meleika chintelemuns wanchee pay larchee dollar, my lettee go?"

Controlling his voice with an effort, Roy answered, "How-fashion you can lettee go? No can fight three piecee number one strong man?"

The boy squatted on the floor again, the shadow of the table half concealing him from the guards. "My no fight. Those men too muchee fool. Fortuneteller give them bad-luck talk; they allee same scare like rabbit. You pay my larchee dollar, my lettee you go. You wanchee?"

"We'll pay you four dollar," Roy said.

"You pay my four dollar; odder chintelemun allee same pay four more dollar." Throughout the conversation the boy continued to count his pile of cash. They could see the grin of anticipation on his face.

Jerry spoke up. "All right. But get along with it; we don't want to be stranded too far from the foreign factories."

The boy seemed to understand. He rose and went around the table, and with his back to the guards leaned across it, speaking low in the fortuneteller's ear. One of the guards was in a half doze, the others talking quietly among themselves; they paid no attention to the old man and his helpers.

They were attracted, however, when the fortuneteller's helper opened a box and took out a scroll. This he opened with a great show of reverence and laid before the fortune-teller, revealing a circle divided into sections bearing Chinese characters. He traced the figures on the chart, mumbling. The boy repeated aloud some words that caused the guards to look with interest toward the table. The fortune-teller gabbled louder, his gnarled forefinger tapping at characters here and there in the circle. He jabbed his finger toward the rivermen. One by one they rose and came close.

Roy and Jerry could only watch like the audience at a play. They guessed that this was the "bad-luck talk" the boy had promised. They waited for the moment that would give them an opportunity to escape.

The men were speaking excitedly among themselves. Again and again the fortuneteller pointed to the chart, then at each of the boatmen. Jerry watched the door onto the deck, apprehensive lest the raised voices bring Ole and Ross back into the cabin. From outside, however, came the noise of exploding firecrackers and the strains of a floating band of musicians.

More and more excited, the rivermen put copper cash in the hands of the fortuneteller, receiving long strips of red paper in return. The fortuneteller's boy lifted a bamboo curtain behind the table, revealing a smaller cabin in the stern of the boat, where a fat wooden image sat in a dimly lit niche, incense rising before him. One by one the rivermen went into the cabin. Behind the last one the boy let the curtain fall. He then came swiftly to Roy and Jerry holding out one hand; the other he pointed to the window above their heads. They sprang to their feet, thrust their silver into his hand, and drew back the sliding oiled-paper panel. They stepped out onto a narrow ledge, took one wild glance about them, and seeing the deck of another sampan a few feet away, made a leap for it.

Confused by the movement, the lights and shadows and reflections, they had no chance to choose their route. They raced blindly the length of the deck on which they had landed, upsetting a crate of chickens. A cock flapped angrily and crowed, and the owner popped his head out of the cabin like a jack-in-the-box, screaming with rage. At the bow of the boat they found the carved prow of a large craft overhanging them. They reached for it and swung themselves up.

Behind them they could hear a general outcry. Among the Chinese voices those of Ole and Ross rang out. "We don't have much of a lead," Jerry gasped. "Which way is the shore? We must gain the shore even if we have to swim."

They crouched a moment in the shelter of the gilded carving, trying to get their bearings. In the bright moonlight they made out the shapes of peaked roofs above masses of trees, quite close at hand. "There it is!" whispered Roy. "Run for it!"

They ran, pounding along the empty deck, which seemed endless. They were on a great, creaking wooden palace built for some mandarin's pleasure, idle now and moored to a pier where stone steps led down to the water. They were almost at their goal when Jerry, in the lead, saw a pack of men running along the shore. He saw Ross's red face and bald pate shining like the moon itself, and two of the Chinese rivermen behind him. He stopped Roy with a gesture. "They've divided up," Roy whispered. "Ole and the other one are behind us. They've got us cornered."

"If we can't go forward or backward, we'll have to go sideways," said Jerry. They leaned over the rail. Under the side of the junk lay a ramshackle sampan, with a family gathered at their evening meal near a small fire. They were eating peacefully regardless of the shouting men on the shore and the clamor that told of Ole's progress across the boats the way the boys had come.

With one accord Roy and Jerry climbed over the rail and dropped down. They had only one chance. If the sampan's occupants cried out, they were lost, for their pursuers were close and watchful for such a clue. And it was almost certain that they would cry out. But the only alternative was to jump into the water, in which case the splash was sure to give them away.

They landed lightly on the deck, and remaining on their knees, made frantic signs to the people not to cry out. Surprisingly, their hosts greeted their appearance in utter silence. They stared at the strangers but went on pushing their rice from bowl to mouth with busy chopsticks. There was an old woman, two young men, and a round-faced girl with an infant fastened on her back.

Emboldened by their silence, Roy sought to enlist their

sympathy. Pointing to the shore and back to the river, he made signs of terror. Jerry mimicked him heartily. Still the sampan folk did not speak, but began making signs of their own to each other. Roy sat back on his heels with a heartfelt sigh. "They're mutes," he whispered to Jerry. "If only we can get them to hide us until those bully boys go away!"

They renewed their efforts, acting out their story as best they could. They had only a moment to convey their meaning. Then Ole's party was heard searching the pleasure junk above them, and Ross hailed the sampan from the shore.

The old woman seemed to come to a decision. She made a lightning signal to her sons, drew Roy and Jerry to the cabin, and thrust them below. By the light of a small candle burning before the family gods, the boys could see two children sleeping on the floor. They had no time to examine their surroundings further, however, for the old woman motioned them to lie down. This done, she gathered an armful of dirty matting and laid it over them. On top of the matting she placed the sleeping children, who slept on as limp as kittens. Roy and Jerry could hardly breathe. They lay face down on the filthy floor, smothered by the weight on their backs. Faintly they could hear voices and footsteps on deck as the two parties of their pursuers closed in. They were caught now like rats in a trap, their lives utterly dependent upon the old woman and her family.

The voice of Ross rasped angrily, but being answered by silence, the singsong harangue of one of the rivermen took its place. This, too, drew nothing but silence, while the boys could only wait and pray.

Footsteps crossed and recrossed the deck, with thumps and thuds when the searchers knocked over a tub or opened a chest to see what it concealed. Soon Roy and Jerry heard men come into the cabin, walk from wall to wall, ransacking every hiding place. One of the children woke and whim-

pered, sitting up to look at the intruders. Her sharp little el-
bows dug into Roy's back. He felt a strong desire to laugh.
Of all the strange places to which their venture had brought
them, surely this was the strangest and the most ridiculous!
Then he heard Jerry draw in his breath sharply. One of the
men had kicked the matting, putting his toe squarely into
his ribs. If only Jerry could hold his temper! Another kick
thudded into his own thigh. A wave of anger swept through
him. If he survived this, he'd repay Cousin Audley for every
humiliating moment. If only he could hold his *own* temper!

At last the men left the cabin, and soon afterward Roy
and Jerry felt the rocking of the sampan as they went
ashore. But for some time no one came to relieve them of
their burden which had become well-nigh insupportable.
Their nostrils were full of foul odors; their joints ached with
stiffness, and their skin itched from the bites of crawling in-
sects. They both began to wonder if they had been betrayed
into another imprisonment. All sorts of fearful fancies played
through their heads. Jerry struggled with a necessity to
sneeze.

The sneeze and a rescuer arrived at the same time. Thank-
fully they felt the children lifted off, and they struggled out
from under the mats, rubbing sore muscles and gasping for
air. The old woman was with them again, cautioning them
to silence. Leading them on deck she pointed out the way
the men had gone, one group up along the shore, the other
down. "Then we must go inland," Jerry said. "We dare not
stay here. We'll be all right when we reach a populated spot,
where we can find someone to take us to the factories."

Roy emptied his pockets of silver, pressing the coins into
the old woman's hand. She looked from him to the money
wonderingly. He patted her arm, wishing he could thank
her for what she had done. Her sons and the girl with the
baby still sat around the few coals in the brazier. The old

woman returned to them, showing her coins. They smiled widely, ducked their heads at the boys, and resumed their strange, mute conversation with their hands.

"Come on, Roy!" urged Jerry. "They'll be back. They know we're somewhere nearby."

Roy put his mind to their course of action. "Blast this moonlight! Well, keep to the shadows wherever you can. Let's aim for that roof straight ahead that looks like a temple."

They stepped ashore, feeling fairly well sheltered by a large, spreading banyan tree. Beyond its shade there was a wall that offered a dark screen, and beyond that a grove of bamboo. A little farther, and they were hugging the wall of the place they took to be a temple. On the other side they could see a glow of light and hear the wild discords of Chinese music. "Good!" breathed Jerry. "All we have to do is follow the wall around to the gate. There will be people there."

Slowly they made their way along the wall, seeing danger in every shadow and hearing pursuers in every noise of the night. Presently they entered a lane with houses on one side and an occasional passer-by: a coolie trotting under his load, a farmer hurrying away from the town, a palanquin borne by two uniformed men and attended by others before and behind. Each time Roy and Jerry took cover by standing still in the shadow of the wall.

The lane opened into a more populous street, with a few lighted shops and people coming and going in family groups. Here was the gate they sought. It opened into a wide courtyard, lighted with torches. A crowd of visitors, priests, and vendors mingled here, amid a constant din of firecrackers, musical instruments, gongs, and voices. Some sort of procession was coming down the broad stairway, the participants carrying enormous paper images of gods and goddesses, lions, dragons, and fishes.

Into the courtyard of the temple Roy and Jerry walked incautiously. They did not realize that among all the fantastic sights of the place, to the natives they themselves were the most extraordinary. Hatless, their straw-colored hair in wild disorder, their fair skins the fairer for their weeks ashore, their foreign garments soiled but elegant, and their blue eyes blazing with excitement, they presented a startling picture to the surprised villagers.

Someone set up a shout, *"Fan-quai! Foreign Devils!"* Others took it up, "Foreign Devils! Red-haired Foreign Devils!" The crowd began to gather about them. One urchin darted close, pulled at Jerry's coattails, and darted away out of reach. A stone whizzed past their heads.

Roy had meant to try out his pidgin English here, in hope of finding a boatman who would take them to the foreign factories. But the crowd was too great and of too uncertain a temper.

They turned and pelted out of the courtyard and down the street. The rabble followed, throwing stones and filth from the ditches. Their flight took them to the outskirts of the village. The street became a narrow lane walled on both sides. They followed it, unable to choose any other direction. Behind them the shouts and footfalls were gaining on them, for as some of the crowd fell away, fresh curiosity-seekers joined in the chase. It was not often that Foreign Devils were to be found away from the protection of their allotted district.

Eyes fixed on the lane ahead, hoping to find some break in the endless walls, the boys pounded on. Suddenly they saw another group approaching them. In the milk-white light of the moon there was no mistaking their identity; it was Ross and Ole and their Chinese ruffians. It was obvious that they recognized the boys and the plight they were in, for they started for them with a rush, brandishing their marlinespikes.

There was nothing to do but to assay the wall. Roy dropped to the ground. "Quick, get on my back!" Jerry did not stop to argue, but climbed on his brother's shoulders and felt himself propelled to the top of the wall as Roy sprang upright. He grasped the rough stone, pulled himself astride the wall, then leaned down to help Roy. With one or two false starts, scrambling, kicking, and grunting, Roy somehow reached the top. They had just time to see the two bodies of their pursuers meet at the place they had been. Then they dropped to the ground on the inside of the wall.

CHAPTER XI

BEHIND THE WALL

OUTSIDE they heard the rabble raise a gleeful cry. "Foreign Devils! Foreign Devils!" They grinned at one another as Ole and Ross replied with oaths. To the crowd, one pair of Foreign Devils would serve as well as another. Ole and Ross would not find it easy to get away with whole skins.

But they had little time to enjoy the predicament of their enemies. They were called upon immediately to face their own. Where were they? It was one thing to be outside of a wall; quite another to be shut inside. They looked around them curiously.

They were in the midst of a grove of small, neat trees, whose dark leaves mirrored the moonlight. "Orange trees," Jerry whispered. "We must be in somebody's orchard."

Cautiously they made their way along a row of trees until they came to the end. They found a flagstone path at their feet. "We will do better to follow the wall," Roy held Jerry back. "Sooner or later it will lead us to a gate."

"But *how* soon?" hissed Jerry. "Some of these estates are miles around. The path must lead to a house, and where there's a house, there's a gate. Come on!"

Roy gave in and they followed the path, which meandered under an arch of willows, and presently skirted a large pond, full of reeds, from which a cold damp air breathed upon them. They were glad when they climbed above it, mounting between jagged black boulders. The path seemed endless, and they began to walk as if in a dream.

103

They seemed suddenly to have grown outlandishly tall, for now they looked down on the tops of old, gnarled pine trees which overshadowed the roofs of moss-grown pagodas. They crossed a bridge so small they had to walk single file, over a river in which was an island village. The moonlight shone through the roofless walls of ancient ruined temples, threw into relief the crouching forms of fantastic beasts sculptured in the rocks, and seemed to have bewitched a whole miniature world through which Roy and Jerry were doomed to wander forever. Their bewilderment was increased by the behavior of the path, which abruptly diverged. They were obliged to choose one direction at random, only to find themselves in a maze of little paths, none of which seemed likely to lead them out of the Lilliputian landscape.

They paused a moment to collect their thoughts. "You see where your path has led us!" said Roy. "I say we would do better to keep to one direction. The moon is toward the east; the river must be to the north. That's our best chance."

"And march up and down these blasted rocks and stumble through these cursed pines all night? I say any path is better than none," Jerry maintained, stubbornly.

In their heat they forgot caution, and stood, in the full moonlight, talking in raised voices. At once they saw their folly, for lights darted like fireflies out of a grove ahead of them, and they heard high-pitched Chinese cries. They did not know whether to hide or to run; they searched wildly for cover, but the tiny trees and infinitesimal mountains offered no shelter. When they did break and run, they knew they stood out like giants against their background.

A squad of giants pursued them, and they were soon surrounded. This time there was no chance to resist. Rough hands grasped their collars, and lanterns were held up to their faces. They were pushed and pulled by their captors into a broader path, and soon they saw more lanterns. The walls of a great house rose before them, restoring the scale of things to normal. They entered an ornamental gate and passed through a series of courtyards surrounded by spacious buildings. Servants scurried before them, vanishing in several directions, and from behind the screens of grillwork that made passageways about the courts, they felt that eyes watched them. At last they were thrust through a door into a well-lighted hall.

At one end was a platform holding a low table set with the apparatus for brewing tea. Other tables stood nearby, with carved wooden chairs and footstools. Although the furnishings were few in the vast room, it and everything in it bore a look of ease and luxury.

Their captors stood like soldiers at attention, all eyes focused on a doorway. Not a word was spoken. Into the breathless hush a slender figure moved quietly. It was a man in a mulberry-colored robe, over which the gleaming jade beads of his rank hung heavily—Fouqua, the hong merchant, smiling faintly.

The leader of the soldiers broke into speech, evidently explaining the disturbance and describing the crimes of the two Foreign Devils who had come tumbling over Fouqua's garden wall. The mandarin hushed him with a gesture and waved him and his men out of the room. He came courteously toward the boys, shaking hands with himself and saying, "My flen Ameleika chintelemun, Lacee, my velly glad welcome you my house. What for you own come, so-fashion? Too much trub', no have China custom, no can do."

Taking turns, Roy and Jerry tried to explain the events of the night in their best pidgin English. Since Fouqua was already familiar with their story, he soon understood what had happened, and looked very grave, shaking his head and muttering, "My think Captain Audley bad chop man. Next time he come China-side my no have pidgin with he!"

"Next time!" Roy exclaimed. "Can he not be punished for what he has done?" He sought to translate his thoughts. "He have kidnap us; he wanchee kill us; why for mandarin no can stop *Thunderbird,* no lettee sail, put Captain Audley in irons?"

Jerry added his plea. "You number one hong merchant, can do all things, must care for Foreign Devils. You send chop to Whampoa, no lettee *Thunderbird* sail, no lettee Captain Audley get away!"

Fouqua shook his head. "No can do. He no have hurt China man; no have broke China custom; my no can stop he. You lettee him go. Maskee, maskee, you allee same sail with you flen Brown; more better you go with he."

He urged them to take chairs; a servant who had remained in the room to replenish his master's pipe at frequent intervals poured tea. They saw that they could not persuade him to take a hand in the matter of the *Thunderbird;* indeed, he could not, for as he said, Captain Audley had not broken any Chinese law. Their complaint against him was merely a quarrel among Foreign Devils, and Fouqua, for all his importance as a hong merchant, had no power over him, as long as he did business under the regulations, paid his debts, and harmed no Chinese subject.

So they resigned themselves to the restful comfort of Fouqua's hospitality. Upheld by danger, they had not realized how tired they were. Now as they sat and inhaled the fragrant steam from their fragile porcelain cups, they felt many aches and bruises, and a coming appetite for the dates and ginger, pastry, and unfamiliar fruits that were laid out for them.

Presently Roy remembered his manners, and remarked to

his host, "Fouqua have number one fine house. Too-much largee! Allee same Emperor's palace at Peking!"

Fouqua chuckled at the compliment. "You likee? My have larchee farmilee, two, three hundred piecee people have chow my house. This land allee same belong my farmilee larchee time. In time of Sung Emperors, my farmilee belong this place."

He talked on while they drowsed in their chairs, content to be warm and comfortable after the exertions of the evening. There was something timeless about the quiet room, with its lofty carved ceiling, its walls hung with painted paper lighted by the soft glow of paper lanterns. Fouqua, too, seemed ageless. They might have been visiting one of his remote ancestors. He spoke of the tea they had just drunk. It was a choice tea, served on special occasions. Only three trees existed, planted by divine hands thousands of years ago, near the Temple of the Silver Moon in the Woo-E hills. Each tree produced one catty of tea each year, nearly all of which was reserved for the Emperor. Small quantities found their way into the hands of the hong merchants and were sometimes passed on as gifts to their foreign friends at the factories.

The mention of the factories roused Roy and Jerry. They must return at once! The party at the Hwa-to Gardens would surely be in great alarm, and their friends would be searching for them everywhere. They sprang up, explaining their haste to Fouqua, who summoned his servants. "You go my sampan, take my coolies, you velly safe now, you no trub'," he assured the boys.

He escorted them across the inner court, but they were stopped by another arrival, who came striding through the moon gate at such a rate that the servant who meant to announce him was left behind. It was Broderick Brown. When he saw Roy and Jerry, he stopped in his tracks and stared.

"Thank God!" he said, feelingly.

The boys never forgot that simple statement and the warmth behind it. Here was one friend—one rock amid their sea of troubles; they went to him, grasping his hand, pounding him on the back, and trying to explain everything that had happened to them all at once.

The young captain took off his hat and wiped his brow, for his hurry had heated him in spite of the night chill. He then explained his own adventures. "After you left the pavilion, I watched Captain Audley like a hawk, thinking I was a jump ahead of him—and all the time he had his plans laid forty fathom deep! A seaman came for him, telling him a boat from the *Thunderbird* was at the landing, ready to take him aboard. He had decided to sail sooner than he'd planned, he said, and we all drank to his health and then someone asked, what about the Lacey boys? Weren't they sailing with him? And the old sea serpent grinned and said you'd already taken a boat and were halfway to Whampoa, you were so anxious to be on board early. That's when I woke up and realized how he'd duped us. I thought for sure you were out of reach of help, but I came all a-fluking for Fouqua; if anyone could help us, he could." He gave them each a look they never forgot, a look of admiration from one man to another. "However, I see you helped yourselves and left 'em with slack sails to whistle for the wind. Ho ho! Wouldn't I just like to see Captain Audley's face when he gets to the ship and finds you missing!"

He burst into laughter, and Roy and Jerry joined in heartily. "He's played his trump card now," Jerry said. "He will have to sail immediately, for fear we might find a way to stop him. He knows he'll not get his hands on us again!"

"He'll race to reach home ahead of us," said Roy.

"He'll have a race he won't forget, then," cried Broderick

Brown. "It will suit my business very well to make a fast voyage. We'll weigh anchor not three days behind him."

Fouqua stood quietly by during their conversation, nodding, smiling, or chuckling by turns. He now accompanied them to the outer courtyard and delivered them into the hands of four stalwart coolies carrying lighted lanterns upon which the characters of Fouqua's name stood out black and bold to be seen and feared by all who passed. Bidding them good night, he gave sharp instructions to his men.

By a short path the coolies led them to a waiting sampan, and once again Roy and Jerry found themselves on the canal, surrounded by celebrants of the Festival of the Full Moon. It seemed a month at least since they had left the pavilion at Hwa-to, yet the moon had not yet reached its zenith. By devious winding waterways Fouqua's boatmen brought them to the gleaming river, and they saw again the plain, square shapes of the foreign factories, many of their windows still lighted.

The coolies did not leave them until they were back in their own quarters in Number Two, with a pair of Broderick Brown's seamen on the alert downstairs and the windows and doors of their upstairs rooms securely fastened. The coolies dismissed, Broderick Brown went to his rooms, and Roy and Jerry sat on their own bed and looked at each other. They were pale with fatigue and excitement, their clothes dirty and in disarray. Although they were convinced that Captain Audley was incapable of doing them further harm for the present, there was danger in the air; they could shut it out of the room, like the moonlight, but it was still there. Mimbo, once the ecstasy of welcoming them back was over, seemed to scent it, too. He prowled uneasily from window to door.

"I can't sleep a wink," Jerry declared. "I don't see how I can ever rest again until we have that blackguard Audley by the throat!" He lay back on the bed, stretching painfully.

"You can take those filthy clothes off," said Roy, tugging at his own shoes. "It may be six months before we lay eyes on our dear cousin again. We'll have a chance of meeting in Batavia, but if we miss him there, it's unlikely we'll have the pleasure again until we get back to Virginia. He will go straight to Mr. Morris, no doubt, and they'll be hatching out goodness knows what plots to keep us from ever regaining Rivergarden. My only hope is that he'll not harm our stepmother!"

He was undressed now, and he turned to climb into bed. "I'll leave the candle for you—" he began, but there was Jerry sprawled on the coverlet, sound asleep. Roy smiled and snuffed out the candle. It was good to be back, good to be alive when not three hours ago they were being carried to their death. It was good to drift off to sleep. . . .

Mimbo, seeing his chance, jumped onto the bed and curled up at Jerry's feet.

CHAPTER XII

THE TRAP

THANKS to Fouqua, the business of readying the *Swan* for her home voyage was carried out with unusual dispatch. Chopboats plied back and forth on the river from his godowns at Canton to the ship at Whampoa, and coolies labored from dawn to dark to empty the one and fill the other. Since Roy and Jerry had just taken part in the loading of the *Thunderbird*, they were able to be of assistance to Captain Brown and to the pursers in the office, who forsook their recreations and burned much lamp oil to close the *Swan*'s account books.

"I believe I am justified in taking you on as supercargoes for the homeward voyage," Broderick Brown decided. "If we make a good voyage, I shall be part owner of the *Swan*, and you shall have your pay. If we fail, the present owners of the *Swan* will determine your worth—which, I warn you, they may view through the wrong end of the telescope. Do you care to chance it?"

Of course they did, and threw themselves with redoubled energy into the preparations. Worth complained that they had forgotten his existence, and did not care whether he was going to be killed in the duel or not.

"That famous duel! I begin to think it will never take place!" said Jerry.

Worth looked hurt. "How can you say such a thing concerning an affair of honor between gentlemen? We are both more than eager to settle the matter; it's only that there are so many difficulties in the way. Our seconds are corresponding regularly; and yet you treat it as a joke. Tell them how the matter stands, Nathaniel."

"Indeed, the matter is far advanced," Nathaniel Miller answered solemnly. "I assure you, no stone is being left unturned in our efforts to find a suitable time and place. It is unthinkable to have a duel until the season is over—you see how busy we are, and we can't risk losing a purser. Afterward, we shall be packed off to Macao, and Mackie absolutely refuses to be killed there. We are now negotiating upon the possibility of Lintin Island."

"We can't have it there in hot weather," Worth protested. "The sand flies are so annoying. Perhaps—"

"Only one thing is certain about this duel," Roy observed to Jerry, "you and I will never see the end of it. Come on, there is work for us, if we are to be ready when the chow-chow chop is loaded."

Dinner was their last meal at the factory, and they felt a pang of sadness as they looked on the familiar faces around the table and thought how unlikely it was that they would ever see them again. The cook and the comprador had put their heads together to produce a masterpiece of a meal, and the servants smiled and bobbed their heads at every opportunity to show their regret at the departure of the "Ameleika chintelemuns." Mimbo was allowed to lie under Jerry's chair as a special treat, and he showed his appreciation by thumping his tail at each sentimental speech. Altogether it was a memorable affair, made more so by the arrival of Fouqua in great state, with servants laden with parting gifts for Captain Brown and his supercargoes.

Farewells were cut short by the news that the chow-chow chopboat, carrying last minute cargo, was ready at the landing. With lumps in their throats the boys marched off behind Captain Brown, their melancholy already turning to anticipation. Still a group of friends followed to shake hands at the landing.

During this last delay Roy murmured to Nathaniel Miller, "Can't you break up that senseless duel?" For he was haunted by the thought that Worth, with his round blue eyes and ridiculous hair, might be destined for an early grave. Miller confided into his ear, "Don't worry; McChesney will delay the thing for another season. If it ever does come to a meeting, we will see to it there is no ball in the pistols!"

Relieved, Roy joined Jerry, who was trying to express his thanks to Fouqua. There was little that either one of them could say. But much was said by their eyes and answered by Fouqua's parting wish, "Good wind and good water!"

At last they were on the river; the two forts dropped astern; the foreign factories sank out of sight; the tiny fluttering flags of the western world disappeared from view. It was dark before they had retraced the familiar track to the *Swan*'s anchorage at Whampoa, and saw her riding lights waiting.

The chow-chow cargo was stowed away by lantern light, and afterward Broderick Brown and his new supercargoes made a merry meal in his cabin. All was in readiness to sail at dawn, and they were full of plans for the adventures ahead as well as memories of adventures past.

With the first light the pilot came aboard, and the anchor chains rattled through the hawsepipes as the men bent to the windlass. Roy and Jerry came on deck in time to see the sails unfurl, swell with the breeze, and move forward into the mist of morning. The Whampoa comprador and his assistants swung over the rail, leaving a cumshaw for the Captain's table—baskets of oranges, jars of preserved ginger, dried lichee nuts and Nankin dates. As his sampan cast off, the comprador performed his last service, exploding a volley of firecrackers at the end of a long bamboo pole to give the gods notice of the *Swan*'s departure.

Through the mist there was little to be seen, the only evidence of land being its smells and noises. After the turn below the First Bar they had the wind just abaft the beam; the pilot bade them be niggardly with their canvas as he felt his way between the narrows and shallows. As the day wore on, the mist gave way, though the sun was yet overcast. Now the boys recognized the slender spike of the Second Bar pagoda and the overhanging hills and rocky islands of the tiger's throat.

The *Swan* anchored just above the Bocca Tigris, the pilot going off next morning to Anonghoy Fort to show his permit to pass. Once through the jaws they were beyond the jurisdiction of the Canton authorities. The river widened, and the *Swan* blossomed with sail. The breeze had freshened to a real blow. "I've never made a quicker passage," Captain Brown told the boys. "We'll be back in Macao roads tomorrow. If I did not have to go ashore to see Mr. Wilson at Macao, we might be clear of the mainland."

Roy was inclined to fret at the idea of marking time at Macao, but Jerry felt his heart give a pleasant skip. Macao meant one thing to him, a girl with pale skin and smooth brown hair and great dark blue eyes—Felicia. He would not mind a bit if he were forced by circumstances to visit her home again. This time, while Broderick Brown discussed business, why shouldn't *he* be the one to be shown the observatory in the garden?

But at noon next day, when the boat stood ready to take Captain Brown and the pilot off to Macao, Jerry's dream met with cruel reality. "I wish you fellows could bear me company," Broderick Brown said. "But if you'll take my advice, you'll remain on board. Although I believe that Captain Audley and the *Thunderbird* are already at sea, it is yet possible that he is at anchor nearby, still hoping to make trouble for you. He can't lay a finger on you as long as you're aboard the *Swan,* so that's the place for you."

Roy accepted this advice equably, turning his mind at once to some sketches he might make for Rosalie of the nearby islands and shipping. Jerry, however, was taken hard aback; he had a moment of black anger at Captain Brown, who, he thought, would not be sorry to have Felicia to himself. This thought he dismissed as unworthy, but he hung sulking at the rail, returning with interest the scowls that the Duke and José García gave him as they pushed off from the ship. The return of the Laceys to the *Swan* as supercargoes had been the last straw to their old watchmates, causing ill-concealed resentment in the fo'c'sle. The Duke, in particular, made it his business to let the gentlemen know, in subtle ways, how little he thought they merited their advancement.

"Oh, ignore him; he's just eaten up with jealousy," Roy said. "They all mean well enough; they just don't understand."

"That's what I complain of!" Jerry grumbled. "We tried to be good seamen when we were thrust before the mast— more than that, we *were* good seamen! Now that we are back in our rightful place, we shall be good supercargoes, and they lose nothing by our gain."

Roy reflected, "It seems to me that sailors fear change worse than the cat. It isn't only our ups and downs of fortune that have unsettled them. I suspect that the same group that holds a grudge against us has never really accepted Captain Brown since he took command of the *Swan.*"

Not feeling too cordial toward the young captain at the moment, Jerry said nothing, but gloomed over the rail while Roy went below to collect his paper and pens. The wind was blowing by fits all around the compass, a cold, nagging wind raising a sea that made the *Swan* roll. Jerry soon retired to the cabin and before long Roy followed, out of patience from trying to keep the paper from whipping off his drawing board. They ate a miserable dinner and whiled away an hour or so studying the charts of their homeward route. Gradually the light failed, and Jerry's thoughts, which had been tugging shoreward all afternoon, parted their mooring and drifted straight into Felicia's drawing room, where they found her doing needle point by the fire and laughing gaily at Broderick Brown's jokes.

Roy, thwarted in an attempt to read by the swinging lantern, gave up and retreated to his bunk. He was roused by a hail outside and the approach of footsteps in the companionway. Jerry hurried to open the door, expecting Captain Brown.

Instead, it was the Duke. His very attitude, stiff as a ramrod, indicated suppressed impudence, but he spoke civilly enough. "Compliments of Captain Brown, sir, and he has decided to spend the night ashore. Since the motion of the ship must be irksome, he says, and it's likely to be some time before you get another opportunity to sleep ashore, he says, will the gentlemen care to join him at Mr. Wilson's home? If so, the boat awaits the gentlemen."

His manner, like a stage butler announcing, "The carriage awaits without, melud," was offensive, but his message was so welcome that the boys had no trouble overlooking his airs. "We'll be ready at once," Jerry said jubilantly. "Stand by the boat!"

The Duke retired, while Roy and Jerry made themselves neat and packed the few articles they would need. "I wonder what made Captain Brown change his mind?" mused Roy. "I don't mean about staying the night—even an old hardshell like him would prefer a good steady bed to this bouncing cockleshell. But what of his warning concerning Cousin Audley?"

"Perhaps he thinks us safe under cover of darkness. Or more likely, he has had news of the *Thunderbird* and knows she has made her final departure. It's my opinion that there never was any danger, anyway, since Cousin Audley is in far too big a hurry to linger here."

Leaving Mimbo disconsolate, they wrapped themselves in their greatcoats and went down the ladder, meeting the boat as it rose on the swell. They huddled silently in the bow while the sailors bent to the oars, conversation being impossible with the wind roaring round their ears. The distant lights of Macao winked tantalizingly at them in the vast blackness. The waning moon had not yet risen, and the place where it would rise was blanketed with clouds.

After a long pull the boat was landed, but at a point far south of the place where Roy and Jerry had gone ashore with Captain Brown. Other ships' boats were moored nearby, and a row of lighted taverns and sailors' boarding-houses beckoned hospitably across the Praya Grande. As the boys mounted the steps to the sea wall, the Duke said, "The Captain has given us shore leave tonight, sir, charging us to be ready with the boat in the morning."

"Very well, then," Roy said, and the men, after securing the boat's gear, went eagerly across the road to the taverns. Roy and Jerry stood a moment to get their bearings; they knew the general direction of Mr. Wilson's house, but were doubtful which street to choose.

"The Captain detailed me and Hosey here to put you on the right street to Mr. Wilson's house, sir," said the Duke. Turning, the boys saw to their surprise that he and García had not gone with the others, but stood just behind them, braced against the wind.

A warning bell rang faintly in Roy's brain. The Duke was so courteous—it wasn't natural. "We'll find our way, thank you," he said rather curtly, and the two sailors touched their caps and started to follow their mates.

"Wait," Jerry stopped them. "If the Wilsons are expecting us for supper, we'd better not waste any time. We'll be obliged if you would show us the shortest way."

Duke and José García turned back and stepped out briskly, Roy and Jerry following them across the Praya Grande, into one of the narrow streets that led off from it into the city. Street lamps at rare intervals guttered in the rising wind; doors were closed and windows shuttered, so that it seemed a sleeping city, though yet early in the evening. Collars turned up, hands deep in pockets, Roy and Jerry did not try to talk. They were busy with their thoughts. Jerry was thinking of a good warm supper and the shine of candlelight on Felicia's hair. Roy was trying to quiet the uneasy feeling that persisted in the back of his mind. "After all, Duke and García are only following Captain Brown's orders," he told himself. "They could not leave us at the sea wall if the Captain had told them to show us the way to Mr. Wilson's. What is there to fear?" His only answer was the whistling of the wind and the hollow ring of their footfalls on the paving stones.

The moon had risen somewhere behind the shifting masses of cloud, giving a sickly intermittent light that did not reach into the narrow streets winding between the dark houses. Here and there a gleam of warm firelight escaped through the cracks of a shutter, or the door of some public house opened for a moment to admit a visitor, or down some intersecting street they caught the glow of Chinese lanterns carried before a palanquin.

Surely, in a city yet astir with life, two able-bodied young adventurers had nothing to fear? But Roy had at last put his finger on a definite fact which explained his uneasiness. There was someone following them.

At first he only felt that vague uneasiness. Then he caught a glimpse of a movement as they turned a corner. Was it the edge of a fluttering garment? Or was it only a shadow? Later he was sure he saw a figure, oriental in silhouette. But what of it? The citizens of Macao had a right to walk their own streets.

They had been making good progress in the right direction, and were warmed by the gradual but continuous climb uphill. They were in a narrow street of mean houses, opening a short distance away into a wider, well-lighted thoroughfare. The Duke and García paused. "There's your street, sir," the Duke pointed ahead. He leaned close to make himself heard. "Follow the wall to your right, and you'll find yourselves at Mr. Wilson's gate." The boys thanked him heartily and counted out a generous tip for them both. Relief nourished Roy's generosity, anticipation Jerry's. At the very moment when they should have been on guard, they stepped as innocently as doves into the trap.

García and the Duke stood close in front of them to receive their tips. Behind them the door of a house flew open, and Ole and Ross lunged out. There was no struggle, no disturbance. Two marlinespikes were lifted and brought down with two thuds. The limp bodies of Roy and Jerry Lacey were dragged inside the house, and the door was shut.

The Duke bowed mockingly to the closed door. He and García tossed their coins in the air, pocketed them, turned, and went whistling back down the street.

CHAPTER XIII

THE SONS OF HAN

I F WE DID not have to await the pilot, we could sail at once, and be quit of China and of these young cockerels tonight," said a familiar voice as Jerry came to life after a long and troubled sleep. His head ached, and when he opened his eyes, the walls, the table and chairs, the fine nautical figure of Captain John Audley, and the ugly face of Mr. Griff all pulsated painfully.

He was in the master's cabin in the stern of the *Thunderbird*. Roy, still unconscious, lay face down on a bench at one side of the room, his wrists tied behind him. His own were bound in the same way, as he proved with a jerk. Captain Audley saw the movement and smiled.

"Well, cousin! You might have saved us all the trouble of that episode in Canton, and come quietly when Ross and Ole were kind enough to offer their escort. Didn't you know you had no chance in the long run against an old sea dog like myself?"

He was flushed with triumph and brandy; bottles and glasses sat on the table between him and Mr. Griff, who looked well pleased with the situation. The mate crossed his legs, drank, and said to the Captain, "Off the Grand Lema we can drop the pilot; after that we can drop the young gentlemen—and there will be no one to hear the splash!"

Jerry staggered up from the chair they had flung him into.

He could tell from the feel of the vessel that the sea had grown quieter. "You can't get a pilot until daybreak, and by then Captain Brown will have found you. When we don't

120

arrive at Mr. Wilson's, he will search for us, and never fear but he will know whom to look for!" He spoke defiantly, but his voice sounded hollow; his tongue felt thick and dry.

Cousin Audley's eyebrows went up over his nose; he shook his head and clucked his tongue with mock pity. "And what makes you think Captain Brown expects you at Mr. Wilson's?" he inquired.

"Why, the Duke said—"

"My dear boy, your faith in human nature is touching. The Duke said what he was paid to say. He and his watchmates had no objection to doing you two an ill turn! But the worthy Captain Brown—and what a sterling character he is, to be sure—is sleeping peacefully under Mr. Wilson's roof at this moment, confident that you and Roy are safe aboard the *Swan*. He will know nothing of your disappearance until morning. By that time we will be under way, and Captain Brown will be delayed in Macao seeking high and low for his lost chicks."

He chuckled at his own humor and took another drink. He looked over his shoulder at the windows, which showed a hint of gray light. "But why do we talk of the morning to come? It is here. Mr. Griff, look lively! Make ready to take on the pilot. The sooner we get the *Thunderbird* home, the sooner you'll collect your wages."

"And mighty fat wages they'll have to be, to close up my mouth," said Mr. Griff insolently. "As to the pilot, Mr. Heflin has this watch, and he's sober for once, so let him take her to sea. I'm due a bit of sleep after this night's work."

Cousin Audley was not to be goaded out of his good humor. "Go sleep your head off, then. You're too drunk to know the difference between the best bower anchor and a chaw of 'baccy, anyhow."

Mr. Griff lurched out of the cabin, and Captain Audley followed, locking the door behind himself. Jerry went to the bench, where Roy was beginning to moan, and knelt beside him. Roy opened his eyes. Meeting those of his brother, he seemed to read in them all that had happened; he groaned and made an effort to get up, but rolled to the floor with a thud. Jerry could help but clumsily. At last Roy got himself into a sitting position on the floor, leaning against the bench, and Jerry was relieved to see him assay a pallid smile. "I'm all right," he said. "And I see you, too, survived the night. What a couple of dolts we are, to fall into such a trap!"

"Oh, I don't know," Jerry protested. "How were we to know that the Duke had any contact with the *Thunderbird*?"

"A child might have guessed that the crew of the *Swan* and the crew of the *Thunderbird* might have become acquainted while anchored at Whampoa. I expect Duke talked of a grudge against Captain Brown and his favorites who lived ashore like fine gentlemen. We had only to exercise half our wits to avoid trouble."

A saying of Benjamin's popped into Jerry's mind, and he smiled wryly. "There's no use beating yourself over the head when there's so many that's waiting to do it for you," he told Roy. "That's what Benjamin used to say when I fretted over a mistake that was over and done. After traveling around the Caribbean and across the Isthmus with Benjamin, I'm convinced that he is wiser than Solomon, so let's take his advice and apply the other half of our wits to our present plight."

Each was putting up a good front in an attempt to cheer the other; but they both knew that this time they were fairly caught. It was but a short run to the Lema Islands. These next few hours were likely to be their last in this life.

Their eyes turned instinctively to the windows. "Feels as if the squall has blown itself out," Roy said. "Still, there'll be plenty of breeze to take us to the Lemas."

They staggered to the windows and saw that the sky was thick with an angry dawn. The *Thunderbird* was between some island and the mainland; they guessed her to be not more than a league from Macao, though the city was not in sight. The sea had subsided to a long, glassy swell. Roy and Jerry leaned against the sill and searched the horizon hungrily. If only they could see the lofty canvas of the *Swan!* But the scattered sails of a fleet of fishing junks were the only signs of life.

No; there was another junk bearing down upon them. Presently it hove to and stood off while a sampan came toward the *Thunderbird*. Three Chinese stood in the bow looking up at the ship as they passed almost under her stern. Roy and Jerry peered down at them with the desperate curiosity of doomed men watching for their executioner.

"This must be the pilot now," Roy said. Then he caught his breath and pressed his face against the glass. "There's Ching!" he cried.

"Ching? It *is!* What can he be doing in the pilot's boat?" Jerry almost butted his head through the window, but the sampan was now out of their view.

"Do you suppose—?"

"No, surely not. It must be just a coincidence. Perhaps he's a friend of the pilot's—or a relative, for all we know."

"He never talked about his family. But coincidence or not, we must get word to him somehow! If he comes back in the boat we'll break the glass and yell. Stand by to help me kick it out."

"Listen; I can hear them coming aboard. The sampan should cast off at once if it's going to return."

They waited in an agony of suspense, but the sampan did not return, and the junk tacked off toward the island. They heard the activity on deck as the *Thunderbird* weighed anchor and took wing. They were off to meet their fate. But now there was a gleam of hope. Ching was on board.

He must, indeed, be on deck near the helmsman, not far away. They could hear voices above deck, and, while they listened, they heard Captain Audley stamping down the companionway singing out for his breakfast. With one accord the boys left the windows and assumed discouraged attitudes upon the bench. In a moment Cousin Audley came in, still in a high good humor, and reported to Roy and Jerry, as if they should be as pleased with the news as he, "Well, lads, we're under way. The pilot is a rascal; he brought four boatmen and two helpers with him to eat our victuals. But I am ready for them. A crate of hens has just died; I'm convinced the coolies at our last anchorage poisoned them. They will do well enough for these yellow sons of Han."

The words, "sons of Han," made Jerry think of Worth, and he wondered if the duel had yet taken place. Hastily he recalled his thoughts to the present, which was all too fleeting. "I don't suppose you intend to feed *us*?" he inquired.

"Why not, my boy? Why not? It's a waste of good rations, but I have never been parsimonious." To their surprise, he came to them and cut their bonds, but stood behind them with the knife unsheathed.

Joe Kent, the steward, came in with the Captain's tray and laid out a handsome repast. "Bring two more of the same for the young gentlemen," Captain Audley directed. "But make sure you do not use any eggs from the hens that just died."

In a flash Roy and Jerry saw the way cleared for their deaths. Word would go around the ship that they had eaten the poisoned eggs; their bodies would be cast overboard, and no one but Captain Audley and his confederates, Griff, Ole, and Ross, would know the truth. Roy could feel his cousin's heavy hand on one shoulder, while Jerry felt the point of the knife against his ribs. They were not to give away the fact that they were captives. Realizing this, they saw one more small gleam of hope. All of the *Thunderbird*'s crew were not concerned in the plot. If they could make their plight known, they might find friends.

"Aye, aye, sir!" Joe Kent said smartly. To the boys he said, "Glad to have you back aboard, sirs. When we sailed without you, I didn't think we were to have the pleasure of your company, sirs."

At a pressure of the heavy hand and a nudge of the knife, Roy and Jerry produced a pair of sickly smiles. "Look lively, Joe," Captain Audley said. "The young gentlemen came aboard in the night and brought good appetites with 'em. Four eggs apiece, Joe."

Soon the boys were provided with breakfasts bountiful enough for a condemned man's last meal, and with Joe Kent out of the room, Captain Audley locked the cabin door again and sat down to enjoy his own. He faced his captives across the width of the cabin, ostentatiously laying his knife on one side of his plate and a pistol on the other. Thus provided against surprise, he tucked his napkin under his chin and fell to. The brandy bottle being still on the table, his glass found its way to his mouth at regular intervals.

Jerry looked at his tray with a queasy feeling in his stomach. Roy, too, felt an antipathy toward the eggs, but he knew there was nothing wrong with them, and he remembered that he had had no supper. If an opportunity came to get out of this death cell, they would need all the strength they could muster. He tasted the food and at once felt ravenous.

Jerry followed his example, lifting his napkin. He stared. Where the napkin had been was a slip of paper. On it was written several lines in Broderick Brown's firm hand.

"Well, eat!" said Cousin Audley pettishly, from across the room. "You needn't be afraid—yet." This sally restored his good humor, and he returned to his bacon, chuckling.

Jerry ate. He managed to push the paper to the edge of his tray where Roy could see it, attracting his attention with a nudge of his foot. Cramming buttered buns into their mouths, they read, guardedly, "Chinese pirates will attack off Dirty Butter Bay. At sound of firing, take care of Captain A. Ching and I will do the rest. B.B."

After that, the food tasted much, much better. Jerry slipped the note into his pocket, and they continued to eat, watching Captain Audley quite as closely as he was watching them.

At last Captain Audley pushed back his plate. He leaned back in his chair and sucked his teeth reflectively, then rose.

"We should be passing Dirty Butter Bay," he said. "I'll just tie your wrists again while I go on deck, to keep you out of mischief. Gerald, bring your tray over here and put it on the table. Stay where you are, Leroy."

It was now or never. They could not wait for the signal. Their job was to "take care of Captain A.," and they could not do that once their hands were tied. Jerry approached the table with his tray, ready to throw it in the Captain's face. Roy sat on pins, waiting for the chance to spring.

Tipsy though he was, Captain Audley was on guard, pistol in hand as Jerry came near. But his eye was caught by a movement outside the windows. "My God!" he breathed, and turned his head to see better.

Jerry leaped forward, swinging the heavy wooden tray edgewise across Captain Audley's throat. He screamed with pain and choked, his eyes popping nearly out of his head. Before he could recover himself the boys were both upon him. They had him tied hand and foot in a trice.

The Captain was getting his breath back, gasping out

oaths with growing fury. "He'll rouse the ship in a minute," Roy said. "We'll have to knock him out."

"I'll do it with pleasure," said Jerry, taking the pistol by the barrel. "He'll know what a headache feels like when he comes to." Down thudded the butt end of the pistol, and Captain Audley dropped back on the floor like a stone.

Jerry turned away. He did not feel pleasure, after all.

Roy was at the window. "Look, Jerry!" The excitement in his voice brought Jerry at once. They saw what had astonished Captain Audley out of his caution. Two great black junks, flying banners from stem to stern, were bearing down upon the *Thunderbird*. They were now so close that the boys looked right into the mouth of the cannon mounted in the bow of the one directly astern. Even as they watched, another glided out from behind a point of land on their starboard quarter. They heard the clanging of gongs and saw a puff of blue smoke. The water spurted up all along their track.

"There's the signal!" shouted Jerry. "Take any weapons you can find. They'll need us on deck."

The only weapon in evidence was a sword that hung on the wall; Roy seized this and followed Jerry out of the Captain's cabin, taking the precaution to lock the door. "Look sharp!" he warned. "Mr. Griff will have heard the noise, and we must pass his cabin."

As he spoke, the door of the first mate's cabin burst open, and a stout Chinese sailor came out, grinning fiendishly. When he saw the boys, his manner changed at once; he bowed from the waist and then leaped up the companion stairs as nimbly as a cat. They followed him onto the deck.

Here there was a strange mixture of order and confusion. At the wheel stood honest Jack, the helmsman, his eyes rolling uneasily toward a middle-aged Chinese who sat close by with an antiquated blunderbuss across his knees. From time to time this man, evidently the pilot, gave a direction, which Jack obeyed with alacrity. In the waist of the vessel stood Mr. Heflin, a bewildered look on his face. He, too, had a Chinese shadow, this one armed with a brace of pistols. Two more sons of Han stood guard at the fo'c'sle companionway. It was closed and barricaded, and from below came a furious outcry from the watch imprisoned within. The watch on deck had gathered about the mainmast, armed with boarding pikes and belaying pins. They urged one another to battle, but the Chinese had the only firearms, and no one wanted to be the first to charge them. As they waited irresolutely, one of the junks bore down upon the *Thunderbird* and grappled her amidships, the high dragon's head prow reaching right over the rail, crowded with Chinese seamen.

As Roy and Jerry made their appearance, they were met by Ching, shouldering an enormous matchlock. The old gentle smile creased his face. "*Thunderbird* allee same belong you," he announced. "Tellee sailor man no fight, no get hurt."

Roy called out to the sailors, "Steady, men; don't resist, and there'll be no trouble."

The men muttered uneasily and hefted their weapons. They kept wary eyes on the pirates, who hung on the prow like grapes ready to fall.

Roy went on, "You know me and my brother, here. You know that we are the owners of this ship. What you don't know is that Captain Audley wants to take it for himself—wants it badly enough to kill us. He had us shanghaied aboard last night. Well, we've turned the tables on him. He's tied up in his cabin right now, and so is Mr. Griff; and they'll be taken in irons to the United States to stand trial for their crimes. If any of you helped them in their dirty work, you'll be punished. But anyone who is loyal to us and willing to sail the *Thunderbird* home for her rightful owners will be treated fairly. Don't offer any violence. These men are only here to see justice done."

Looking at the junks surrounding the *Thunderbird* and at the piratical crew ready to board her, Roy almost doubted his own words. But Ching nodded approval. "No fightee, no get hurt," he repeated. "Captain Brown wait in Dirty Butter Bay."

Roy turned back to the men. "Well, who is ready to work for the rightful owners of the *Thunderbird?*"

There was an uncertain silence. To Roy and Jerry it seemed to last a lifetime. Suddenly Mr. Heflin spoke up. "I'm with you!" As always, he was as pale as death, but for the moment he had lost his hangdog look.

Jack echoed from the wheel, "I'm with you!"

One by one the sailors called, "Aye, aye, sir!" or touched their forelocks. Among them were old Hawks, Fat Pork, Codder, Jock, Joe Kent, and the bushy-haired mulatto the men called Charleston. Ole and Ross were not in the group, having been in the watch imprisoned below.

Roy and Jerry vaulted over the poop and shook hands with everyone. "Very well!" cried Roy. "My brother and I will not forget the men who work for us. Mr. Heflin, take the ship into Dirty Butter Bay!"

CHAPTER XIV

DIRTY BUTTER BAY

THE *Swan* awaited them in Dirty Butter Bay, a most welcome sight; and a most welcome sound was heard, the fervent barking of Mimbo greeting his lost master. As soon as might be a boat came off from the *Swan,* bearing Captain Brown, Mr. Hart, Mimbo, and a well-armed squad of sailors, among whom the Duke and José García were conspicuously absent.

The junks had fallen back, only one accompanying the *Thunderbird* into the bay. This was under the command of the pirate the boys had first met coming out of Mr. Griff's cabin, and whom Ching introduced as his brother, Ching Fong. "Him number one first-chop fisherman," Ching proclaimed. "S'pose fish go 'way, him number one first-chop pirate."

Fong bowed and smiled. He was larger than Ching and younger. He bore a scar from forehead to chin, which had cost him an eye and made a twisted mask of his face. A benevolent gleam brightened his one eye when he looked at Ching. "My brother." He bowed to Roy, Jerry, and Captain Brown in turn. "My brother allee same dead. You bring him China-side. My thank you."

Captain Brown told the boys, "Fong and his men were ready for any kind of a fight. I believe he would have taken on the British Navy singlehanded if need be, to show his gratitude for Ching's return."

"But where did he come from?" asked Jerry. "And how

did you know where we were? How—? Oh, I don't understand any of it!"

Roy said, "We understand well enough that Captain Audley set a trap for us at Macao, and that we fell into it, head
over heels. But how on earth did you find us in time to save
us from the sharks?"

"You have Ching to thank for your lives," Broderick
Brown answered. "Ching had just got back from a fishing
cruise up the coast, and, hearing at Whampoa that the *Swan*
was sailing for home, came to Macao to say good-by. He
overheard talk in a waterfront tavern that put him on the
alert, and he followed when García and the Duke led you
up the street."

"I *thought* someone was following!" Roy exclaimed. "If
only I had known it was Ching!"

"Well, Ching saw them turn you over to Ole and Ross,
and he followed again until he knew where they were taking you. Then he routed me out at Mr. Wilson's and told
me what had happened. He cooked up the scheme to take
the ship."

Ching nodded toward the pilot, who, still comfortably
seated, had exchanged his gun for a long-stemmed pipe.
"Him number one pilot, my olo flen. My go on board with
he, take Fong, take number one strong fishermans; bimeby
we lock fo'c'sle, show gun to mate, show gun to helmsman,
knock Mr. Griff on head. You allee same take care of Captain; all finishee, all things plenty fine."

Broderick Brown slapped his knee. "I never saw a neater
trick. A ship taken by Chinese pirates, and not a man lost.
It wouldn't have been so simple if all the ringleaders hadn't
been below and half drunk. I was standing by to lend a hand
if there should be a battle, but thank God there was not!
The rascals are all in our hands, and the ship is yours if you
can get her home."

"We'll be shorthanded, and Mr. Heflin is our only officer, but we'll get her home!" Jerry declared.

Captain Brown rose. They were in the big cabin Roy and Jerry had occupied when they sailed from Norfolk so long ago, with Mimbo established under Jerry's bunk, as of old. "First we must have all shipshape," he said.

With his usual energy he soon had the two ships humming with activity. He had Ole and Ross taken to the *Swan*, to keep the Duke and José García company in irons, while Captain Audley and Mr. Griff were confined to Mr. Heflin's cabin on the *Thunderbird*. Mr. Heflin was asked to serve as master on the home voyage. He swallowed hard, turned even paler than was his wont, and accepted in an almost inaudible voice. Mr. Hart, first mate of the *Swan*, was transferred to the *Thunderbird* to act as first officer.

Roy and Jerry were well satisfied with the results of the morning's work. A cheerful air seemed to blow through the *Thunderbird*, ridding her of the foul deeds and ill feelings that had flourished there. Only in Mr. Heflin's old cabin the infection persisted, where Captain Audley and Mr. Griff nursed their headaches and meditated on revenge. Every precaution was taken to make sure they remained there. Their ports were locked, their wrists were shackled, and a guard was told off to stand regular watches before their door.

Two of Fong's fishermen were found who were willing to sign on to work the ship as far as Batavia, where Captain Brown hoped to recruit more seamen. Batavia was to be the rendezvous for the *Thunderbird* and the *Swan*, either ship reaching the port first agreeing to wait for the other at least ten days.

"And now, nothing remains to be done but to set sail. However, let us spare one hour for pleasure. We have much to celebrate. Come to the *Swan* for dinner, and you shall see why I showed such reluctance to take part in the great Battle of Dirty Butter Bay," Broderick Brown invited.

Accordingly, Roy and Jerry, Ching, Fong, and Mr. Heflin accompanied the young captain to the *Swan*. Dinner was spread in unaccustomed style, and just as the company prepared to sit down, Captain Brown went out and returned with Felicia on his arm. He laughed at their thunderstruck expressions.

"Yes, the *Swan* has the honor of carrying a lady this voyage," he explained. "Mr. Wilson put his daughter in my charge, thereby putting me at the same time in a quandary. I could not tell him that I was planning to turn pirate! As a member of the firm he could never countenance such a scheme! Neither could I refuse to give Miss Felicia passage. In the end I decided to confide in her, make known the whole affair, and abide by her choice as to whether she should undertake such a featherbrained voyage."

Felicia laughed—a silvery tinkle that enchanted Jerry's reddened ears. "I told him he should change the name of his ship from the *Swan* to the *Wild Goose*," she said.

"But she came; no words of mine could deter her. And thanks to Ching and Fong, our voyage is well begun. God grant that it will continue under His guidance and protection, and that He will see us safe in our home ports." For a moment all heads were bowed; then dinner was begun in a clatter of dishes and conversation.

How pleasant it was to have a lady at the table! The food tasted better; the talk was more interesting; everyone looked more handsome and more cheerful than usual. Watching the gentle movements of Felicia's small hands, Roy thought longingly of his stepmother, who presided with such grace at the Rivergarden table. Her beauty was never far from his thoughts, symbolic of the beauty of Rivergarden and of all lovely women. And Rosalie! Of course he thought of Rosalie.

Felicia was perhaps even younger than she, almost a child, but having served as companion and hostess for her father, she had acquired a precocious dignity. Beside her, Rosalie would seem a harum-scarum tomboy. But oh! how Roy wished that Rosie were seated across the table from him at this moment, instead of Felicia!

Jerry raised food to his mouth mechanically, swallowing without knowing what he ate. He had never dreamed of such a wonder. Felicia was so much lovelier than he had remembered! And she was not going to stay in far-off Macao. She was going to the United States to visit an aunt; she would be in Boston, where he perhaps might see her. Half the meal was spent basking in these golden thoughts. But then he suddenly saw the other side of the coin. She would not be on board the *Thunderbird*, but the *Swan*. Broderick Brown, not he, would see her every day. And Boston was a long, long way from Rivergarden. The last half of the meal was spent in gloom.

But it was not Jerry's nature to be gloomy long. By the end of the meal he had remembered a cheerful fact. He would see Felicia when they met the *Swan* at Batavia!

It was time for farewells. Farewell to Ching, their faithful friend, to whom they owed possession of the *Thunderbird*. "If our venture is successful, we will owe it all to you, Ching," Roy told him, on the verge of tears.

"No, no," said Ching. "You save my life in Meleika. My help you China-side. Have settee counter." Tears overflowed his crescent eyes, but he wore his broadest smile. "My take number one care Kowí-bird. My catch bugs for he; he have plenty chow."

Fong had been taken aside by Captain Brown and discreetly offered a generous cumshaw for his services. Fong, however, tucked his hands in his sleeves. Grinning like a gargoyle, he refused. "Meleika chintelemuns bring Ching China-side, bring back from dead. You no pay. My pay."

The first vessel to leave Dirty Butter Bay was Fong's junk, which took its departure amid a blue haze of smoke from exploding firecrackers. Next went the *Swan*, with a flutter of Felicia's white handkerchief. Then it was the *Thunderbird's* turn. Slowly she spread her sails and committed herself to the northeast wind. Her young owners stood on the poop near Captain Heflin; the pilot stood ready at the wheel. Soon his duty was done, and the Lemas dropped astern. Now, indeed, they were rolling down the China Sea. Roy and Jerry watched the receding shore line. With a short-handed ship, a drunkard of a captain, and two prisoners plotting against them, they must bring the *Thunderbird* safely to port on the other side of the world.

Before dark they made the rounds of the ship together. They found old Hawks in his workshop, ready for a yarn. He showed them some of the toys he had bought at Canton for his grandchildren, and told them heartily that he was glad they had recovered their ship. "Captain Audley, he knows how to sail a ship. I've served with him before, and no complaints," he said. "But this trip was different; he looked the same, and he sounded the same, but his insides were different, somehow—like as if you took down a bottle that had always held molasses, and it turned out to be vinegar, instead."

When they left him, he followed them to the door, shaking his head. "You watch him and Mr. Griff; watch 'em like you would a couple o' sharks. They ain't run out o' tricks yet—don't you think it."

They found Fat Pork in the galley, with Mimbo in attendance, just as in the old days. The cook beamed and joked and flattered them, but the boys felt no confidence in his good will. "He'll be our friend as long as we're on top," Jerry said as they made their way aft against a freshening gale. "That's all I can say for *him*."

Mr. Hart was on deck, obviously quite as much at home on one deck as another. He was a big ox of a man, slow of thought and speech. He had already been over the ship and formed his own opinion of how she should be handled. The boys felt awkward at first in talking to him as owners, when they had so lately served under him as seamen on the *Swan*, but Mr. Hart exhibited no resentment, or even surprise. He spoke briefly of the ship, the wind, and the course, hitched up his trousers, and went on with his work.

A visit to the prisoners came next. They found Jock, the Cockney, on guard before the door, carrying a musket almost as tall as himself. He saluted Roy and Jerry smartly, unlocked the door, and stood aside with a fine military air, but as they went in he spoiled the effect by a confidential wink.

Mr. Griff was sprawled in a hammock, the very picture of a villain suffering from the effects of a blow on the head and an excess of drink. Captain Audley, on the other hand, sat at a table playing solitaire, his dress neat, his manner easy, the only evidence of his recent misadventures being a white scarf wrapped about his throat. He spoke first. "Well, Mr. Griff, we have visitors." He went on playing, ignoring the boys, and talking over his shoulder to Mr. Griff. "Pirates, Mr. Griff. I'll wager you thought pirates were rascally fellows with great black beards and drawn cutlasses. Not so, nowadays. Nowadays piracy is practiced by dimpled milk-fed boys, damn their pretty eyes!" Without looking up from his cards he began to curse venomously.

Jerry took a step forward, but a look at Roy's face stopped him. For once he took upon himself the role of peacemaker, placed a hand on Roy's arm, and led him out of the room.

Their last call was on Mr. Heflin, the man upon whom so

much depended, and of whom they knew so little. They found him seated at Captain Audley's big desk, in front of the wide stern windows in the master's cabin. A troubled sea rose and fell outside the windows, rearing white heads to look into the cabin, then sinking back, leaving nothing in view but the threatening sky.

Mr. Heflin, who had been fingering a small object, put it hurriedly in his pocket and lit the lamp. "We're in for a blow," he said, making an obvious effort at conversation. "We will be lucky if we meet with nothing worse. This is a season of change in this part of the world."

The boys had seldom heard him put two sentences together before. As if exhausted by the effort, he returned to his chair and sat on the edge of it, looking ill at ease. His colorless face was seamed and crumpled into curious folds and creases, like the forehead of an old hound. All the life in the man seemed to be concentrated in his eyes, which glowed with such dark intensity that they were hard to meet.

Roy felt at a loss as he searched for the right words. He could hardly ask the question that was in his mind, "Are you capable of keeping sober long enough to sail the *Thunderbird* safely home?" Yet it was necessary to come to an understanding with the *Thunderbird*'s new master. While he hesitated, Jerry solved the problem by saying, frankly, "We want to thank you for undertaking the responsibility of master, Mr. Heflin. There is no one else capable of navigating the ship. We must depend upon your skill and your loyalty, or we are lost."

Mr. Heflin winced and dropped his eyes. One hand lay on the desk, trembling slightly. The other fumbled in his pocket.

"Indeed we are grateful," said Roy.

The words unlocked Mr. Heflin's lips. He began to speak

in a rusty drawl, gathering momentum as he went. "There is no call for gratitude," he said, earnestly. "If I do my duty now, that does not wipe away the fact that I failed to do it earlier. No; I did not help Captain Audley in his crimes against you; but I closed my eyes to them; I pretended to myself that I did not know what was going on."

He looked so miserable that Roy broke in. "Don't reproach yourself. You could have done little to help us, then, in any case. Now you can help us a great deal; it's the present we are concerned with, not the past."

Mr. Heflin's appearance was quite ghastly. He had gone a pasty white, and was sweating profusely. He rose to his feet, and pulling his hand out of his pocket, leaned across the desk holding it out to the boys. On his trembling palm was a small key.

"Take it," he whispered hoarsely. "Take it and keep it away from me. Throw it over the side if you like. It's the key to Captain Audley's liquor supply. I cleared the cabin, locked it all away. I was trying to find courage to give it to you when you came in."

Roy took the key, and Mr. Heflin sank back into his chair with a long sigh. The boys made a move to go, but he stopped them. "Wait!" he said. His voice was tired, but clear. "That's over. If you knew how many years I have been trying to do that! I've been master of ships before, you know. Then the habit of drink took hold of me, and I went back to first officer, then second. I could not get any berth at all when Audley found me; that's why I kept my mouth shut, for fear of losing my job." He looked them squarely in the eyes, with the ghost of a smile on his lips. "You've made me master of a ship again. But you can't make me master of myself. Can *I* do it? Can I bring the ship home safely? That's what you wish to ask. I would to God I could give you the answer." He spread his arms out from his sides. "God knows."

"God has brought us thus far," Roy said, holding out his hand. "We can trust Him for the remainder."

Mr. Heflin shook Roy's hand, then Jerry's. Then in a matter-of-fact tone, he said, "Maybe you'd like to look at the charts." He traced with his forefinger the track of the *Thunderbird*, almost due south down the map of the China Sea. "Nothing to worry about here but typhoons. But here, we begin to find our way among a thousand islands—and every one of 'em is inhabited by Malay pirates."

CHAPTER XV

THE SPICE ISLANDS

ONE NIGHT a sudden squall struck the *Thunderbird*, bringing rain in such quantities that it seemed likely to hammer the decks under the sea. The main topsail yard snapped in the slings, the fore and mizzen topsails split into shreds, and the jib was carried away; all in the space of a lightning flash.

The noise brought all hands on deck. Officers and men tumbled into a quaking world of darkness, and for the next few hours they shouted and struggled amid the howling wind, the crashing thunder, and the wild glare of lightning. Roy and Jerry worked beside the sailors, jumping to the commands of Mr. Heflin and Mr. Hart, glad of every trick of seamanship they had learned. The *Thunderbird* did her part, too, shaking off the weight of water valiantly, responding to the efforts of the men to ease her. A new main topsail yard was crossed, the sail bent on, the fore and mizzen topsails and the jib replaced.

Out of the confusion she emerged triumphantly with all sail set. The sea subsided to a murmuring ripple along the hull. The stars reappeared as big as lamps against the deep velvet blackness of the sky. One watch went below, but Roy and Jerry paused at the rail before leaving the deck. On the mild air came the strong smell of spices.

Jerry sniffed like a bird dog. "The Spice Islands," he said. Roy followed in his thoughts some of the ideas conjured up by the words: shoals and freak currents; fresh water, coconuts, and chickens; Malay pirates; Batavia. They were entering the perilous waterway between Sumatra and Borneo and must move carefully if they were ever to make their escape into wider waters through the bottleneck of the Straits of Sunda.

For the next ten days they were never out of sight of those islands so well known to sailors as the source of pirates and spice. Mr. Heflin and Mr. Hart had both navigated these waters before, and proceeded with proper respect from bearing to bearing and sounding to sounding. Jerry got his fill of casting the lead at last, and Roy was forever jumping to the tune of "Ready about!" and "More beef!" Shorthanded as they were, the owners must work like fo'c'sle hands, and the sailors thought the better of them for it, knowing that while they rested in their hammocks, Roy and Jerry spent more hours over the charts. Even when they slept they felt the progress of the ship, and anything untoward in her motion brought them on deck.

Every weapon on board was overhauled and made ready for action. The cannon were cleaned and oiled, and the crew was drilled in their use. The officers and owners went armed at all times and the Captain's cabin became an arsenal.

Fat Pork put a keen edge upon his cleaver, brandishing it with such bloodthirsty enthusiasm that the seamen gave the galley a wide berth. Old Hawks made shift as an armorer, working overtime at his anvil, with the help of one of the Chinese who had some skill in metals, to repair old weapons or make new ones from scrap iron.

They had not sighted the *Swan* for many days. Now and then they caught sight of other sail, and spoke several: a Dutch Guard of Coaster, a stately East Indiaman, and a pepper ship nine months out of Salem.

Mr. Heflin proposed to touch at North Isle off the coast of Sumatra for water and provisions. The islands multiplied. Past Pulo Timon, Pulo Aore, Pulo Tissang, Pulo Saya they sailed; then on between Saya and the Seven Isles, bringing still more islands into sight. At sunset Mr. Hart saw land he believed to be the island of Banca, and the *Thunderbird* was made to lie off and on through the night in soundings from eight to sixteen fathom. At daylight they bore off toward the straits, and at noon saw the Sumatra shore, feeling the pull of a strong southward current. Next day they were well within the strait between Banca and Sumatra. Jerry was in the starboard lead chains, sweating under the sun as he swung the lead with the rhythm of an old hand. Codder was in the port chains. They cast alternately, singing out:

"By the mark thirteen!"

"By the deep twelve!"

"Quarter less twelve!"

"By the mark ten!"

"And a half five!"

"Mark under water three!"

By this time the deck was alive with men as the ship was brought about. As she bore off to the south and west, the leadsmen sang:

"By the mark seven!"

"And a quarter!"

"By the deep eleven!"

"And a half eleven!"

Roy, standing a trick at the wheel, took time to mop his brow. Jerry grinned but did not lose his steady rhythm. Mr. Heflin went to his cabin and sat down. He had almost run the ship on the Fredrick Hendrik Shoal. He wet his lips nervously. Roy found him there an hour later when he sought him to say that a number of Malay proas were in sight. Mr. Heflin rubbed his hand across his forehead. "We've nothing to fear from them," he said, in such an exhausted voice that Roy asked anxiously, "Are you ill, sir?"

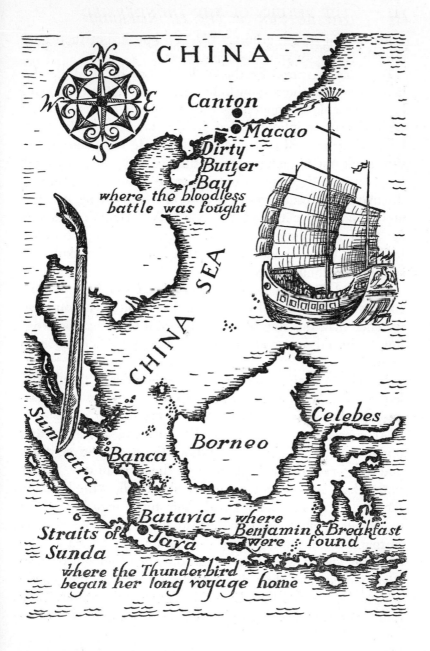

Mr. Heflin smiled grimly. "Ill? Yes, I'm ill, but there's no remedy for me in your medicine chest."

Roy was reassured by the smile. As one of his duties he had taken over the responsibility of the medicine chest, and he rather enjoyed matching the symptoms of his patients with the prescriptions listed in the medical book. Jerry laughed at his zeal and said that he made everyone on the ship stick out his tongue three times a day; and Mr. Hart often had a coughing fit after supper, until his stratagem was discovered, in order to get a dose of syrup, being inordinately fond of sweets. But the look in Mr. Heflin's eyes was far from reassuring. They had lost none of their burning brilliance, but they had sunk farther back into his skull and spoke of bottomless misery.

Roy said, "Mr. Heflin, you have gained weight, and your color is that of a healthy man who lives outdoors. You have watched over this ship like a mother bird teaching her fledgling to fly. I'd say you were a well man and a fine sailor, to boot."

Mr. Heflin straightened his sagging shoulders. "Thank you, lad," he said. "Come, let's have a look at those proas of yours—perhaps they have some foodstuffs to trade."

At sunset they came to on the Sumatra shore, getting under way at daylight to stand down the straits. Strong tides and dangerous shoals kept them on the alert all day, and at night they lay off and on under short sail, with lookouts doubled. Roy and Jerry stood their turns together at the masthead, feeling close enough to the great tropical stars to touch them. During these long hours they talked a little of home, and of what they would do when they got back to Rivergarden; and they thought a good deal of the people who had come into their lives during their adventures. They had met with wicked people, and much villainy; but when they reckoned it up, they discovered that they had met with more benevolence, and their hearts were filled with gratitude. Often they merely watched and listened, drinking in the sounds of the night, many of which could be heard at the masthead although inaudible on deck.

Early in the evening they heard the domestic sounds of villages of the Sumatra shore. When these had died away, they became aware of unfamiliar jungle voices from the uninhabited islets between Sumatra and Banca. "I wonder how a tiger sounds?" Jerry asked, after a spine-chilling cry. "Fat Pork says there are tigers in these islands and snakes as big as those of the Amazon. I wonder if there are monkeys, too? Roy, I wish you could have seen Breakfast."

He had often told Roy about Breakfast, the little monkey he had adopted on his journey with Benjamin across the Isthmus of Panamá. "I wonder where they are now?" he mused. "Benjamin swore he would follow me if he could, but I almost hope he didn't try. He was happy in the Serranía del Darien. Once he left there he would be a runaway slave again, with every man's hand against him."

"But he is the only witness to the murder of our father," Roy reminded him, somberly. "Without him we can prove nothing."

"We have his story, written down and signed by him. And in any case, our story must speak for itself. It will be our word against Mr. Morris' and Cousin Audley's, that's all." Jerry broke off suddenly. "Roy! Look! Look! What is it?" and flung his hands over his face.

The stars were hidden by great, pointed, flapping wings. Silently they brushed by, one actually touching Roy's sleeve. A moment of terror, a taint of animal smell, and they were gone, darting, flapping, zigzagging toward the nearest islet.

"Bats! But such big ones! Did you see them?" Jerry cried.

"Yes, I saw them," said Roy, rubbing away the gooseflesh

on his arms. "If that's a sample of the life in those jungles, I'm glad I'm aboard ship, with nothing but pirates to worry about!"

Next day he had to eat his words. From the shelter of the isle of Lucepara a sloop appeared. Mr. Heflin and Mr. Hart looked her over through the glass, and said, "She's well armed and well manned, with a heavy swivel gun amidships." The *Thunderbird* showed her colors but got no reply, the sloop continuing her course toward the *Thunderbird*. "Man the guns!" ordered Mr. Heflin.

"She's better armed than we; can't we run for it?" Mr. Hart asked.

"Not a chance. Bear down on her. Steer directly for her, Jack! Run her down!"

The boys had brought up the cutlasses and passed them out among the crew. They listened to Mr. Heflin in amazement. His face flushed with anger, his voice rang out with a vigor they had never suspected he could muster.

The sloop checked, and the men near the wheel could be seen huddling and gesticulating as if in argument. Steadily the *Thunderbird* came on, until Roy and Jerry could see the crew of the sloop; dark, sinister, turbaned fellows wearing long knives that flashed in the sun.

"Drum to quarters!" shouted Mr. Heflin.

Charleston set to on his drum. The men stood ready at the cannon, and Mr. Hart deliberately loaded his pistols.

Activity increased on the sloop. For a moment battle seemed inevitable; then the sloop quickly came about and glided out of the *Thunderbird*'s path, retreating the way in which she had come.

"Keep your stations!" Mr. Heflin called out. "She may have gone for reinforcements."

They waited tensely, and soon saw a number of vessels hovering among the islets ahead. Not a word was spoken, though the same thought was in every mind: "We're in for it!"

Just then the lookout sang out, "Sail on our larboard quarter, sir!" And in a moment they could all see a ship under a crowd of sail fast overhauling them. Ahead, the lurking vessels scattered like quail.

When the ship was near enough to speak, they heard a welcome British voice ringing across the water. She was an East Indiaman bound for home. She paused just long enough to say, "Look sharp if you go ashore. Our shore party was attacked yesterday, and we lost two men."

Mr. Heflin put his sword back into its scabbard. "She arrived just in time to save our gizzards from those Malay krises."

"I don't know about that, sir," Jerry said. "You already had them scared to death. Would you really have tried to run 'em down?"

Mr. Heflin smiled; the first real smile the boys had ever seen on his face. "There's an old saying about what to do if you meet the devil," he said. "If you can't go around him, go through him. I was going to try it."

A few days later the *Thunderbird* came to in the North Isle Roads, lying well out until morning, when she was brought in nearer to the watering place. Immediately upon coming to anchor, all the boats were hoisted out, and since the officers were needed aboard to supervise some repairs to the ship, Roy and Jerry were charged with the task of filling the water casks. They did not need to be reminded of the East Indiaman's warning. Every man was armed, and the boats well supplied with ammunition.

The shore was only dimly visible through a thick vapor. The boats were kept close together, and Codder, who had visited this coast before, and had a smattering of the language, directed their course. "The Malays would find our ship a pretty prize, sir," he observed. "They attack out of pure meanness, but they love firearms—firearms and money."

Jerry suggested, "We'd better keep the boats out of their reach and swim the water casks off."

Roy agreed. "We'll land, while the rest keep a good space between them and the shore. Surely if we give no offense, we will have no trouble."

But Codder took a gloomy view. "You don't know these fellers, sir. They don't need no offense nor no reason to run amuck. Some says they takes dope before they starts their killin', but it's my opinion it's meanness that makes 'em do it. Nothing but meanness."

The sun was already hot and drank the morning mist so thirstily that they could now see the low-lying shore. It was covered with trees; indeed, the water overflowed the land and washed between the tree trunks. Codder pointed to a place where slightly higher ground formed a beach fit to land on. Already there were native proas there, and as their boat was brought up on the sand, Roy and Jerry had their first close view of the Malays.

They had visualized a race as gigantic and as ugly as the Cyclops, but instead they met a smiling people, a clear yellow brown in color, of active but delicate build. They had poultry and fruit for sale and willingly directed the boat's party to the watering place, which lay back a few hundred yards from the beach.

Roy remained on the beach to direct the landing of the water casks, while Jerry proceeded with Codder to the spring. It was a beautiful spot, a deep, clear pool fed by a tinkling stream. The earth was much beaten down around it, however, by the feet of foreign sailors, who had left their marks in the felled trees, the remains of old fires, broken casks, and the wide worn path to the beach.

Another path led to a native village. One or two thatched huts could be seen half hidden by trees, and the villagers were much in evidence as they went to and fro from the beach or passed on their way to the day's work in the rice paddies. A score or more of idlers had gathered near the spring. They squatted on the ground in the shade, smoking and talking peacefully, but one and all armed with the long, formidable knives that seemed to be the most important part of their dress.

Jerry felt a thrill of apprehension. As two of the men rose and came toward him, he stood his ground, reminding himself that his party had the advantage of firearms. One of the men was evidently a person of some consequence, for he wore a striped robe and shoes with upturned points at the toe, whereas the others were content with little more than loincloths and turbans. His companion was one of these; he wore also an ingratiating smile.

"Salaam, master," he greeted Jerry. He went on to say in his own language that he was the servant of this man, Po Qualah, who was a leader in the village; that his master could tell the American captain, for a price, where a good cargo of pepper could be obtained.

Codder translated this speech, and Jerry was flattered to learn that he was taken for the Captain of the *Thunderbird*. "Very civil of him," he told Codder. "Thank him, please, and say that we have no need of pepper, since we already have our cargo, but we can use a quantity of fresh fruits and vegetables, fish, and poultry, and will purchase bullocks at a fair price."

Codder entered into negotiations with Po Qualah and several other villagers who came to take part in the bargaining, while Jerry signaled to Roy and the business of watering got under way. The sailors rolled the empty casks up to the spring, showing the natives the whites of their eyes, but the

Malays responded with smiles and offers to trade for tobacco. Jerry kept them at their work, however, hoping to complete it without delay. The sooner they were supplied, the sooner they could sail for Batavia, and the sooner they reached Batavia the sooner he would see Felicia. If only Broderick Brown were not so young, and not so brave and capable and strong! If only he were not so near Felicia!

Ah, well, this Malay chieftain had taken him for a captain, too, and he was only a few years younger than Broderick Brown, and he had learned a thing or two about ships, himself.

The morning wore on. No hint of mist remained; the equatorial sun seemed to stand for hours directly overhead. Jerry would have liked nothing better than to call a halt to the watering and take a long nap in the shade. The sailors, pickled in brine and seared in the sun, cast longing glances at the grove where the villagers lounged, eating cool crescents of papaya; and one or two of them took to strolling that way to do a little trading while the water casks were being filled.

About noon Jerry was leaning against a tree, drowsily listening to the gurgle of water into the casks, when a sudden clamor brought him awake with a start. A knot of men in the grove had gathered about Jock and Joe Kent, and their voices could be heard disputing in a mixture of languages.

Jerry weighed the situation in his mind. Both the sailors and the natives were armed. He could summon the rest of the men from the boats; on the other hand, the Malays could count on unlimited reinforcements from the village. No doubt the firearms of the Americans would rout them in the end; but it was equally certain that the long daggers of the Malays would do much harm.

He recognized Jock's voice rising furiously, though he could not hear what was being said. The man with whom he was quarreling was Po Qualah's servant. He screamed an answer and raised his kris. Jerry could see the white face of Joe Kent looking around the circle of onlookers, who muttered and fingered their weapons.

Codder stepped to Jerry's side, hefting his gun. Jerry laid his hand on the barrel. "Wait. Don't fire. Whatever happens, don't fire. Come with me." As he strode toward the grove he told the rest of the sailors, "Go back to the beach and wait. If we don't return in fifteen minutes, my brother will give you your orders."

He walked into the fringe of the angry crowd, shouldering his way to the seat of the disturbance. His appearance surprised the group into silence, but the silence was threatening. Jerry faced Jock. "Give me your cutlass!"

Jock blustered, " 'E called me a dirty name, 'e did, the bloody 'eathen!"

Jerry repeated, "Give me your cutlass!" And Jock reluctantly handed it over. Then Jerry turned to Codder. "Ask Po Qualah to disarm his man."

Codder gulped, for Po Qualah stood opposite Jerry with his kris drawn. He somewhat falteringly addressed the leader, and to everyone's surprise the Malay surrendered his kris, and Po Qualah sheathed his own. Jerry went on. "Tell Po Qualah that we do not wish trouble; that we come in friendship and will buy many provisions if we are treated with friendship. But if any of us is attacked, I will bring the ship close to his village and will destroy it with her guns."

Codder wiped his hand across his sweating face, planted his legs apart, and delivered this ultimatum with some zest. Po Qualah listened gravely, then spoke to the excited natives. One by one they fell back and walked away, or returned to their former positions of ease. The Malay chieftain then spoke to Jerry, translated by Codder as follows: "He says there'll be no trouble, sir, but that his man don't like bein'

called a bloody heathen, and it'll be better if the sailors keeps
to themselves. He says he'll meet you on the beach before
sunset with all the bullocks he can muster, and sir, he says
the captain is a brave man, meanin' yourself."

Codder grinned, and Jerry blushed like a rose. To hide his
discomfiture he ordered Jock and Joe Kent back to work on
the double, and they found little time on their hands during
the rest of the day. The villagers dispersed at Po Qualah's
command to collect what livestock they had for trade.

Jerry took his turn at the boats, Roy at the spring, and
before sundown the watering was completed and the transfer
of provisions from the beach to the ship began. Mr. Hart
came ashore to take charge of this task, and Roy and Jerry
took a well-earned rest, sitting a little way apart from the
bustle on a driftwood log.

A grateful coolness came with the descent of the sun. The
stir and color of the improvised market, the cackle of hens,
the squealing of pigs, and the nervous snorting of the water
buffalo were entertainment enough. Adding to their con-
tentment was the sense of a job well done and the knowledge
that by morning they would resume their journey, and would
soon meet the *Swan* at Batavia.

Their reverie was interrupted by Po Qualah, who came
toward them, followed by his servant. The chieftain bowed
slightly as they rose to greet him, and made a short speech.
Seeing that they did not understand, the servant used his
scant English to explain that his master wished to say good-
by, that he considered the American captain a good friend,
and that as a parting gift, he presented him with his kris.

Jerry took the weapon and examined it curiously. He was
pleased at the idea of having it as a souvenir, in memory
of the occasion when it had come so close to his own ribs.
Drawing it from its sheath, he started to touch the blade with
his thumb to test the edge.

Po Qualah cried out and seized his hand. The servant said calmly, "No touch. Him poison."

Jerry's legs almost gave way. He said weakly, "Thank you. Thank you very much."

"My friend," said Po Qualah, using English for the first time. "Brave man."

When he was gone, Roy burst out laughing. Placing the kris gingerly on the log, he clapped Jerry affectionately on the shoulder. "Brave man, indeed!" he chortled. "But I never saw a brave man's knees shake quite so hard before!"

CHAPTER XVI

BATAVIA

JERRY MET Felicia again in the central hall of the Royal Batavian and Foreign Hotel, under the glitter of candle flames in thirty chandeliers, multiplied by looking glasses into a myriad. He was dazzled, and quite speechless, which was a pity, since this was the only occasion on which they met during their stay in port. On the very next day she was affected by one of those fevers so prevalent in Batavia, and was whisked away by a friend of her father's, Mr. Allerbrook, to his house on one of the islands in the bay. In the purer air of this place she rapidly recovered, but was not allowed visitors before the day designated for the *Swan* to sail.

These events were still in the future, however, and their supper that night at the Royal Batavian Hotel was an occasion of great festivity. Each of those present had particular reason for satisfaction.

Broderick Brown was pleased because of the safe arrival of his young friends, the Laceys, whose trials and triumphs he had so cordially embraced. There was also the matter of a purchase of coffee and sugar, which, if completed, would fill the *Swan*'s cargo to advantage. He had high hopes of his venture with the *Swan*, which might very well lay the cornerstone of that substantial fortune that he meant to possess some day. As he looked around the table, he realized that not a little of his pleasure was due to the presence of Mrs. Allerbrook and Felicia, representative of all the charm, elegance, comfort, and companionship that a sailor was obliged to deny himself for years on end. Mrs.

154

Allerbrook was an imposing matron, gowned in the latest European mode, the like of which Broderick seldom met, even in Boston. It was gratifying to him as host to see the heads turn to follow her as his party progressed to the dining room. As for Felicia, she was only a child, but she could pass for a young lady tonight. If Gerald Lacey only knew how foolish he looked, whenever he looked at her! No, that wasn't quite true; he was a fine-looking lad, an honest, loyal lad, and a brave one. There was nothing wrong with him that time wouldn't cure. Why, three years ago, when he himself was as young as Jerry, he had made quite a spectacle of himself over a girl not half as pretty as Felicia.

Roy, of course, had reason to be pleased, with his homeward voyage so well begun, and his friend Broderick Brown sitting beside him at such a well-appointed table. His eyes were charmed by the handsome architecture of the hotel, with its piazzas and porticoes, its mirrors and paintings, its arched hallways and sweeping staircases. The company to be seen there also delighted him. Besides the Europeans present, there were members of every Oriental race, each wearing the garb of his country. He was pleased with Jerry, and thought how proud their father would be to see him so well grown and purposeful. Although he was only a year older than his brother, Roy sometimes felt quite paternal towards Jerry. Under all his satisfaction, however, some apprehensions stirred when he remembered Cousin Audley imprisoned on board the *Thunderbird,* nursing his black thoughts. And Mr. Heflin—what of him? He had elected to remain on the ship tonight, rather than expose himself to the temptations of the shore. So far he had comported himself manfully. But would it last? After tonight, Roy resolved regretfully, he must forgo these pleasures, too, and keep Mr. Heflin company. It might mean the salvation of the *Thunderbird;* perhaps even of a man's soul. These solemn thoughts gave the gay scene an added glitter.

Felicia had her own happy thoughts. It was exciting enough to be bound for America, that far-off homeland she had not seen since she was a child. Added to this was the excitement of being escorted in a public place by three such handsome young gentlemen. Of course, Broderick Brown was really too rugged of feature to be *handsome,* but there was an air about him no one could mistake. And Leroy and Gerald Lacey—now, they were really a good-looking pair, with their fair hair and frank blue eyes; so tall, too, and broad-shouldered. Their soft, drawling voices and their gentle manners would recommend them anywhere, and when one thought of the incredible adventures they had been through! She really did not know which one she liked the best. Leroy, perhaps, was a shade handsomer, but he had a faraway look in his eye which was not very flattering. Gerald—well, he said very little, but his eyes followed her wherever she went. Mrs. Allerbrook was too elegant for words, and Mr. Allerbrook was genial; the food was delicious, and the surroundings were romantic. The whole voyage was romantic. She would have a great deal to write in her diary.

Jerry's thoughts were too incoherent to record. The supper was over before he knew it. Felicia was borne off by the hospitable Allerbrooks. He and Roy returned to the *Thunderbird,* and the heavy hand of responsibility fell again on their young shoulders.

There was much to be done to ready the ships for the next lap of the voyage, for the only stop they expected to make at any civilized port between Batavia and Norfolk was the island of St. Helena, thousands of miles away. While the necessary preparations were going on, Broderick Brown was busy with the purchase and loading of his consignment of coffee and sugar. Mr. Heflin stayed aboard the *Thunder-*

bird, still resolved not to venture ashore, and Roy became his right-hand man. Mr. Heflin had grown to depend upon him in countless ways, moral as well as physical. Roy cast many a longing glance at the thirty-foot wall across the bay behind which lay the teeming city of Batavia, with its shady canals and lofty houses. But when Mr. Heflin's unhappy eyes turned to him, he did not have the heart to refuse their unspoken appeal.

Thus it came about that to Jerry and Mr. Hart fell one of the most important tasks, the recruiting of seamen to fill the depleted crews of both ships. The two Chinese supplied by Fong were dismissed, according to agreement, in Batavia. Three men aboard the *Swan* and two aboard the *Thunderbird* were so sick as to be unable to perform their duties, and if the reputation of the place was upheld, more could be expected to fall victim to the diseases that seemed to pollute the very air of the tropical metropolis. The matter was, therefore, urgent, taking Jerry and Mr. Hart ashore at the earliest opportunity.

They first visited the uncle of Yu Kee, one of the Chinese who had come with them from Dirty Butter Bay. Yu Tai Wa operated a public house near the quay and received them in his upstairs apartment overlooking the roads where the two American ships lay among the vessels of many nations. He was a venerable person of some consequence in the large Chinese population of Batavia. In his presence Jerry felt he must have been transported suddenly back to Canton. The scent of sandalwood was strong in the room, mingled with the tobacco in Yu's pipe and the steam from the little cups of bohea tea brought in by Malay slaves.

After the inevitable courtesies and refreshments, Yu gravely considered the problem presented to his attention. After some deliberation, he advised them to consult a relative of his, Yip Man, who also owned a tavern. His own establishment, he assured them, was completely respectable —too respectable to be frequented by those who might be helpful to his visitors. That of Yip, on the other hand—well, a few dollars planted there might bring forth much fruit. They had only to wait a few moments in this miserable room, and he would send word to Yip. Their host left them, and they passed a quarter of an hour contentedly enough, Mr. Hart puffing on his cigar, while Jerry examined the curious objects to be found in the room. At the end of that time Yip Man entered, bowing and smiling, and announced, "My chin-chin you."

He was small and skinny and slightly cross-eyed. He looked fit for any sort of villainy, but Mr. Hart was not disposed to be particular, and Jerry always expected the best of everyone. Yip Man came to the point at once. "How muchee sailor you wanchee?"

"We can use a dozen if we can get them, even more if they're able men," Mr. Hart answered.

Yip proceeded to the next question, "How muchee you pay?"

Mr. Hart mentioned a figure that seemed to wound Yip's feelings. He suggested twice the amount, and they haggled a while, finally agreeing upon a figure that both insisted was robbery. "But you'll be paid only if they're sound; none of your lame, halt, and blind, you understand?" Mr. Hart warned.

"My savvy." Yip smiled.

"And I don't expect 'em to be sober, but they got to be conscious," Mr. Hart went on. "And we need 'em at once."

"My savvy. You come my place tomollo night. You got money, my got sailorman."

On the following night Jerry and Mr. Hart set out for the tavern of Yip Man. They were armed and accompanied by two armed seamen, others remaining with the boat at the

quay. Jerry, who had misgivings about the nature of the
transactions in which he was engaged, gave voice to them
as they walked toward the public house of Yu Tai Wa.
"Look here, Mr. Hart, do you intend to shanghai these men?
If so, I'll have nothing to do with it. I was treated so once,
myself. There must be an honest way to hire an honest seaman."

Mr. Hart rumbled, "There's no need to get your hackles
up, lad—I mean, sir. There's nobody like a tavern keeper
for making the acquaintance of sailors ashore. We're only
paying Mr. Yip for introducing us to his sailor friends, you
might say. Is there anything wrong with that?"

"Not if you put it that way. But why the weapons, and
why the bodyguard, if that's all there is to it?"

"Why, sir, surely you've heard of the wicked ways of this
port. No man goes alone and unarmed after dark in Batavia,
and nobody knows it better than I. I was waylaid myself one
night six years ago on one of the principal streets."

At Yu's tavern they were furnished with an escort of slaves
carrying lighted flambeaux to conduct them to the house
they sought. The expedition was taking on an increasingly
formidable character. As they tramped along, Jerry was
thinking hard. He was not as ingenuous as he sometimes
appeared, for his experiences during the past year had
taught him a good deal about the seamy side of life. His
good sense told him that Yip was a common crimp, and
that Mr. Hart was not as shocked at the idea of shanghaiing
a crew as he professed to be. On the other hand, it was
possible that Yip might put them in the way of obtaining
a crew by legitimate means. He decided that his only
course of action was to go along and find out.

The street they were traversing bore little resemblance
to the broad paved avenues of the central part of the city.
They were now in that suburb without the city wall called

the Chinese Town. The houses here were low and mean, the canals were stagnant and odoriferous beyond description. Added to the stench of these ditches were the smells of the bazaars, which, though closed for the night, revealed their presence pungently. Almost overpowered by the odor of fish, Jerry and his party hurried past the fish market and turned with some relief into the open door of the Pavilion of Everlasting Felicity, which the slaves indicated was the tavern of Yip Man.

In the outer room a group of Chinese sat at a table, eating, while a pair of Dutch seamen gloomily drank at another. Yip appeared at a door at the back of the room, and Mr. Hart, Jerry, and the two seamen followed him through. This room was more crowded and noisy with Oriental music and conversation in many tongues. "Too-muchee people tonight," Yip explained with satisfaction. "French ship, English ship, Dutch—all sailorman allee same come Yip Man house."

"Let's be about our business, Yip," Mr. Hart said, brusquely.

"Too muchee hurry," smiled Yip. "Sit down, have number one first-chop drink. My make all things ready."

Mr. Hart sat down, not too reluctantly, and the sailors went grinning to the bar. Jerry left his glass untouched while he sat alert and watchful. It was not easy to be either; the room was dark, full of smoke and the smells of sweat, sour wine, and strong spirits.

Mr. Hart grunted and drank his drink down. He, too, seemed watchful and ill at ease. "Where did Mr. Everlasting Felicity go?" he muttered. "I'll give him ten minutes to keep his bargain, no longer."

Just before his time was up, Yip was back at their table. "You pay," he said, "twelve piecee sailor."

"Do you take me for an idiot?" Mr. Hart demanded. "We'll pay when we see what we get."

"You come."

Signaling their men, Mr. Hart and Jerry followed Yip through still another door. This led out of the house into an overgrown garden. They made their way gropingly toward a light that feebly revealed a small boathouse built at the edge of a canal. Yip pushed the door open, and they went inside, every man's hand upon his weapon.

"Number one first-chop sailor," Yip announced proudly.

In the dim light of a hanging lantern, seven figures could be seen. Two drunken men sat leaning against the wall humming a drowsy tune, while another snored lustily at their feet. Four bodies were heaped in a corner like cordwood. Mr. Hart went forward to examine them, followed by his sailors. Yip and Jerry stood just inside the door. Suddenly Jerry saw a fist descend heavily upon the tavern keeper's head, dropping him in his tracks. He seized his sword to defend himself from a black figure that sprang out of the shadow, but was thrown off balance by something—a small, hairy, chattering something—that hurtled onto his chest and hung, clawing and kicking, around his neck.

The others came at once to his aid, and while he struggled with the nightmare creature that had fastened itself upon him, they battled with the man who had felled Yip Man. The quarters were too close for firearms, too close, even, to swing a sword, and their antagonist was powerful, and as slippery as an eel. Jerry subdued his attacker first. A memory broke through his fright, and he stopped struggling, to find two little arms hugging his neck with pure affection. Gently he pulled the creature off and looked at him. "Breakfast!" he cried. "Is it you?"

It was a little monkey, chattering with excitement. At the name, "Breakfast," he danced with joy. This was the pet that Jerry had left with his father's slave, Benjamin, on the

Isthmus of Panamá. If this was Breakfast, then the other must be Benjamin.

Jerry leaped into the fray. "Wait!" he cried. "Hold off! Fall back, I say! I know this man. He is my friend!"

A knot of knuckles struck his nose; a knife sliced the sleeve of his jacket. Still he persisted, and at last succeeded in separating the men. They stood back, panting, while he shouted, "Hold off! It's Benjamin! Ah, Benjamin!" They grasped each other's hands.

Benjamin was bruised and bloody. His clothes hung in rags. A knife had gashed his hand, which bled profusely. But his eyes gleamed as he looked at Jerry. "Mahs' Jerry! Ah've found you again! Ah've found you at last!"

Mr. Hart wiped his face and neck, and wrung out the wet handkerchief. "What *is* this?" he demanded angrily.

Jerry explained as best he could. "This is Benjamin, my father's body servant. He helped me to follow the *Thunderbird*, but he got sick crossing the Isthmus of Panamá, and I had to leave him behind. He promised to meet me when he could—and here he is!" He pounded Benjamin on the back, while the Negro grinned in reply. He was much the same as when Jerry last saw him; his wool a bit frostier, perhaps, and his body leaner, but the same Benjamin. Jerry turned to Breakfast. "And this is Breakfast. He's traveled a long way from Panamá."

Yip Man was sitting up, blinking. His oblique eyes evidently took in as much of the situation as he needed to know, for he stood up and held out his hand. "You pay. Must go, chop chop."

The drunken men had not stirred throughout the hubbub, but still the one slept and the others sat humming their tuneless tune. The sailors pulled them to their feet, and reported, "They can walk."

"Take a look at the others."

The sailors pulled at the limp bodies, but there was no response. "They're alive," said one. "But they won't know it for a while."

Mr. Hart growled to Yip, "I told you I wouldn't pay for men you'd doped."

"English captain allee same pay," said Yip unconcernedly.

"He's right," Mr. Hart told Jerry. "If we don't take 'em, the next ship will. What do you say?"

If he had not asked Jerry's opinion, Jerry would very likely have refused to take the men. But his mind was too full of the return of Benjamin and Breakfast to be much concerned with anything else. And, he reasoned, would he be doing these poor wretches any kindness to leave them in the grasping hands of Yip Man? He nodded. "Very well."

"Load 'em into the boat." Mr. Hart counted out the coins into Yip's extended hand. "Call the slaves to light us. You can get your boat from Yu tomorrow." The boat, a Malay proa, was pushed off, and they set off down the canal. Mr. Hart leaned back with a sigh. "God knows what kind of shark bait he's sold us," he said glumly.

Jerry hugged Breakfast and smiled at Benjamin. "Never mind about them," he said. "We got a bargain. I promise you that Benjamin is worth a whole boat's crew, all by himself!"

CHAPTER XVII

STORM

THE *Thunderbird* passed in the night between Prince's Island and Pulo Krakatao, narrowly missing the menacing Qu Klip rocks. Then she was through the Straits of Sunda and homeward bound.

She was alone. The *Swan* was somewhere in the same ocean, on the same track; but they might not meet again. Broderick Brown was obliged to go direct to Boston, while Roy and Jerry were determined to leave the *Thunderbird* at Norfolk while they made all haste to Rivergarden with their prisoners, Cousin Audley, Ole, and Ross. The latter two had been returned to the *Thunderbird* at Batavia and were now confined in an empty cabin near enough to that of Captan Audley and Mr. Griff for one guard to keep an eye on both doors.

It had been arranged that Mr. Heflin should take the *Thunderbird* on to Boston, where Broderick Brown undertook to sell her cargo along with his own. Roy and Jerry had not forgotten that a large part of their patrimony was invested in the *Thunderbird,* and they knew that Broderick Brown could handle their interests more profitably than they could themselves.

All this, however, seemed far ahead as the *Thunderbird* met one hard squall after another. In spite of the "recruits" added to the crew at Batavia, the ship was undermanned. Four of the men were now confined to their quarters by sickness, while others were showing symptoms of disease. Mr. Griff came down with an ague and had to be dosed with great quantities of Peruvian bark, of which there was only a small store aboard. Of the four recruits who had fallen to the *Thunderbird's* lot, one was a Malay who had never left his native isle before and knew nothing of seamanship. Two were fugitives from a French man-of-war; they had been in hiding three months in Batavia's Chinese Town and were debilitated by drunkenness and disease. They were pathetically glad to be quit of the place and tried their feeble best to be of use. Benjamin, of course, was the fourth, and as Jerry had promised, he did the work of six men, in spite of his wounded hand.

The supercargoes' cabin was now enlivened by the presence of Breakfast, whom Mimbo welcomed as an old friend. "If Kowí were only here, our menagerie would be complete," Roy said. He was much taken with Breakfast, and while at Batavia had amused himself sketching his antics and describing his tricks in letters to Rosalie.

"Kowí wasn't much of a sailor," Jerry observed. "I'm sure he's much happier back in China with Ching—that is, unless Ching turns pirate like his relatives and takes to the sea."

"Not he. He wanted nothing but to go back to his carpentry. I must say, I shall have had my share of seafaring myself, when this voyage is over." Roy made a grimace as the motion of the ship threw his chair against the wall. The floor was slimy with the water that found its way through her upper works. Books and papers, bedding and clothing were packed away or bundled in canvas to keep out the wet.

"There's nothing wrong with a sailor's life that can't be cured by a good night's sleep," said Jerry.

"Speaking of sleep," Roy yawned, "it's time you turned in. But only a sailor could sleep through this racket."

The boys had been standing watch and watch since leaving Batavia, so that one of them would always be on guard against the uncertainty of the elements, the temptations of

Mr. Heflin, the sickness of the crew, and the menace of Cousin Audley and Mr. Griff.

"I can sleep through any storm, nowadays," Jerry said. "It's the sense of responsibility that weighs upon the mind. Roy, sometimes I feel as if we were sitting on a powder keg, which is bound to explode at any moment."

Roy laughed, but he understood exactly what his brother meant. He went on deck. Although it was the beginning of the first dogwatch, the sky was as dark as night. The squall had blown itself into a tempest, raising seas higher than any Roy had yet seen. He clung to the nearest support, all but overpowered by the wind. The ship was under close-reefed topsails, and all able hands were engaged in taking in sail amid the awful play of lightning and the crashing of thunder. Roy took a step forward to go to their assistance, when a blinding flash struck the main topgallant mast and ran down the mainmast with a force that shook every timber in the vessel. The men were knocked to the deck like ninepins; some lay stunned, while others staggered to their feet, blinking. For several moments there was the greatest confusion, but the fury of the storm brought them all back to their senses more quickly than discipline could have done. A tremendous gust of wind split the foresail, requiring immediate attention, and while that work was going on Roy and Benjamin struggled across the deck, dragging those men injured by the blast to safety.

When it appeared that no one above decks was seriously hurt, Roy sent Benjamin to see what had happened in the fo'c'sle, while he returned to the cabins. With a great throb of relief he caught sight of Jerry coming from his cabin, armed with cutlass and boarding pike. Without a word they turned and went together to the cabin where Cousin Audley was imprisoned. The door was ajar, and from within came a billow of acrid smoke.

Kicking the door open, they burst into the cabin, to find the lantern fallen and the bed on which Mr. Griff lay ablaze. The guard was lying face down on the floor, rolling from side to side with every pitch of the vessel; and Cousin Audley was missing.

Hastily they dragged the unconscious men outside, and shouted for help. The hissing of flames added a new note of terror to the tumult of the elements. Roy yelled in Jerry's ear, "Go get some men to put out the fire. I'm going after him."

Jerry did not pause to ask who "he" was, but thrust his cutlass into Roy's hand and pounded off.

Before he reached the stairs, however, the door of the cabin where Ole and Ross were imprisoned swung open, and the two ruffians lunged out. Behind them Roy caught just a glimpse of the smiling face of Cousin Audley; then there was a loud report and a bullet sang past his ear. He saw Jerry desperately parrying blows from both his assailants, but he could not go to his aid. Cousin Audley, not waiting to reload, charged straight for him with sword drawn. Roy went to meet him with his cutlass.

Jerry stumbled backward to the stairway, favored by the narrow space in which his opponents must fight. They could not flank him, and hindered each other when they pressed forward together. They were armed with the weapons Captain Audley had taken from the guard; Ole wielded a knife with his long arm, while Ross hacked with a cutlass. Jerry swung his boarding pike like the arms of a windmill, and had the satisfaction of feeling it thud against flesh more than once.

The companionway was filling with smoke. Tongues of flame ventured from the burning cabin, licked at the varnished walls, and spread greedily. And while the boys battled for their lives in an inferno of smoke and heat, the storm raged as savagely as ever; the ship tossed helplessly; and the men above deck struggled to keep her afloat.

Roy was no match for Cousin Audley's sword. All his will and agility, all his lessons, even the recent fencing practice at Canton could not keep that flickering blade from coming closer and closer to his throat. His breath rasping from the smoke, he gave way, tripped over the groaning body of Mr. Griff, and went tumbling. As he went down, he saw Cousin Audley poised for the kill.

A terrific roll sent the *Thunderbird* almost on her beam ends. For an interminable space of time she seemed borne down, inert; then she righted herself with a lurch. A cataract of salt water flooded the companionway. Roy, Jerry, their attackers, and the two unconscious men were swept into a struggling tangle. They were all fighting a common enemy. The weight of it pressed them down; brine filled their eyes, their mouths, their lungs. The fire hissed like a tiger, sending out clouds of scalding steam. Jerry, at the foot of the stair, was able to find the rail and cling to it. He shouted for help as loudly as he could croak. Another roll of the ship broke his hold, his head hit a corner of the stair, and he sank into oblivion.

The boys came back to consciousness in their own cabin. The ship was still tossing violently, and Mr. Hart stood braced in the doorway watching them. Benjamin was swabbing the floor. At the opening of Jerry's eyes he dropped the swab and bent over him.

"What happened? How is the ship? Is the fire out? What about Cousin Audley?" Jerry asked. He sat up, rubbing his head.

Roy struggled out of his bunk, feeling himself all over. He could not believe that he was really alive and unhurt.

"Your precious cousin is in good health," Mr. Hart said. "He's back in his cabin and asking for his supper."

"Is Mr. Griff alive?"

"Just barely. He was badly burned. I doubt he'll last the night."

"What about the others?"

"Ross swallowed enough salt water to bathe a whale, and he's out of his head. If he lives, he won't be fit to give you trouble for some time. Ole put up a fight when the men tried to take him in custody, and he got shot. I don't know who did it, and I ain't going to ask. He's dead."

For two days the storm raged unrelentingly. The motion of the ship was violent, and it was almost as wet below as above decks, although dead lights were fixed in all ports. A legion of cockroaches drowned and washed about the cabins. Mimbo and Breakfast clung shivering together in a bunk, refusing the cold rations, which were all that could be had, it being impossible to keep a fire in the galley. On the third day the wind decreased, but the sea remained tremendous. The tortured *Thunderbird* took in so much water that the pumps were set to work at least part of every watch. Mr. Hart, seeing prodigious numbers of fish about the ship, predicted, "We'll be fairly into the trade wind before the week is up."

Three days later he was proved a good prophet, and the *Thunderbird* set a pace of one hundred and thirty miles of ocean a day in her race toward the vast continent of Africa. Life aboard was once more supportable. Daylight could again enter the cabins, and the comforts of dry clothing and hot food were again available. For Roy and Jerry, however, every waking hour was filled with anxiety. Even in their dreams the charge of the ship weighed heavily upon them. Roy often thought longingly of those carefree nights during the voyage out, when he and Jerry lay idly watching the unfamiliar stars of the Southern Hemisphere wheel into view, trusting the ship to Cousin Audley's capable hands, which had not yet been raised against them.

Mr. Griff died at the height of the storm, and his remains were committed to the deep as soon as the weather permitted. Just before the service, Ross, too, gave up the ghost, so that there were two weighted sacks to tilt over the side. Mr. Heflin read the burial service, looking very much like a corpse himself; indeed, the faces of all those assembled took on a ghastly greenish pallor from the reflections cast upon them by the sea and stormy sky.

A week of fair weather was welcome; still disease stalked the ship. Roy's watches began to be a continual round with the medicine chest, a continual ache in his heart because he could do so little to restore health to these once strong men. One of the sick was Battoo, the Malay, whose illness was aggravated by a severe mental distress. He lay in his hammock moaning incoherently, at times crying aloud. Roy begged him to be quiet for the sake of his fellow sufferers, but to no avail.

Codder, who lay nearby, spoke up. "There's nothing you can do for him, sir. I've seen fellers like him before. They gets an idea and it eats on 'em till they dies."

"But what does he want?" Roy asked. "He seems to be begging for something."

"You won't believe me when I tell you what he wants, sir. He's calling for a crocodile what he thinks is his twin brother."

"What?"

"I'm only telling you what he says, sir. He says when he was born, a crocodile was born along with him and was put in a certain river, and it's his duty to feed him at certain times. Well, the time for feeding the beast has come around again, and he ain't there to do it, and he believes he'll die because of it."

The Malay had grown quiet and appeared to be listening to their conversation, his bright, feverish eyes going from one to the other. He spoke rapidly to the sailor, who reported, "He says that his crocodile twin is beautiful, with a red nose and spots, and he wears bracelets and rings in his ears. He lives in a beautiful river on his home island. . . ." Battoo's voice went on dreamily, describing who knew what wonders, but breaking off with a childlike sob.

Roy stood up abruptly. He felt desperately tired. He was tired of sickness, tired of responsibility, tired of the ship and the everlasting sea! How many more men must die, before the oceans were crossed?

That day a cow that they had taken on at Batavia died. Cousin Audley complained bitterly because he would now have to do without cream. Joe Kent had a quarrel with Fat Pork, who turned sullen and served up an inedible dinner. Mr. Heflin developed a racking cough and took to his bunk. Jerry and Roy met during the dogwatch, each seeing in the other's face the reflection of his own anxiety.

"Mr. Hart says we must be nearing Madagascar," Jerry said, with forced cheerfulness. "We have put a good distance behind us." Roy managed a smile. Neither of them spoke of the tempestuous weather to be expected in this latitude. On the horizon, however, black clouds piled up, grumbling with thunder.

In spite of threatening weather, the *Thunderbird* had favorable winds for another week. Roy and Jerry were now in charge of the ship, for Mr. Heflin was confined to his cabin. He was still able to give instructions, which Mr. Hart and the boys carried out. Roy and Jerry worked wherever they were needed; they did the tasks of cabin boy, guard, fo'c'sle hand, surgeon, and chaplain. Jerry's special charges were the livestock, the provisions, and the working of the ship. Roy dealt with the navigation, kept the log, read Sunday services, and nursed the sick.

In this latter capacity he spent much time with Mr. Heflin, hoping to arouse him from his depression. Mr. Heflin, like poor Battoo, seemed almost to invite death. His cough had improved, yet he took less and less interest in the ship, ate scarce enough to support life, and sat for hours at a time staring into space.

He seemed to want Roy with him; only Roy could persuade him to eat, or rouse him to go over the charts. Roy sat often with him when he was off duty, though he was dead for sleep. One Saturday night, to keep himself awake, he took up his Prayer Book to familiarize himself with the Collect, Epistle, and Gospel to be read on the morrow. That done, he leafed through the service of Morning Prayer. He began to read aloud, without knowing it, his voice growing louder as the sonorous phrases of the canticles rolled off his tongue:

> O all ye Works of the Lord, bless ye the Lord: praise him, and magnify him for ever.
>
> O ye Angels of the Lord, bless ye the Lord: praise him, and magnify him for ever.
>
> O ye Heavens, bless ye the Lord: praise him, and magnify him for ever.
>
> O ye Waters that be above the firmament, bless ye the Lord: praise him, and magnify him for ever....
>
> O ye Sun and Moon, bless ye the Lord: praise him, and magnify him for ever.
>
> O ye Stars of heaven, bless ye the Lord: praise him, and magnify him for ever....
>
> O ye Winds of God, bless ye the Lord: praise him, and magnify him for ever....
>
> O ye Nights and Days, bless ye the Lord: praise him, and magnify him for ever.

O ye Light and Darkness, bless ye the Lord: praise
him, and magnify him for ever.

O ye Lightnings and Clouds, bless ye the Lord: praise
him, and magnify him for ever. . . .

O ye Seas and Floods, bless ye the Lord: praise him,
and magnify him for ever.

O ye Whales, and all that move in the waters, bless ye
the Lord: praise him, and magnify him for ever. . . .

Mr. Heflin asked suddenly, "What are you reading? If
you please, read it again."

Roy looked up, surprised, and found Mr. Heflin's eyes
fixed upon him attentively. Gladly he read the passage
again. When he finished, he let the book fall to his lap while
he sat thinking how the words were much more meaning-
ful now than they were before he went to sea. Surely no one
lived as intimately with Nights and Days, Lightnings and
Clouds, Seas and Floods as did a sailor! No one but a sailor
could know their full might. And knowing them, who else
could sense so vividly the might of their Creator?

His thoughts were interrupted by Mr. Heflin. "You are
tired," he said gently, a new note of awareness in his usually
lifeless voice. "Go to bed." As Roy rose, he added, "Would
you—will you leave the book here?"

In the morning the wind was higher; there was a heavy,
confused sea under a dismal sky. The service was almost
drowned out by the war of the elements, but to the surprise
of the company Mr. Heflin attended, and the sight of him
seemed to put heart into the men. After that, he again put
in an appearance at meals, saying little, to be sure, but
seeming less withdrawn. In his cabin he read the Prayer
Book from cover to cover, and then he took down the Bible
and started methodically at the first page of Genesis. Sometimes he asked Roy to read the Psalms to him, but more

often he read away by himself, and Roy was glad enough to be allowed to retire to his bunk. The weather was frightful, and it grew steadily worse.

Through day after day of heavy weather, the *Thunderbird* was doggedly approaching the Cape of Good Hope. Within four degrees of its latitude the wind moderated, and all aboard were cheered by the sight of many birds flying about the ship. Next morning they had a light breeze from the east, which freshened as the sun got higher, backing to northeast. Just after noon the wind backed three points more, then suddenly fell dead calm. The men on deck looked fearfully at the sky, which bore a dreadful appearance, and predicted a gale. A gale it was, sweeping upon them from north-northwest, whipping the seas into mountains. Like a living barrier this adverse wind barred the way to the Atlantic.

One sight of the coast of Africa, and a few moderate days raised their hopes, but the gale returned with even greater fury and continued without interval for fourteen days. The ship was made as snug as possible with the spritsail and spritsail topsail yards rigged in and stowed over the main hatches. Still she pitched tremendously, and there was no refuge from the motion and the wet anywhere. Poor Mimbo gave up hunting rats, and Jerry said they must all be drowned. Breakfast was the picture of misery. Jerry made him a cloak from a piece of blanket and a bit of old sail. Tied around his middle, it kept him warm and dry. "He looks more like a monk than a monkey," Roy said, hoping to get a laugh, but laughter was not plentiful on the *Thunderbird* these days. Even Benjamin found it hard to force a dry chuckle.

Strangely enough, the stanchest spirit aboard was Mr. Heflin, whose voice was heard on the poop proclaiming above the wind in the darkest hour of the night, "O ye

Winds of God, bless ye the Lord: praise him, and magnify
him forever!"

"Has he gone mad?" Jerry asked when he first heard this
phenomenon.

"On the contrary; look at his face. He is the sanest man
aboard," Roy answered, and indeed, even in the stress of
the storm Mr. Heflin's face was calm. The lines and furrows
of his face had smoothed out, and his eyes looked directly
at the objects close at hand, instead of staring afar off.

"Perhaps he has found himself at last," Jerry mused.

"He's done better than that," said Roy. "He has found
God."

The end of the gale was marked by the sight of land, identified by Mr. Hart as False Bay. Shortly thereafter the unmistakable shape of the tableland above the cape was recognized, bearing northwest some four or five leagues. Jerry
was on deck at the time, and he routed Roy out of his bunk
to look at the famous landmark, which they must pass before they could turn north toward their home port. They
breathed a sigh of relief.

Their satisfaction was premature. Hard squalls played
with the *Thunderbird* like a cat with a toad; large hailstones
pelted her, and the wind blew stubbornly from the northwest, as it had been doing throughout the month.

Jerry, in a fit of depression, declared to Mr. Heflin, "It's
like a nightmare. We'll never round the cape. The ship can't
take this pounding forever, nor can I!"

"On the contrary, according to my reckoning we are already past. The current has carried us around in spite of
the wind," Mr. Heflin said. "Don't try to defy the elements;
put your mind to something that will be of use. We are short
of water for the livestock. Do you think you can set up a still
to make sea water fit for the purpose?"

Thus challenged, Jerry went back to work, but the long

ordeal was telling on him. Roy, too, felt the strain. Sometimes he glimpsed himself in the mirror on the cabin wall and wondered to see his face still unwrinkled. "I wouldn't be surprised to find my hair turned white," he told Breakfast. "Every day is like a year. I didn't know it would be as hard as this." Yet when the boys were together they strove to be cheerful. Each one depended upon the other. Each of them felt that if the other should falter, it would be the end of them both.

One day of sunlight! How joyfully the great warm orb was greeted! But its appearance was brief, and an observation brought discouraging news: they were a degree to the south of the latitude their dead reckoning made them. The *Thunderbird* labored on, through unsettled weather and confused seas.

The Malay, Battoo, died and was buried at sea, far from the warm river where waited his crocodile brother. The foul weather continued; but at last the wind came from the right quarter; at last the ship was running free toward St. Helena.

One night Jerry was waked by a loud crash, and found his bunk awash. An immense sea had struck the starboard quarter, beating in the sash frame of the quarter gallery, bursting open the door, and filling the cabin with water. Knowing that Roy was on watch, his first thought was for Mimbo and Breakfast. The former was splashing frantically somewhere in the dark, and he could hear piteous cries from the latter in the upper regions of the ceiling. Wading toward the door, he met Mimbo heading for the same escape, and getting him to safety on the companion stairs, he returned with a lantern, followed by Benjamin and Jock. While they repaired the damage and fixed in the deadlights, Jerry tried to catch a very frightened monkey. From beam to hanging lantern Breakfast swung, chattering with

terror, with Jerry leaping from table to chair in close pur-
suit.

Balancing as best he could against the motion of the ship,
Jerry reached out desperately, managing to grasp one of
Breakfast's arms. The little monkey, however, held on to the
lantern chain with his tail, and the harder Jerry pulled, the
more tightly he clung. The vessel gave a lurch, Jerry lost his
footing, and he dived for the lantern chain. For a moment
they both hung from the ceiling, boy and monkey; then the
hook gave way and they tumbled in a heap. Jerry clutched
Breakfast triumphantly, and stood up amid roars of laughter. He saw that the doorway was filled with onlookers;
Roy, Mr. Hart, and several of the sailors had come to investigate the commotion, and stayed to enjoy the spectacle.
Roy was laughing; Benjamin was laughing; Mr. Hart guf-
fawed and slapped his thighs. The sailors whooped with
mirth. Jerry, after a blank moment, joined in. The ship rang
with laughter as those who had been present described the
scene to the others. It was the first good laugh the *Thunderbird* had heard in many a day.

A few days later the weather also smiled—the deadlights
were removed, and ports were thrown open fore and aft.
Everyone fell to with a will to spruce up the ship for port.
When the island of St. Helena was sighted, it appeared to
be a mountain of barren rock, rising precipitously from the
sea. Forbidding as were its overhanging precipices, it was
none the less welcome to the sea-weary eyes aboard. When
well in toward the land, the ship was hove to and Mr. Hart
was sent in a boat to ask permission of the governor of the
island to anchor in the bay. This done, they made sail and
rounded a bluff promontory, standing in so close that Roy
and Jerry looked inquiringly at Mr. Heflin.

"We must hug the shore or miss our anchorage," the Master explained. "The island rises so steeply from the ocean

floor that only a narrow shelf is left to anchor to. If we miss it, or if the land wind forces us off, the strong leeward current makes it the devil of a task to beat up again."

The next moment they felt the wind of which he spoke. Rounding the point of rock, a verdant valley opened to sight. Down the valley the wind rushed with such force as almost to lay the ship on her broadside, although she went only under double-reefed topsails. Another great shoulder of rock, and the *Thunderbird* was nearly becalmed but glided past to the opening of another valley, where she again felt the force of the wind.

Such was the approach to St. Helena, the tiny rock in the wide Atlantic where the boys looked for respite from their labors, comforts for the men, and repairs for the ship. They had hoped, too, to find the *Swan* there before them, but when they passed the third mountain and saw the pleasant town in still another valley, they let go the anchor with the regretful knowledge that they were still alone.

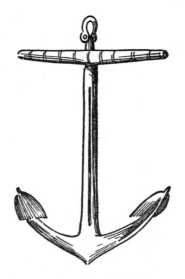

CHAPTER XVIII

CALM

ST. HELENA lay astern; six days later the island of Ascención was passed. When the lookout sang out, everyone gathered at the rail to look longingly at its rocky heights and gleaming white beaches.

"Too bad it's too late in the year for turtle," Mr. Hart said. "I've been here when we took a hundred of 'em, weighing four hundred pounds apiece."

"Dat's a lot of fresh meat," sighed Fat Pork.

Jock rubbed his middle. "Fresh meat! Wot yer talkin' about?" He whined, in an attempt at humor. "Never heard of it."

"I et fresh meat once," Joe Kent joined in. "But that was ten years ago, before I went to sea."

Roy and Jerry heard and sympathized. The small amount of beef they had been able to purchase at St. Helena was now gone, and of the livestock they carried, only a few chickens and the goat survived.

"We'll have fish," Jerry said. "The weather is so favorable, we can keep a fishing detail on the job all day."

The fishing detail was a popular one. It was much better sport than tarring down the standing rigging or calking the deck, or any of the thousand and one other tasks with which Mr. Heflin and Mr. Hart kept the men busy during fair weather. Benjamin was one of the most enthusiastic anglers aboard. Whenever a school of bonito was sighted, he was sure to be astraddle the jib boom, his legs locked between the guys, dangling a hook wrapped with white rag

179

so cleverly that it skipped from wave to wave. When one of these forty-pound fighters took the bait there was a good show, which Benjamin made better by his whoops and sallies.

"Hooray!" he would shout. "Here's a big 'un!"

The men who could avoid an officer's eye would come to look on. "What you foolin' with dat li'l bitty minnow for?" Charleston would scoff. "Let 'im go home to his mammy!"

"Minnow! You can't see straight, man! Dis is de gran'-daddy of all de fishes. Whoah dere! Whoah, Ah say!"

The harpoon was kept ready, and at the cry of "porpoises under the bow!" there was a rush forward. The harpooner, balanced under the bowsprit on the back ropes, had the waves right beneath him, the porpoises racing just ahead of the cutwater. The men above him shouted instructions, "There you are! No, that one, to the starboard—you lubber! You let him go!" When the harpoon did lodge in the animal's back, the work was not done, but all hands must haul with a will to hoist it to the block seized to the end of the bowsprit. Someone must run out on the bowsprit to pass a rope with a running bowline in its end to the harpooner, who slipped it over the porpoise's tail. Some of the men then hauled on this line, while others slacked the harpoon line, and so it was brought on deck, meat fit for the Captain's table.

The Captain's table, however, saw little of it. Mr. Heflin and the boys agreed that what fish was caught by the men should go into their own mess kids. Mr. Hart, not seeing eye to eye with them in the matter, had his own private arrangement with Fat Pork.

In any case, there was never enough to go around. Mimbo was the only creature aboard who thrived, for the rats had not been drowned after all, but appeared in greater numbers as the heat increased. The men who had recovered from the fevers of Batavia now began to complain of new symptoms—swollen feet, aching joints, bleeding gums. Men who had hitherto escaped ill health began to decline. Roy did not need his medical book to tell him what the dreaded signals meant: scurvy. Hopelessly he looked up the remedies, and was informed that earlier mariners had found spruce tea to be of great benefit, as well as all kinds of greens, fruits, and vegetables. Recoveries were said to be quite rapid after merely smelling the turf, and in severe cases, burying the patient up to the hips in earth was recommended.

Cousin Audley had provisioned the *Thunderbird* with a lavish hand, since Roy and Jerry had supplied the money, but toward the end of the long voyage there was little left of the original store. Supplies taken on at Batavia had been consumed in the long passage around the cape, and there had been few available to replace them at St. Helena. Fine white rice from Manila, coffee, sugar, and salt meat they had in abundance, but though these filled the stomach and pleased the palate, they did nothing to arrest the advance of the sailor's ancient enemy.

The *Thunderbird* crossed the equator for the fourth time. King Neptune did not appear on this occasion, but a more terrible visitor did. The watches were assembled for a funeral instead of a festival.

It was a funeral without a corpse. The afternoon before, one of the Frenchmen, whom the men called Lafayette, had been working on a staging hung over the stern, repainting the name and home port of the *Thunderbird*. He was a clever painter, who liked to mess with colors and brushes, and he embellished the work with flourishes in spite of the menacing fins of the sharks who cruised below. The sea was glassy, the airs light and fitful; Lafayette painted away without interruption, whistling happily, until dark.

When he climbed over the rail and gathered together his gear, he discovered that he had forgotten his favorite brush. Roy and Jerry, Mr. Hart, and the helmsman were nearby, and most of the men were on deck for the sake of the air.

"Why go back now, man?" Mr. Hart asked. "The brush will keep."

The Frenchman shook his head. "He fall off. He good brush. Good brush, I not 'ave, only one."

He went back over the rail.

There was a splash; then, like lightning, the swishing sound of a great fish. Then silence. Mimbo, lifting his nose toward the stars, began to howl.

Horror-struck, those nearby ran to the rail. In the darkness nothing could be seen. The mainyard was backed and the ship hove to. A boat was lowered as quickly as possible, but no trace of life could be found in the black waste of waters.

Next day Mr. Heflin read the service for the burial of the dead at sea. Lafayette had been popular with the crew, and some of the sick asked to be brought on deck to listen. At the close of the service Benjamin raised a hymn, and all who were able joined in.

Listening to the voices, among which so many were quavering and feeble, Mr. Heflin's face was grim. As the days passed, the expression became habitual. The *Thunderbird* was all but becalmed.

Like the rats, the human beings were driven from below decks by the heat. Windsails were let down into the forepeak to ventilate the hold. Through this funnel the stink of the bilges rose. The cockroaches multiplied by millions. The pitch boiled up out of the seams. The sick lay under an awning rigged on the fo'c'sle head, while the men still active went about their duties languidly.

"We must keep 'em busy," Mr. Heflin said.

He was sitting with Roy and Jerry after supper on the poop, their feet propped up on the port quarter bitts, hoping for a breath of air. Jerry mopped his forehead. "How long can this last?" he asked. "What has happened to the wind?"

"I thought I'd had enough of wind rounding the cape," Roy said ruefully. "But I'd do anything now for a puff of it—just one little puff!"

Mr. Heflin looked up at the slack canvas. "You've come through the storms with courage, but it's the doldrums that try men's souls," he said, half to himself. "In these latitudes a ship will drift like this for days, perhaps weeks—sometimes, months."

The boys heard him with sinking hearts. He had spoken aloud the fear that they had tried to hide from themselves during these last days. After all they had been through, after all their efforts and all their prayers, were they to be delayed forever so near to home? Must they stew helplessly in the middle of the shark-infested ocean with a ship full of sick men? They felt sick themselves—sick at heart, sick of mind.

Roy suddenly put his hand over his eyes and groaned.

Jerry cried out, "What can we do?"

In all their adventures they had never come so near to despair.

Mr. Heflin said quietly, "Boys, this is the time to have faith. When I was lower than you will ever be, you showed me how to find it. Now it's your turn. Read the Bible and pray. Keep the men's spirits up. Get the ship ready for port. We'll get there."

Roy uncovered his eyes and looked at Mr. Heflin long and steadily. Jerry rubbed Mimbo's ears and gulped as if he had swallowed some bitter medicine. It *was* a bitter dose, but once taken, he felt better.

Mr. Heflin went on, "You'll hear terrible tales of ships becalmed here until all aboard died of starvation and thirst. I suppose there's truth in these stories, but don't let 'em prey on your mind. The currents are working for us all the time, and they'll carry us to where we'll find wind. Just don't be in a hurry."

Both boys grimaced at his last remark. Don't be in a hurry? When the men were dying of scurvy? When their stepmother needed their protection? When the whole future of Rivergarden depended upon them? But Mr. Heflin was right. They had turned to him for help, and he had told them the truth, and they were grateful to him.

And so the *Thunderbird,* her wings clipped, drifted day after day. Mr. Heflin was now in full command of the ship, and he carried out his own advice to keep the sailors busy. He had them calking the deck and bends, painting, scrubbing, polishing brasswork, and varnishing brightwork. On Sundays he made them tidy themselves up, attend Morning and Evening Prayer, wash and patch their clothes, darn their socks. If there was nothing else to do, they picked oakum or made chafing gear.

Roy and Jerry took part in all these tasks, but their chief concern was another bit of Mr. Heflin's advice: to keep up the spirits of the men. There were frequent rains, which, caught in an old sail over the gallows frame in the main deck, kept a tank full of fresh water for bathing. Jerry led off with the daily bath for the Captain's watch, Roy for the Mate's, and every man who could stand was obliged to follow their example. Once established, bathing became a popular pastime, though old Hawks grumbled that it "warn't natural," and Fat Pork attracted so much comment upon his size and shape that he took to carrying his cleaver with him when he bathed, threatening battle against all comers.

The dogwatches were the time for games, tall tales, and singing, the latter led by Benjamin in the one watch, Jock, the Cockney, in the other. Jock could not match Benjamin's melody, his voice being likened by his companions to the sound of a rusty gate; but he had a fund of songs in his memory that no one else could match. On occasion the two watches met together and held a contest in singing, which Jock's crowd always won because they could hold out longer. For pleasure, however, they listened to Benjamin, with Mr. Hart a close rival. He was discovered to have a deep bass voice that might have belonged to Davy Jones himself.

Fat Pork was the champion teller of tales, but nearly every man had at least one story in him, which was drawn out by the influence of the tropic nights. The *Thunderbird* rolled on a glassy sea, with the stars above and below her, only a few dim lanterns burning about the deck. The men lounged on the deck or the fo'c'sle head, the sick on their pallets. Presently one said, "You talk about scurvy. Pshaw, you ought to 'a been on the *Kite* the time the yellow fever come aboard at Guadeloupe. Ten of us went to sleep in one watch and only three woke up again."

Jack asked dryly, "Which bunch was you in?" and raised a loud guffaw.

Aft, the owners and officers of the *Thunderbird* took their ease, listening dreamily to the voices of the men. Cousin Audley came out on deck and began his nightly promenade, one wrist chained to his guard. He was allowed now to spend much of his time on deck, a space having been allotted him under the awning of the poop. Twice a day he was given an opportunity to walk for his health's sake, and he seemed to thrive upon captivity.

Roy insisted that their prisoner be fed from the Captain's table, with the addition of whatever fresh fish was caught; he wished to give him no excuse to complain of his treatment at their hands. Jerry fumed to see him so sleek and comfortable and swore that if he had his way Cousin Audley's fare would be reduced to bread and water.

He fumed now as he saw the portly figure of his cousin saunter forward, trailing a fragrant thread of cigar smoke and chatting pleasantly with his guard.

"I still say he should not be allowed to talk," he grumbled.

"He's not allowed to talk to the men, only to the guard on duty," Roy said. "It would be inhumane to condemn him to perpetual silence, and he has to make his wants known, in any case. What harm is there in that?"

"He might cook up some scheme for escape."

Roy laughed shortly. "If he can escape from this place he is welcome to do so."

Cousin Audley was now within earshot of the men, several of whom touched their caps in greeting. He bowed his head affably, and went on with his conversation with the guard in a slightly louder tone. "As to the Sargasso Sea, that's real enough, and we're at the edge of it now, as you can see by the weed we sight daily. Did you know that the weed on the surface is only a bit of the whole, and the roots go down to eighty fathoms?"

"I've heerd of ships that got caught in the weed, sir," said the guard.

"I'm inclined to doubt the truth of such tales," Cousin Audley said. "It is not the weed that imprisons ships in these waters, but the calm."

By this time Cousin Audley had reached the knightheads, paused to gaze forward over the bowsprit, and turned to complete his circuit of the ship. Talk had died out among the sailors, and some of the loungers sat up to hear better.

Seemingly oblivious to his shadowy audience, Cousin Audley went on, his voice just loud enough to be audible, "I know what the calm will do, for I witnessed it myself, and not far from this very point on the map."

"Did you, now, sir?" gaped the guard, who knew his fellows were envying him. Guard duty was considered a soft assignment. The violence attending the outbreak of the prisoners on that night of storm was attributed by the men to Ole and Ross. The Captain—for so most of the crew still thought of John Audley—always behaved like a gentleman. He wasn't above slipping a cigar or a glass of wine to a fellow who'd stood on his wet feet four hours at a stretch. And as for his conversation—well, that was a treat! The Captain always had been a man as could make men listen to him.

"Yes, we were becalmed then, just as we are now, when the lookout sighted a strange-looking vessel. Her rigging was dismantled, her hull thick with barnacles and trailing seaweed. I had a boat lowered and went myself to board her. I'll never forget what I saw." Cousin Audley paused, and there was no sound but the faint creakings in the frame of the ship, the ripple of water, and the irregular tapping of the reef points on the sails.

The guard had stopped, forgetful of his instructions to keep moving when exercising the prisoner. "What did you see, sir?"

"Why, man, I saw a ship full of skeletons—yes, from the cabins to the fo'c'sle every man was dead these many years. Even the rats were dead. I saw their bones and the bones of the ship's cat. Lord knows who ate who."

Cousin Audley resumed his walk, recalling his guard to his duty with a jerk. Behind them the men began to mutter uneasily. One of the sick men turned face down with a groan. Over Cousin Audley's face spread a slow, self-satisfied smile.

Bracing and hauling to catch every feeble flutter of air, drifting in the warm invisible river of the Gulf Stream, the *Thunderbird* inched her way to the northwest. Mr. Heflin kept a tight rein on the men, who were sun-seared ghosts of themselves, limping on swollen limbs and plagued with boils. Still he kept them holystoning the deck, patching sails, painting and polishing in preparation for the port they had all but given up hope of reaching. There were some sour looks and much grumbling. No one wanted to go over the rail to clean the ship's side. One look at the plank slung beneath the mizzen channels made them all sick men. Those who were forced to do the job talked long and loudly about it when out of earshot of the officers.

On his daily promenades Cousin Audley dropped a word here, a word there, casual words, spoken with the greatest good humor. They acted upon the men like drops of whale oil upon a flame.

Short rations, short tempers, but what long, long days and nights! A deputation from the crew waited upon Mr. Heflin to complain about the food. He called all hands together and made a short speech, telling them that their lot was sure to improve soon. "We are now not many leagues southeast of Bermuda," he said. "It is a region of calms, but we have caught what airs there are, and any day we will fall in with a breeze. In the meantime, we are sure to sight other sail hereabout, and if we come close enough to speak, we will be able to purchase some provisions. Be of good heart, lads, you've served well, and you'll all get shore leave in Bermuda."

This speech had some effect, but it did not last long. That night one of the sick men died, and the service was held at once, the climate allowing no delay. The call to service bell gathered the men in the waist once more. The melancholy farewell over, Mr. Heflin closed his book and started aft together with Mr. Hart, Jerry, and Roy. Behind their backs the men huddled in groups and whispered.

The bos'un ordered them to disperse, but they gathered about the boats, their voices rising to a threatening grumble. The words, "Take the boats," "Row to Bermuda," could be heard.

The bos'un went aft. "They're workin' up to somethin', sir," he told Mr. Heflin. "They've not done nothin' fatal yet, God help 'em, but they're close to it."

"Get the pistols, Mr. Hart," Mr. Heflin commanded. To the boys he said, "Arm yourselves!" But he went unarmed to where the men waited.

As if he saw nothing unusual in their demeanor, he ordered Charleston to the masthead. "And look sharp for St. David's Head Light!"

A sudden silence fell among the men. Then the word went around. "St. David's Head Light!" "We must have made the Bermudas!" A thrill of joy went through the crew. "Thank God!"

Taking out his knife, Mr. Heflin went to the mainmast and cut a neat cross. "That's for a breeze," he said. "With a breeze, we'll see St. David's Head Light tonight."

The men dispersed, those on watch falling to their tasks with a will, the others finding vantage points for themselves from which they could gaze ahead. They saw the same sea which had filled their eyes for weeks. The same glassy sea, the same stars, but gilded by hope.

The boys met Mr. Heflin as he returned to the quarterdeck. They were jubilant from what they had heard. "The Bermudas? At last? Why didn't you tell us?"

Mr. Heflin's shoulders sagged. "Because I didn't know," he said. "I don't know. It's true enough that we are very close. It's true enough that I scent a breeze. There's one somewhere; I feel it in my bones. But will it come tonight?

If it doesn't, those poor souls forward will be guilty of mutiny, I fear."

The boys' hopes faded, but Mr. Heflin's calm courage kept them from despair. They remembered the wreck of a man he had been when the command of the *Thunderbird* was thrust upon him. All other feelings were lost in gratitude and wonder.

A faint, faraway sound made them turn their heads, searching. Again it came, the sound of a giant stirring in his sleep, the rumble of distant thunder. Their eyes swiveled around the horizon. Was it blacker than the night on the port quarter? Were the lowest stars blotted out?

The thunder growled once more, louder, unmistakable. Then, as all eyes watched, the dark area boiled upward, spread into ballooning clouds, illumined by internal lightning. A ripple kissed the salty old side of the *Thunderbird*.

With a hiss and a gust of spray the squall swept upon them with incredible swiftness. The sails filled with a gulp. Jock, at the helm, braced his legs wide apart and grinned as he felt life in the wheel. Orders rang out, and men who had been too sick to rise a few minutes ago sprang to obey.

With a white bone in her teeth, the *Thunderbird* raced like a hound. At five bells of the midwatch St. David's Head Light was sighted, and at evening the next day the ship was anchored at Five Fathom Hole.

There was much to be done, but Roy and Jerry had been useless for the past few hours, doing nothing but leaning on the rail looking at the green landscape. Drawing a deep breath, Jerry laughed to see Mimbo sniffing as ecstatically as he. "Your medical book was right," he told Roy. "Just the smell of the turf makes a well man of me!"

CHAPTER XIX

THE RETURN

NATURE had no more tricks in store for Roy and Jerry. The remainder of the voyage to Norfolk was as uneventful as a voyage could be, with both ship and men refreshed by their stop at the Bermudas and blessed by favorable weather. Human nature, however, was still capable of pulling a rabbit out of a hat.

Once docked at Norfolk, Roy and Jerry went ashore directly to arrange for the journey to Rivergarden. Jerry was for leaping upon horses and riding posthaste to their goal, but Roy pointed out, "That's all very well for us, but what about Breakfast and Mimbo? What about Cousin Audley? And the baggage?"

"The baggage could go on to Boston, for all I care," Jerry replied. "But I don't know where we could leave a dog and a monkey. Nor would it be easy to keep Cousin Audley under control on horseback."

"We'd look like a circus traveling through the country. We want to avoid attracting attention, not seek it."

In the end it was decided to hire a coach and pair. By stopping only to change horses they could make almost as good speed as on horseback; and they, their menagerie, and their prisoner could have the necessary privacy.

Mr. Heflin also went ashore, having it in mind to make a small personal venture in tobacco if it could be purchased at a price that would allow a profit in Boston. He returned to the *Thunderbird* in the evening to have a farewell supper with the boys, who planned to spend the night aboard the ship and make an early start next morning.

Supper was served in the Captain's cabin. Mr. Hart was on leave ashore, so there were only the three of them, with Benjamin in attendance.

"I didn't know it would be so hard to say good-by," Roy said, looking around the room. "I have been looking forward to this moment for two years, but now that it has come, I am sorry to leave the old *Thunderbird* and her crew."

Jerry said, "I hope to see her again. If Broderick Brown has her way, Wilson and Company will buy her."

"She's a worthy craft." Mr. Heflin had spoken little during the meal. A feeling of melancholy oppressed them all. The sufferings and the successes they had experienced aboard the *Thunderbird* had knitted a bond between them that was difficult to sever. Even Mimbo seemed to feel the threat of some change in the air. He stayed close to Jerry's feet and looked often into his face, seeking to read the future there. Breakfast clung to Benjamin's shoulder and gazed pensively into the dishes he served.

"You cain't act like this when you gets to Rivergarden!" Benjamin scolded him. "Mistress won't put up with any such goin's on at *her* table!"

At last the boys rose to go to their own cabin. As they crossed the companionway, they felt the emptiness of a ship with most of her crew on shore leave. They missed the motion of the hull, the pulsating life they felt in every plank when she was in the open sea. Now the *Thunderbird* was inert, drowsing at her moorings like a tethered horse.

Their cabin was quiet and unfamiliar, too. All signs of their occupancy were neatly packed away in the chests and valises that stood ready in one corner.

Roy's eyes went for the hundredth time to the great box that held Rosalie's tea set. He was concerned lest its contents suffer on the journey to Rivergarden, but he knew better than to mention his fear to Jerry. He could only trust to the skill of the Chinese packers to get it there safely.

He stood staring at it absently, while Jerry prowled restlessly about the room. Both had a vague feeling that something was wrong.

Suddenly Jerry stopped in his tracks. "I know what's the matter!" he cried. "The guard! There wasn't any guard at Cousin Audley's door!"

They rushed into the companionway. It was quite empty. They tried the door of their prisoner's cabin. It was unlocked. The room was deserted.

Mr. Heflin was called, the ship was searched, and every soul aboard was questioned. No one knew anything of the matter. No one had seen the guard or the prisoner. There had been no violence. Nothing was disturbed. The boys were forced to the conclusion that John Audley had simply walked ashore with his guard and disappeared. Questioning along the water front brought no result.

Wearily Roy and Jerry returned to the ship. "It's our own fault," Roy groaned. "We should have known he'd get at the men some way. He bribed 'em, or tricked 'em with that silver tongue of his."

"What does it matter? He's gone. But we'll see him again. Let him find *us!* I'm going to get some sleep."

Before daylight they were on their way. A hasty handshake for the few men aboard, a word with Mr. Heflin, whose eyes were luminous with tears, the heaving of baggage, the clatter of hoofs on the cobblestones, and the *Thunderbird* was left behind. Benjamin drove the horses, Mimbo sniffing the air joyously from the seat beside him. Roy, Jerry, and Breakfast huddled inside, taking the jolts without complaint. Benjamin had orders to make speed.

They were soon out of the town. As the sun rose, Roy and

Jerry thrust their heads out of the windows to see the familiar Virginia countryside under the blue sky of a crisp Virginia winter day. The sun brightened hourly, warming them to the bone, and bringing out the brilliant colors of late leaves that still clung to many of the trees. A buzzard sailed high in the limitless blue; a squirrel dashed from limb to limb of the trees that arched over the road, and the tang of wood smoke came on the sharp air. "Virginia air!" breathed Roy.

"Virginia mud, too!" Jerry grasped for a hold as the coach skidded sidelong into a rut.

Benjamin urged the horses through the mud. This part of the road was overshadowed by the wood and was still deep with mire. His thoughts, however, strayed from his work. He, too, felt a deep happiness at the familiar sights and sounds and smells of home. But he had fearful memories of his last trip over this road, riding by night on Mr. Morris' horse, hiding by day because Mr. Morris had made him a thief and a runaway. Since then he had been to far places and had lived as a free man. What was he doing here, coming back now to stick his head in a noose? Why was he doing it?

"Why, because Mahs' Gerald and Mahs' Leroy needs me, that's why," Benjamin answered himself. But how could he help them? What could they do against the two men who had robbed them of their home?

In spite of doubts and questions the coach rolled on. Meals were eaten as they went, with only brief stops to water or rest the horses after a hard pull. The boys slept, or took turns at the reins to relieve Benjamin. The food Fat Pork had provided from the galley was consumed; the miles, one after another, were devoured by the wheels of the coach; noon faded into afternoon, afternoon into dusk. Once again it was night.

The horses were dragging their hoofs, their heads nodding wearily as they stumbled along the dark track. At a turn in the road they lifted their ears. Their heads followed, and their steps quickened. "We must be nearing the Rainbow Tavern," Roy said, peering ahead.

"I would prefer another inn—any other inn," said Jerry. "The Rainbow is no place for honest men."

"It has one virtue, however; it is the only inn on the road," Roy reminded him. "In any case we shall not enter the house. We'll stop just long enough to change the horses in the yard. I'll handle the matter; you stay out of sight with Mimbo and Breakfast. I will probably pass unnoticed, whereas you and Mimbo are sure to be recognized."

"Very well, but look sharp! If Cousin Audley is waiting for us anywhere along the road, it will be here. I'll have my pistol loaded and cocked."

The lights of the Rainbow Tavern could now be seen, and soon they were rattling into the stable yard. A black stableboy came out with a lantern, but when Roy told him his business he merely opened his eyes and his mouth wider, the picture of incomprehension. After another unsuccessful attempt, Roy told him to go get his master, and he went off to the house, leaving Roy and Benjamin to stamp their feet in the frost. Jerry, peering from the coach, laid his pistol on his knee. Cowering on the floor, Mimbo shivered in silent misery. His nose told him that he had been here before. The opening of the back door let out a rich fragrance of roasting venison. It awakened memory in Mimbo's mind—the memory of hours of scorching labor at the turnspit. In that kitchen he had blistered and starved and borne the heavy hand of the Indian cook. An agonized whimper was wrung from his very soul. Breakfast shivered in sympathy.

The boy returned with a surly hostler, who made it plain that he could not be hurried save by the application of money to his palm. Roy had anticipated this, however, and gave him a tip that had him stepping briskly, cuffing the stableboy and ordering two other servants to the work. Fresh horses were brought out and harnessed; the jaded horses were taken to the stables, and the coach was off again. Little time had been lost, but such a stir had been raised that several loungers had been attracted to the yard to look on, and faces could be seen pressed against the tavern windows.

"Well, that is safely over," Roy leaned back with a sigh of relief, pulled up his greatcoat collar, and prepared for a nap.

"I'm not so sure," Jerry muttered uneasily.

"I don't believe Cousin Audley has any intention of following us," Roy said. "He knows that our letters have warned our stepmother against him. He will not go to Rivergarden, but to Baltimore to meet Mr. Morris. Together they will brew some poisonous scheme, but we will be in possession of Rivergarden, and with Benjamin as a witness, we will prove our case before the law."

Jerry fingered his pistol. "Maybe so. But—"

"I must spell Benjamin in an hour, so I'll catch a wink of sleep." Roy stretched and shifted from one uncomfortable position to another. He chuckled at a memory. "When I came this way before, I couldn't sleep sitting up. I was fresh from those big soft beds at Rivergarden then. But after two years at sea—" He closed his eyes and dozed off.

Jerry had never had difficulty sleeping anywhere. But for some reason he stayed awake now. It was not that he really expected Cousin Audley to spring out of the darkness. Roy's reasoning seemed sound. And yet . . .

They had not gone far when he realized that the coach was coming to a halt. He put his head out of the window and called to Benjamin, "What's the matter?"

Benjamin was climbing down from his perch. "One of the hosses has gone lame, mahstah."

Jerry stepped out, followed by Roy, who woke with a start. Mimbo squeezed out at their heels, glad of a chance to exercise his short legs. Breakfast remained in the warm nest Jerry had made for him among the baggage. He hated the cold.

Jerry stood at the head of the team, his pistol ready, while Benjamin bent over the lame horse's hoof. Roy held a lantern for him to see by. "Heah 'tis!" announced Benjamin presently, holding up a pebble he had pried out of the hoof. "Ah'm mighty glad to find that. That hoss ain't been actin' right since we left the tavern, and Ah was afraid they'd given us a worthless animal." He patted the horse's shoulder. "He'll do better, now."

"He's still fretting about something," Roy said. "They're both nervous. Look at their ears."

Then they heard what the horses had heard before them— the steps of another horse somewhere in the darkness outside the circle of light cast by their lanterns. Jerry raised his pistol, but a voice rang out, "Drop it. Drop your weapons in the road."

It was the voice of Captain John Audley. Jerry aimed deliberately at the sound and fired. As the reverberations of the shot died away, a laugh replied. "Drop your gun, you young fool, or I'll shoot it out of your hand."

Jerry dashed for the coach, in order to reload. He and the others were stopped by the appearance of the Captain riding boldly into the light, his pistol aimed at them. "Drop it!" he repeated. "That means your knife, too, Benjamin."

They dropped their weapons in the mud. "Put the lantern down and stand against the coach," Cousin Audley commanded.

Roy stooped as if to obey, but instead swung the lantern directly in the eyes of Cousin Audley's horse. The animal reared and pawed the air; the Captain, more of a sailor than a horseman, was unseated. With a thud he struck the ground, and Mimbo sprang snarling upon him.

"Mind the horses!" Roy shouted to Benjamin, for they were all snorting and dancing with fear. Jerry tried to gain possession of the pistol that had fallen from Cousin Audley's grasp, but the lunging of the frightened horse and the frenzied attacks of Mimbo made it difficult to get near. As the boys strove for a chance to seize the bridle, flying forefeet struck the fallen man. With an oath and a dreadful groan, Captain Audley lay still.

At length Jerry got Mimbo away from the body, and Roy caught the sweating horse. With the one confined within the coach and the other tethered to a tree, the boys were able to examine their fallen foe.

He was a pitiable object, muddy, bruised, his hands and neck bearing the marks of Mimbo's teeth. He was breathing, however, and when they lifted him, he opened his eyes and groaned with pain. His right arm hung useless from the shoulder. The venom in his sky-blue eyes, which had once beamed at them so benevolently, was terrifying.

They got him into the coach, first placing Mimbo on the seat outside with Benjamin. Then Roy took the driver's reins, and they started their interrupted journey, the Captain's horse trotting behind. Jerry sat opposite his cousin in the coach, armed and watchful. All night they rode, taking turns at driving and guard duty. The jolting of the coach was torture for the man with the broken arm. Now and then he lapsed into unconsciousness, and when he woke, it was always to face the sleepless guard, and the beady glittering eyes of Breakfast.

Daybreak found them not two miles from Rivergarden. They met no one on the road, but they saw smoke rising from farmhouses here and there. Then they were at the entrance of Rivergarden, where the avenue of oaks began.

When Roy and Jerry rode through the entrance, they rode back into their childhood. How often had they chased each other down this winding drive? How often had they climbed the trees in the orchards, rolled down the slope of the lawn, gathered acorn cups for Rosalie's dolls, or paddled at the edge of the river? Ah! They caught their breath. There were the mellow red-brick walls of the house. Smoke rose from the chimneys. Benjamin stopped the coach at the mounting block with a scattering of gravel. They were at home.

Roy and Jerry bounded out and up the steps. Their knock at the door was answered promptly, but by a servant they did not know. "Why, where's Anthony?" Jerry demanded.

"Wheah's who, suh?"

"Never mind," Roy interposed. "Please tell Mrs. Lacey we are here. Tell her—"

He was interrupted by a low exclamation. Mrs. Lacey stood above them on the stairs, just as they had often seen her in their homesick dreams: tall, queenly, and beautiful.

She wore a white gown in the fashionable Grecian mode, which gave her the look of a piece of classic sculpture. She glided rapidly down the stair to meet them, her arms extended, and embraced them tenderly. They bent over her, overcome with the warmth of her body and the sweetness of her perfume. This was the woman their father had loved, who had presided over their home and mothered them for a brief half year, who in her desire to protect them, had been cruelly deceived by Richard Morris and John Audley.

After some incoherent words, Roy was able to ask, "Did you receive our letters?"

Mrs. Lacey nodded. Jerry said, "Then you know about

Cousin Audley and his treachery. He's outside in the coach, now. He tried once more to kill us, and got a broken arm for his pains. He needs medical attention."

"Bring him in," said Mrs. Lacey. "Take him upstairs to the schoolroom. He can rest on the day bed until the doctor comes, while you and I can make ourselves comfortable for a good, long talk."

The boys went back for the injured man, who allowed them to assist him into the house. Benjamin was charged with the care of the coach, animals, and baggage, and drove off to the stables. Cousin Audley painfully climbed the stairs, and the boys opened the door to the big front room that had been first their nursery, and later their schoolroom.

They let Cousin Audley down upon the day bed none too gently and looked around them. Through the windows they could see the dark cedar trees around the summerhouse at the edge of the lawn, and beyond a glimpse of the river, just as they remembered. The boughs of the old oak tree at the front door still arched across one of the windows, the rusty leaves clinging to the twigs. The ivy still crept over the window sills and tapped against the glass.

But inside the room everything was changed. The mellow old carpet, where Jerry had napped away his study hours; the drawing table by the window, where Roy had tried to give form to his castles in Spain; the overflowing bookcases, the old brick hearth upon which they had sharpened their knives—all these were gone. It was now a sitting room for a fine lady—and gentleman. On a table lay an open box of fragrant cigars.

The door opened and their stepmother came in, smiling. "Our breakfast will be brought to us here," she told them. "The doctor has been sent for. There is nothing to prevent our spending a pleasant hour together. Ah! Here is your host. Richard, here are the boys returned at last from their voyage. They have come a long way to congratulate us on our marriage."

The man to whom she spoke had entered quietly from an adjoining room. He was a slender, sallow man in his middle thirties, fastidiously dressed. It was their former tutor, Richard Morris, the murderer of their father.

CHAPTER XX

THE RESCUE

W ELCOME to Rivergarden," said Mr. Morris.
The truth burst upon the boys with a blinding flash:
Mrs. Lacey had plotted with Richard Morris to kill their
father. They had both plotted with Cousin Audley to kill
Roy and Jerry. She had never loved them; she had never
loved their father. From the first she had been scheming to
get Rivergarden for herself and her lover.

Richard Morris had a pistol in his hand. It looked odd and
ugly in his tapering, well-manicured fingers. He came close
to Roy and Jerry, and, feeling them over, relieved them of
the gun Jerry carried in his greatcoat pocket. This he handed
to Cousin Audley, who smiled with white lips and laid it
across his stomach. "Now then," Mr. Morris said. "Sit down
and tell us about your voyage. I understand from your letters to my wife that it was an eventful one."

He escorted Mrs. Lacey—no, she was now Mrs. Morris—
to a chair, and, seating himself opposite her, turned to the
boys with an expression of polite interest.

Sick with fury, Roy cried, "Enough of this play-acting!
You are *not* our host. You are *not* the owner of Rivergarden."

"That is for the law to say," replied Mr. Morris equably.
"I am the husband of Mr. Lacey's widow, and I was the win-
ner of the estate in a game of cards. You are free to question
these facts, but I understand that lawsuits cost money, and
that you and your brother have none."

"We have the *Thunderbird!*" Jerry declared. "She made a profitable voyage."

Cousin Audley propped himself up so that he could view them better and inquired, "Why do you say *you* own the *Thunderbird?*"

"Because we bought her! We outfitted her. Every penny that went into her voyage was ours!"

"Have you examined the papers regarding these matters?"

Jerry faltered, and Roy looked grave. "N-no. We turned them over to Broderick Brown."

"Did *he* read them?"

"No, he put them in his strongbox until he should need them."

Cousin Audley chuckled. "When he does read them, he will find that he is working for me. It was not difficult to deceive two such innocents as yourselves. You were willing to sign whatever I asked. The *Thunderbird* and her cargo is in *my* name, not yours."

Roy took a deep breath, collecting his thoughts. "Never mind. We have friends in the county, and we will not be denied a hearing. You will have to prove your claims in court. As for you"—he turned to Richard Morris—"*you* shall stand trial for murder."

"If you insist. But what jury in the world would convict a man on the unsupported accusations of two downy-cheeked lads?"

"We have a witness!" Jerry blurted out.

"Do you?"

Something in his tone chilled their blood. Both boys advanced upon him in spite of the pistol he held. "What do you mean?"

"I mean that Benjamin is safely in my care. Even now he is being taken to the place where recalcitrant or runaway slaves are confined."

"Did you harm him?"

"No more than was necessary to subdue him. My overseer is familiar with such cases. The dog and the monkey escaped, however; I am sure they will be happy to testify for you in court!" Richard Morris laughed, glancing at his wife for appreciation.

Roy put his hand on Jerry's arm. "Let's get out of here."

Jerry, red-faced and sick at heart, followed his lead. They could gain nothing by remaining. They must take their story to Mr. McAllister and other friends of their father. And the sooner they could get away from this house, the sooner they could breathe pure air again.

Mr. Morris nodded toward the door. "We will excuse you."

But Captain Audley struggled to a sitting position on the couch. "Just a minute. You may be ready to set our foxes free, Dick, but I am not. Your cleverness does not impress me as much as it does you. I say now what I have said all along: our success depends upon the elimination of these two. Their yapping mouths will bring about our ruin, if they are allowed to leave this house."

"*You* say so! Yes, when you set out on your voyage, you said it would be so simple! We would never see them again! Ha! They have returned, two years older and two sizes larger, with you their prisoner, and disabled to boot. I am not inclined to listen too diligently to *your* counsel."

Captain Audley's drawn face flushed an ugly purple. "I'll take no sneers from you, Dick," he cried. "You have done nothing but sit at home at your ease. What do you know of the hazards of the sea? I said I would put the lads out of our way, and I will! You shall not let them walk out of that door to spread their poison."

Richard Morris rose and came toward the Captain. " 'I will!' 'You shall!' " he mimicked. "Quarterdeck language, no doubt, but it won't do here. You were paid handsomely to carry out your part of our plan, and you have failed completely. I am through with your methods. From now on I shall make the decisions. You may depart as soon as you are able. Enjoy your ill-gotten gains, and be thankful!"

Roy and Jerry listened to this conversation in amazement, edging all the while toward the door. The two men were now menacing one another with their pistols, looking quite angry enough to fire. They stood between the boys and the door, and while Roy and Jerry weighed their chances of reaching it, Mrs. Morris' low, musical voice arrested them all. "Come," she said, "there is no cause for quarreling! We are in perfect agreement as to the end we seek; surely we can agree on the means. Richard, I am cold; will you stir the fire? Cousin, do not excite yourself. You will bring on a fever."

Her husband hesitated, flung a black look at Captain Audley, and went reluctantly to the fireplace. Captain Audley leaned back against the wall, but remained seated, his pistol watchfully on his knee. The boys took some tentative steps toward the door, but he motioned them back.

"There is no need to be hasty," said their beautiful step-mother—no, they would never have to call her that again! "Come, Richard, sit beside me, and let us talk quietly."

A knock at the door brought Mr. Morris to his feet. "That will be breakfast," he said. He motioned sharply to the boys. "We will retire to my room until the table is laid. The servants are new, but there is no need to give them fuel for gossip."

Roy and Jerry, directed by the pistol, went into the adjoining bedchamber and stood waiting in uneasy silence while Mr. Morris listened to the sounds in the schoolroom. Their old tutor had taken possession of their own bedroom; there was only one large bed in it now, and the two wardrobes seemed to be bulging with Mr. Morris' apparel. The dressing table was burdened with jars and bottles like a theatrical star's, and looking glasses reflected their faces from every wall. The smell of spirits, cigars, and pomade hung in the air, together with a lingering trace of the feminine perfume the boys well remembered.

Presently they returned to the schoolroom—Roy and Jerry could think of it by no other name—and found a fine breakfast for a winter's day spread before the middle window. How the past rushed back at them as they saw the old familiar favorites! Fried corn-meal mush, and bacon, and sausage, and griddlecakes, and syrup, and butter and eggs, and more besides! Yet somehow they had no appetite. They were made to sit at the table, one armed man on either side, the beautiful lady they had once loved opposite. They could eat nothing in the midst of all this plenty, but stared out of the window at the wind-whipped trees, noticing that long, streaming mare's-tails were sweeping across the sky. The sun was obscured, and the river took on a leaden hue. Their minds were busy. One enemy wished to let them go. Another was determined to take their lives. With which one would Mrs. Morris agree? They sensed that her advice would decide their fate.

At last the men pushed back their plates and rose as Mrs. Morris left the table. The three of them took their former positions, Captain Audley half-reclining on the day bed, Mr. and Mrs. Morris in their chairs before the fireplace at the other end of the room. Roy and Jerry were told to turn their chairs around. Thus they sat between the two factions, facing the door.

"When will that infernal doctor be here?" Captain Audley demanded.

"I don't know, cousin. He lives at some distance and may have been absent when the servant arrived with my message. Are you in pain?"

Captain Audley gritted his teeth. "Pain? Of course I'm in pain."

His cousin came to him. "Let me see what I can do. If I make a sling for your arm—"

"No. If you move it, I might faint, and if I close my eyes for a moment your clever husband is likely to release the lads and bring his house of cards down in a heap upon us all."

Mrs. Morris turned back to her husband. "Richard, there is reason on his side. You are no doubt right in believing that our case will stand up in court. But need we put ourselves at the mercy of scandalmongering tongues and prying eyes? Would it not be better if the boys' story dies with them?"

Roy and Jerry heard her with expressionless faces. But inwardly they groaned. This was the verdict, then. This was their death sentence.

Captain Audley was clever enough to keep silent and let his cousin plead his cause. Richard Morris, mellowed by a good breakfast and the warm, dark glance of his wife, wavered. "Well, if it could be done discreetly. . . . But the time for such action is past. At sea, thousands of miles away, yes. But here? That's a different matter."

"You can think of a plan, dear," Mrs. Morris said, softly.

The room was so still the boys could hear the ticking of the clock on the mantel. It was the same clock that had ticked away the minutes during the boys' lessons in happier days. Roy could not help thinking that Richard Morris must have been happier, too, in those days before he became enslaved to the beauty of a wicked woman, who had already led him to commit one murder and now urged him toward two more. Jerry was thinking, "We must distract their attention somehow. Roy can disarm Captain Audley, while I attack Mr.

Morris. We can handle them easily, if we once get behind those guns."

At that moment he heard a stealthy footstep on the stair. He felt Roy tense beside him, and saw the eyes of the other occupants of the room drawn to the door.

"I dismissed the house servants. They were not to come back until called," Mr. Morris said to his wife in a low tone.

"It's not one of the servants," she replied, almost in a whisper. "Richard—?" For the first time there was a flicker of fear in her eyes.

He rose and went toward the door. "It must be," he reassured her. "I'll get rid of them quickly."

Jerry saw his chance. Kicking Roy's ankle, he lunged at Richard Morris' unguarded back. Roy, understanding at once what was expected of him, leaped for Captain Audley. As he struck him he screamed with pain and went limp. His pistol dropped from his hand. Roy picked it up and went to help Jerry. Under their combined weight Richard Morris went down, and Jerry, astride his fallen body, pommeled him enthusiastically. Mrs. Morris watched the scene briefly, then moved for the door.

It was flung open almost in her face. There, on the threshold, stood a girl in a green riding habit, her boots muddy, an oak leaf caught in her wind-blown hair. In her arms she carried a small, frightened monkey.

"Rosalie!" cried Roy.

Jerry scrambled to his feet, holding Mr. Morris' gun. "Breakfast!"

Mrs. Morris, gathering her skirts, tried to pass through the door, but Rosalie stood her ground. "If you force your way through, I shall send this monkey at you!" she threatened, holding out poor Breakfast, who chattered and mouthed and reached out for Jerry. Mrs. Morris drew back, catching her breath sharply. Rosalie ignored her, then, and spoke to Roy and Jerry. "I *knew* you were here! I knew it when I found this little creature. And I knew you were in trouble." Her bright red-brown eyes snapped with excitement.

"Trouble? What trouble?" Jerry asked airily. Hefting the pistol, he nudged Mr. Morris' body with his foot.

"Rosalie—" said Roy.

Rosalie let Breakfast go, and he scampered for Jerry's shoulder. "I'm so glad you're back," said Rosalie. "You've been gone a long time." She spoke to both of them, but she looked at Roy.

"How did you find us? How did you happen to come here?"

"Why, I found the monkey near the entrance to the avenue, while I was out riding," Rosalie explained. "I thought at once of the letter Roy wrote me from Batavia, telling me about discovering Benjamin and Breakfast there. I knew there couldn't be another monkey anywhere near River-garden. I *knew* you all must be somewhere near. And I knew that something was wrong in this house. I never trusted that woman." Rosalie looked at Mrs. Morris, who clenched and unclenched her fingers. "When she married that man—well, then I was sure something was wrong!"

Roy could find no words. He walked straight to Rosalie and hugged her hard. She emerged from his embrace blushing like a poppy. He backed away. "So you came here at once to help us!" he said. "You didn't think of the danger. Ah, Rosie! Bless you. You haven't changed a bit!"

A moan from Richard Morris recalled the boys to their situation. They hoisted him from the floor and thrust him into a chair. Mrs. Morris went to him. "These young ruffians shall pay for this, my dear! We shall see what sympathy they get for assaulting a gentleman in his own home!" she cried.

The drumming of galloping hoofs was heard on the drive.

"We shall, indeed, madam," Rosalie announced, grandly. "I sent the groom for my father. Here he is, and from the sound, he must have brought half the gentlemen of the county with him!"

CHAPTER XXI

THE TEA SET

IT WAS the last night of the year 1801. Rivergarden was ablaze with lights, for the young gentlemen were entertaining guests.

The doors between the parlors had been thrown open, giving an uninterrupted view through the house from front to back. The company was still at supper, but the rooms were not completely deserted. On the hearth rug lay Mimbo, comfortably at full length, but with watchful eyes upon the door. And on a footstool perched Breakfast, busily eating raisins from a dish on the tea table.

The table was covered with the cups and saucers, the bowls and pitchers and little dishes that had been made in faraway Ching-teh-Chen, painted in Canton, and brought across leagues of ocean in the hold of the *Thunderbird.* The rosy light of the fire glowed through the delicate porcelain, and the candlelight picked out the touches of gold in the skillfully wrought design.

The door opened, and Roy ushered Rosalie into the room. Her eyes fell at once upon the waiting table. "My tea set!" she cried, and flew to examine each piece with eager hands. "My tea set! I thought you'd forgotten! It's beautiful! Look, everyone, how beautiful! Oh, Roy, you had my initials put on!"

The rest of the company poured into the room in answer to her cries. The tea set was thoroughly admired; then the elders of the party retired to the front parlor for music and

211

backgammon, while the young people remained grouped around the tea table.

Besides Rosalie, Roy, and Jerry, there were three young ladies and three young gentlemen. Some of them were cousins of Rosalie's, and some were cousins of the cousins. They were eager to hear the story of the tea set and asked countless questions about the boys' incredible adventures. Miss Lucia was enchanted when she learned that they had spent last New Year's Eve in the Sandwich Islands.

"Oh, do tell us," she entreated, "I have heard— That is, it is common knowledge— Is it true what is said about their dances?" She dropped her eyes.

"They dance the minuet, now," Roy informed her, solemnly. "Jerry instructed them."

Jerry blushed fiercely. But he turned the tables by saying, "They swim quite as well as they dance—especially the girls."

Roy looked apprehensively at Rosalie from the corner of his eye, but she was following her own thoughts.

"Last New Year's Eve I didn't know whether you were living or dead," Rosalie recalled. "It was a sad time. We did not even have a party. And the one before that—" She broke off. She and Roy and Jerry were remembering that last night of the eighteenth century, when the boys' stepmother brought her Cousin Audley into their lives. Now the three conspirators were in prison, awaiting trial for murder and fraud. The thought of them seemed to darken the cheerful room. A curtain at one of the long windows stirred as if an unseen figure passed.

Jerry crossed to the window and drew the curtains securely. He was drawn back into the circle by more questions. "How does an iguana taste?" "Do the Chinese really walk on their heads?" "Say something in Spanish!"

Benjamin came in with a tray of teapots and chocolate pots, cakes and tarts and fruit. Rosalie established herself prettily at the table. Her eyes lifted to the clock. "I have just time to pour. Then it will be time to drink to the New Year!"

The clock began to strike. In both parlors the guests stood and raised their cups and glasses. As the last stroke of twelve sounded, the toasts died out on their lips. All of them heard the same unexpected sound: the vigorous hammering of the knocker on the front door.

Roy and Jerry were unable to move. The sound had taken them back to that other New Year's Eve two years ago. Rosalie looked from one to the other, her eyes wide. They read in them the same fearful memories that haunted their own. Mimbo, his ears cocked, watched them anxiously.

Benjamin quietly left the room, and they heard him speaking to Anthony at the door. Another voice joined in, and directly they heard Benjamin returning along the hall. The footsteps accompanying him were familiar; Mimbo's tail began to thump. With a flourish Benjamin flung the door wide and ushered Broderick Brown into the room.

Roy and Jerry shot forward at once. They seized the young captain, dragged him to the fire, pounded his back, shook his hand, introduced him all around, and asked him a thousand questions, all at once.

The questions they really wanted answered, however, could not be asked, because the cousins, enchanted with the appearance of the young captain, hung upon his words.

Miss Lucia declared that she would have known him for a sailor anywhere, for did not sailors roll when they walked?

Broderick Brown obliged her by assuming a nautical stance, describing a storm at sea so vividly that she complained she would be quite seasick if he did not stop!

Miss Amelia was concerned because she could never seem to remember the difference between a binnacle and a barnacle. Would the Captain please explain it to her?

The Captain would, and did, accepting her promise never, never to forget again.

Miss Harriet remarked that his brig, the *Margaret,* had a very pretty name. Perhaps it was named for some lady of his acquaintance?

Miss Lucia observed that Captain Brown's acquaintance must be very wide indeed; a sailor must have many opportunities to enlarge his circle, not enjoyed by landsmen.

Broderick Brown agreed that this was so, and the girls fluttered their eyelashes at him outrageously.

"I say, let's have some music and a dance," suggested one of the young men, who was tired of nautical competition.

Accordingly they moved off to the music of the pianoforte, the girls being whirled away on the tune before they noticed that Captain Brown remained by the tea table with Roy, Jerry, and Rosalie.

Roy said, "Rosalie, this is the man you have to thank for your tea set. Without him the *Thunderbird* would never have come home."

"Nonsense," said Broderick Brown. "The *Thunderbird* has done more for me than I for her. Her cargo sold at a good profit, and as soon as the legal complications are straightened out, she will make another fortune for Wilson and Brown."

"Wilson and who?" cried the boys.

"Wilson and Brown. Doesn't it sound well? And I have the business of the *Swan* and the *Thunderbird* to thank for my partnership."

He had to be pounded on the back and shaken by the hand all over again, and Rosalie insisted that he have another cup of chocolate from her beautiful pot. Breakfast climbed upon his shoulder and pulled his hair. "I shall sail the

Thunderbird on her next voyage," Broderick Brown went on. "Mr. Heflin is sailing before then, as master of the *Swan.*"

"When will you sail?" asked Jerry.

"I shall be delayed by several matters of business. It will be perhaps six months before all is in order. By that time Miss Wilson will be ready to return to Macao. She and her maid will be in my charge. I can't say I relish the prospect of having two females aboard for a trading cruise along the Northwest Coast."

Jerry fell silent during this speech and remained so for some time.

Broderick Brown slapped his knee. "Well! I have spoken enough about myself. What of you and your plans? Where will you two adventurers be next New Year's Eve, while I am inhaling the fishy fogs of the Northwest Coast?"

"I expect to be right here," said Roy. "Here at Rivergarden, where I belong. However, between now and then I shall be at my books. Father intended that I should continue my education, and I have decided to go to the college at Williamsburg to take up my studies."

"I have fifteen cousins—no, sixteen—in Williamsburg," Rosalie remarked. "I shall be kept busy visiting them."

When their laughter died down, Broderick Brown asked, "And Jerry? What of your plans?"

"I have been thinking of learning a business."

"Then think of Wilson and Brown. There will always be a berth for you with us. And as for training, there is no better way to learn the business than a few voyages as supercargo. How would you like to sail with me on the *Thunderbird*'s next voyage?"

"I was just waiting for you to ask me," Jerry said, simply, and there was another round of laughs, under cover of which Roy smothered a word of protest. He had half-expected this decision and made up his mind to accept it, but it was hard.

Catching sight of Benjamin, Jerry added, "How about you, Benjamin? You are a free man, now, you know, and may choose for yourself. Will you return to the Serranía del Darién?"

Benjamin grinned broadly. "No, suh, Mahs' Jerry. Ah cain't let you go traipsing back around the world alone. If you sail in the *Thunderbird* again, Ah'll go along."

Just then the dancing came to a stop and Roy stood up, cup in hand. "We didn't complete our toast," he called out to the company. "Let's do it now. Happy New Year, everybody!" and his words were echoed through the parlors of Rivergarden. "Happy New Year!"

The room had become warm, and Benjamin opened a window. From the quarters behind the house came the tinkling of a gourd banjo. Breakfast yawned and settled down on the hearth rug beside Mimbo. Mimbo opened one eye, then closed it with a long, contented sigh.

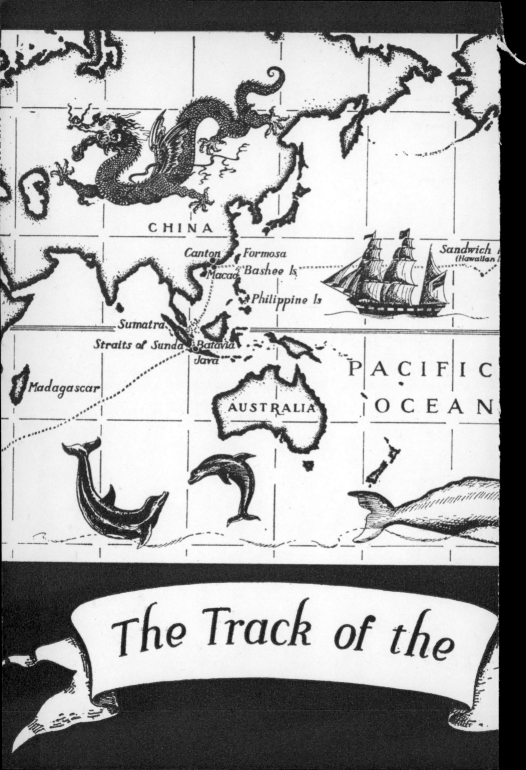

CHINA

Canton   Formosa

Macao   Bashee Is

Philippine Is

Sandwich I.
(Hawaiian I.)

Sumatra

Straits of Sunda   Batavia

Java

Madagascar

AUSTRALIA

PACIFIC

OCEAN

The Track of the